D1733453

DEADLY FORTUNES

THE FORTUNE TELLERS
BOOK 1

TERRY SPEAR

PUBLISHED BY: Terry Spear
Book Cover Art by Nichole Witholder at Rainy Day Artwork

Discover more about Terry Spear at:

http://www.terryspear.com/

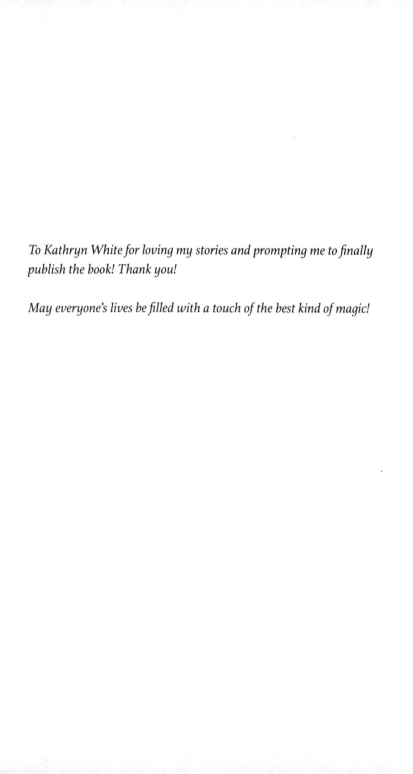

To Kathryn White for loving my stories and prompting me to finally publish the book! Thank you!

May everyone's lives be filled with a touch of the best kind of magic!

ABOUT DEADLY FORTUNES:

A rags to riches fairy tale where a fortune telling can spell doom.

Katrina Landry is not your everyday fortune teller. She's a substitute teacher who longs to work at it full time. But when she substitutes for her cousin at her fortune telling booth at the fair, Katrina meets a man who she foresees is in danger. So what's a girl supposed to do but sneak into a by-invitation-only dance and save the TX Stud's life?

Prescott Worthington hasn't had this much fun in a long time when on a whim he takes his girlfriend to the fair where Sascha the Sensation predicts he will have twins, and that his girlfriend will find someone else to marry. But when the woman shows up at the dance with some nonsense about saving his life, he's totally irritated and utterly bewitched. Maybe she can bring a little magic into his life.

She insists someone's trying to kill him and he thinks it's her boyfriend...only Prescott has no intention of giving up the woman who he's sure needs *his* protection. And a whole lot more.

1

————

Hazy killer visions. That's what plagued her this morning.

Katrina Landry twisted the crystal-beaded necklace between her fingers while potential customers sauntered in front of her booth at the annual Perrytown, Texas fall fair. All morning she'd hawked her fortune telling powers to passersby. By the end of the day's festivities, she wilted, slumping in her chair. Only twenty-four and she felt like ninety. But it was the sense of dread that filled her stomach, foreshadowing of something evil that was to come, that exhausted her the most.

She attempted to quash the rising apprehension worming its way into her system by thinking of the fortune telling role she now played. How could she tell one more person what phony futures lay ahead for them when she knew full well she could give them the real thing? Most just couldn't handle the truth. That was the problem. Then she caught sight of a six-foot James Bond lookalike... the sexy Brosnan version, his hair as rich a brown as freshly turned Texas soil and his eyes, almond shaped and brown sugar colored, the dark variety. She perked up.

Now *he'd* suit her just fine as her soul mate for life... at least from outward appearances. Dressed in perfectly creased navy trousers and a pinstriped shirt to match, the man looked out of place compared to the denim-clothed crowd. The woman who clung to his arm, a tall, chemically-perfected blond, dressed in a designer azure crepe creation that reached mid-thigh, was probably his intended. A guy like that was way beyond accessible.

Katrina poked a curl behind her ear. She stood several inches shorter than Miss Blond Bombshell and not half as sleek. Chuckling to herself, Katrina ran her fingers over her crystal ball, the typical prop of a classical gypsy fortune teller, and worth as much as a used piece of bubble gum.

Her heart fluttered with surprise when 007 caught her eye and steered the blond toward her booth. The canopied table dripped with colorful tassels, and drapes of green, gold, blue and violet silks ruffled slightly in the breeze. Katrina wore a blousy green silk shirt and a colorful broomstick skirt that reached to her gold sandal-clad feet...just the sort of costume that gave her the look of a wild gypsy. An unwieldy mass of naturally dark brown curly hair rested at her breast, and she imagined she looked like one frumpy woman as the couple approached. Before she'd caught sight of them, she'd felt dressed up compared to the jeans crowd.

The woman gave her a cagey-eyed look as if Katrina belonged to a clown show, and for the moment, she felt like it, too. Then she smiled inwardly, noting the woman wore no engagement or wedding ring. Though Katrina hadn't wished to see the blond married happily-ever-after to the hunk, she might see something else that would needle the woman. If not, she could always make something up.

The man pulled out his billfold and handed Katrina the money for a reading. They were *supposed* to buy tickets at the ticket booth. Then the fair's management would collect ten percent on all of the sales. She waffled. She didn't want to lose possibly her last sale of the day, but she'd never cheated on anything in her life. Taking the money, she vowed to buy the tickets later to make it right with the fair's management. She hoped none of the other vendors noticed her taking the cash at her booth.

Then for show, she ran her hands over the crystal ball, her long painted shimmering fingernails mesmerizing her clientele. She paused. "Ooh," she said for dramatic effect. She glanced up at the woman. Her face, an unyielding stone statue, was deeply tanned. Should she tell her, wrinkles and skin cancer would soon follow? Nah. Everyone knew that. Didn't need a crystal ball to tell her so. The woman folded her arms.

Okay, time to get real. Katrina reached out her hand. She rarely read palms. The experience took a lot out of her and tons of customers on a busy day would have put her into a trance.

The woman held out her hand, and Katrina touched the lines in her palm. "Ahhh," she said, again for fun. Rules had to be followed for every professed fortune teller. Otherwise, the medium would be labeled a phony.

"Hmm." Well, for having a male model for her date, the woman was boring as all get up. Except for enduring a comb out on her hair, a nail job, and a teeth cleaning later in the week, nothing else came to mind. All of the images appeared as if Katrina had visited the scene at the time they occurred—the smells, the sounds, and the sights—the women's nonsensical chitchat at the beauty parlor, what this woman wore, and who so and so dated, dull as Perrytown's society news.

The woman's manicure and pedicure was another boring venture, same chitchat, same women, different smelly chemicals. And then came the teeth cleaning. Okay, so that turned out to be a little more interesting as the dental hygienist gagged Miss Blondie with the water suction hose.

Katrina definitely had to conjure something up to make

things more interesting. "I see a strawberry blond in your future who strikes your fancy, Madam. He's tall, like your brother here, and just as broad shouldered."

The woman's cheeks turned cherry as she blustered, "He's my *boyfriend*."

Katrina knew she shouldn't have done it. She meant to give everyone dreams to look forward to, but the woman grated on her. The hunk's pearly whites shown as he grinned. And dimples to boot. He was one handsome devil of a man. He didn't seem to mind her pulling the woman's leg one bit. Katrina loved men with a sense of humor.

She smiled at Handsome, then raised a brow when she reconsidered the woman, who frowned back at her. "Ahem, sorry, Madam, but this gentleman doesn't appear to be in your future. Now the fair hunk of a man—"

The woman jerked her hand away from Katrina. "We want our money back."

Katrina couldn't win them all. She handed the twenty to the gentleman, though she didn't normally give refunds. But something about him made her want to put on her best show. Then she noticed he stared at the dip in her blouse. Her body warmed instantly.

He reached his hand out, palm upturned with no intention of taking the money as he avoided it. "You haven't given *my* fortune yet, Madame Sascha," he said as he read the name on the booth, *Sascha the Sensation*.

Sascha, her cousin, who she now filled in for. Her comical fortune-telling friend, who could have won an academy award for her acting ability in the world of the unreal, had laryngitis so bad that morning she'd croaked a plea to Katrina. Though Katrina rarely manned the booth, she wouldn't have left her in a lurch. Plus, sometimes, she really had some fun. Like now.

She reached for the gentleman's hand, hoping the woman

who clung to him truly wouldn't be marrying him anytime soon, if only for his sake. What she saw made her draw her hand back from his, *quickly*. Her heartbeat sped up at an alarming rate as her hands grew clammy.

Somewhere, someone would make an attempt on his life. He'd be knocked unconscious, his head hit hard against the asphalt as a faint light poked into the dark. That's what she saw as vividly as he stood before her now. How could she tell him by nightfall he'd be in the worst kind of danger? She couldn't. That was the problem. He wouldn't believe her anyway. Nobody would.

Somehow, she had to save him.

She shifted her focus to a more pleasant notion. "You will have a set of twins—" The woman who'd linked her arm with his snorted.

Katrina raised her brows. "And a wife whose hair is as rich a brown as yours." The first part was true, the one about the twins —a boy and a girl. The second she definitely fabricated. Maybe wishful thinking, as she hadn't seen any indication of what his wife would look like. Certainly she only wanted to provoke the blond. Though, if she hadn't colored it, perhaps she had dark hair underneath. Katrina couldn't tell.

She hadn't had that much fun since telling a snot of a woman her husband was gay. It was true of course. What she said didn't count though. No matter what fortune tellers told folks, they knew they made it all up in fun and jest.

The man seemed pleased to hear the news about having a brunette for a wife. His mouth turned up in an amused fashion, despite having a blond clinging vine who grasped his arm, cutting off the circulation, Katrina imagined.

The woman reached for the money, but the man shook his head. "She earned it. Thanks, Madame Sascha, for the enlightening reading. Twins, eh?" He chuckled as his date snorted again.

When they strolled off, he gave a backward glance and winked at Katrina. She smiled, tickled she'd amused him. Done for the day, she pulled the flap down over Sascha's booth.

Despite it being a little early as the fair wouldn't end for another twenty minutes, *she* had finished for the day, well, at least as far as telling fortunes was concerned. For now, she had to find out who the tall dark stranger was and save his life.

First though, she had to buy the tickets for her booth with the money the man had paid. He hadn't wandered far with his blond babe and she figured as much as the two stood out in a crowd, she couldn't lose them.

She was wrong.

By the time she reached the lady at the ticket counter, James Bond and his girlfriend had vanished from sight.

Katrina could kick herself. Sascha could lose her lease if anyone had seen Katrina take cash from the man. Her cousin needed the extra money so she'd *had* to exchange the cash for the tickets. But there was no way she wanted to lose sight of James Bond either.

With tickets in hand, she shoved them into her purse, then dashed through the dwindling crowds. She saw no sign of him as she searched the myriad of faces. Her heart thumped hard. She'd lost him for good.

Maybe they'd already left the fair and had headed for the parking lot. She hurried her step toward the acres of cars parked in the grass.

Then she spied them. He opened the door to a high-priced model silver sports car. She had no idea what the brand name was, but she assumed it cost plenty as sleek as the vehicle looked. He whipped around the front bumper, then headed for the driver's door. She focused on his license plate.

TXStud.

Was he advertising, or what? Her admiration for him plummeted to lower than low. But what had she expected? The real James Bond starred as a stud, so why not this guy? Still, she had to rescue him, despite the notion. *A stud. Right.*

She yanked her car door open. The silver vehicle, turned gray, had been well-loved, owned by three different people already. She twisted the key in the ignition. *Nothing. Not a sound.* The starter had died.

"Need a ride, Katrina?" a bald-headed man asked. The man, who shaved his head for the look, not to conceal the loss of hair, stood next to her, smiling sweetly. She hadn't even heard his approach, though the pungent pine-smelling cologne he bathed in would have reached her first if she hadn't been upwind of him.

"Sure, thanks, Baldy." She slammed her door shut, then walked with him to his vehicle.

Acting as the fair's coordinator of booth sales, and despite her disinterest, he wanted to date her. "Guess Sascha couldn't make it in today."

"Out sick."

He opened his tomato red SUV's door for her. "Are you going to fill in for her tomorrow?" "If she needs me to."

"Any plans for dinner?"

"Yes."

Not really. Chasing after the hunk was her only plan for the evening, but without a vehicle, she worried she couldn't even do that. Maybe, though, she could borrow Sascha's car.

"If you change your mind, you know where to reach me." He winked.

"Thanks, Baldy. I really appreciate your help." She couldn't let him know how much she liked a man with a full head of hair she could run her fingers through. Or that his cologne overpowered her keen sense of smell to the point of being nauseating. Or that when he drew close, his raw onion breath or the wad of tobacco he often chewed didn't make him kissable. And yet in the looks department, he could have been a model for some high-priced men's magazine. Still, she'd never been interested in him the way he seemed to want to take their nonexistent relationship further.

When they arrived at her apartment, she thanked him again. She'd only substituted for Sascha three times at shows that year, and twice her car had given out on her. Financially, she just couldn't see splurging on a new vehicle. Not yet.

She waved goodbye to Baldy, then hurried to Sascha's apartment. When her cousin opened the door, Katrina smiled. Sascha sported a head of riotous red curls and wore an even wilder orange outfit with splashes of aqua and purple flowers. She whispered, "How did it go today, Katrina?"

"Busy. How are you feeling?" She didn't want to seem insensitive and rush her, but she needed a car. *And quick.* She crossed the living room and dumped the fortune telling sales tickets on the coffee table.

"So, so. If my voice doesn't come back by tomorrow morning, could you work my booth again?"

A sure-fire way to lose a prime booth location at the fair was to leave it unmanned during the three-day weekend show. And a waiting list long enough to cover from one end of the state to the other included all kinds of eager shopkeepers just waiting to replace Sascha the Sensation, if given the opportunity. "Certainly, Sascha."

"I noticed Baldy brought you home again." Her cousin collapsed on the red vinyl couch and waved for her to sit on any one of the eclectic mix of seating she had in her living room. They ranged from a well-worn wooden lawn chair to a white fur-covered footstool, the vinyl couch taking center stage.

"Starter problems." Katrina sank into the feather-filled cushions of a winged-back chair, her favorite of all Sascha's pieces of furniture. "Listen, would you mind if I borrow your car for a bit?"

"What's up? You rarely go out at night."

"There's a really good looking guy who came to the fair whose life is in danger. I have to save him."

Sascha coughed as she laughed. "Okay. His name?"

"Texas Stud."

Sascha laughed again and grabbed a tissue to wipe her eyes. "You have all the luck," she whispered. "So does Texas Stud have any other name?"

"Actually that was the name on his license plate."

"Camden Worthington?"

"What?" Jeez, leave it to Sascha to know the guy.

"Big shot in Dallas. Owns several businesses. Who'd ever have thought he'd go to the

Perrytown fair. Surely he wasn't alone though."

"No, he had a blond dame Super Glued to his arm."

"Blond? Yeah, that's the way he likes them."

"Lots of them?"

"Yeah, like his license plate states, he's a stud." Sascha took a sip of orange juice.

Katrina tapped her fingers on the arms of her chair. Now she really wasn't in much of a mood to save him. She shifted on the antique cushions. "How do you know about him?"

"His family hired me for a reading for a party they threw last year. That mansion of theirs is really something. I gorged myself on caviar and lobster... hmm, pretty great stuff. They loved my show and asked me back. In fact, I'm scheduled to go there next week. They had over a hundred people at the last gathering, and it overwhelmed me a bit. I certainly could have used an assistant.

Want to go with me this time?"

"Well, if I don't save the stud's neck, they may not be having the party at all."

"So where is it you're supposed to rescue him?"

Katrina shrugged. "Haven't a clue. Thought maybe you could tell me... give me a hint from your crystal ball."

Sascha's orange painted lips broke into a grin. "Didn't I tell you... the crystal ball's been on the blink the last few shows?" She grabbed another tissue from the box. "While you're out, can you get me some more orange juice and another box of tissues?"

"Sure thing. Thanks a bunch."

Katrina hopped up from the chair, though she wasn't sure what made her so exuberant about her mission. Not that she wanted the stud to get hurt or anything, but she wasn't certain she'd ever find him. And what was she saving him for anyway? The blond with the pedicure?

Then she suddenly had a recollection. "Oh, in my vision he wore a tux when he faces trouble."

Sascha rubbed her chin. If anyone knew about the happenings in Dallas, she did. She had attended enough rich kid birthday parties to always be in the know. "Tonight," she raised her finger in the air, "there's a gala event at Lemoyne's."

"Lemoyne's?"

"By invitation only, though. If you're thinking of crashing the party, don't. They're very careful to check the invitations. Don't want to give out free drinks and hors de oeuvres to the masses after all. You know how rich folks are."

"I guess they don't want a fortune teller there."

Sascha smiled. "Well, if you don't go in the front entrance and come in as part of the wait staff, there might be a way."

"You don't mean like serving drinks and the like. I'd never be able to balance a tray of beverages, not in a millennium."

"The owner will let you in, if I ask him. Damon owes me a favor."

"Not as wait staff."

Still grinning, Sascha shook her head. "No, but all the women wear black. You'd think you joined a funeral procession the way the women dress." She sipped her orange juice. "Got anything black?"

"No. I don't wear it... doesn't do anything for my complexion or hair color."

"Anything dark at all?"

"I have a dark brown suit."

Sascha wrinkled her nose. "No. I mean, it's perfect for office work, but not for evening wear."

"I guess that shoots that down." Katrina dropped back into the well-worn cushions. "Any other ideas?"

"You can take a look at my wardrobe."

Katrina had never seen Sascha wear anything sophisticated, only broomstick skirts and splashy colorful blouses. She was a wildflower in a sea of denim blue. Always noticeable in a crowd. If Katrina wore her clothes to the gala event, she'd definitely be out of place. "Probably a little colorful for the affair."

"Fresh out of ideas, Katrina."

"I'll take a look at my things." Then she considered a possibility. "I do have that burgundy gown. Do you think maybe that would do?"

"Sounds like a winner. Looked great on you the time you wore it to our cousin's birthday party. Off the shoulders, cut nice and low. At least the guys will never notice the color. Hand me the phone, and I'll make a call to Damon. You should arrive about an hour earlier than the event. He'll hide you away until it's time to let you in. He probably can give you some kind of job, like overseeing the placement of flower bouquets or some such thing. Then you can just blend in with the guests when they arrive."

"Okay. Thanks so much for everything."

"You're welcome. I have to warn you though, if you save Camden's life, it won't mean squat to him."

Katrina rolled her eyes.

"That's the way it is with those high breeds. If you were a princess, he might take notice, but without papers, he wouldn't take a second look at you. Even if you save his well-built hide."

"I'm not interested in settling down with the guy. I just have to rescue him, that's all."

"Yeah, I know. You've rescued what? Three dogs and two cats in the past month. Not one of the pet owners offered you a dime. Not even when you ruined your clothes climbing into that septic tank for one." She took a deep breath of exasperation.

Katrina knew Sascha could barely wait to regain her powers again. "Just a few more days, Sascha. You'll have them soon."

"Yeah, well I won't make the same mistake again. Two long years. You know it's like losing one of your senses. For all those years, I've had to readjust to not having it. And I've hated every minute of it."

"We'll celebrate big time when you have full use of them." Katrina felt badly Sascha had lost them due to her involvement with Damon. She should have listened to their family. Having relations with someone other than her soul mate, brought about her loss of powers. She should have been more careful. But Sascha still had a place in her heart for him.

"Yep, at the party at the Worthington's. The two of us will be invincible." Sascha pointed her painted orange nails at the kitchen. "Car keys are on the center counter."

Katrina stood, then crossed the living room to the kitchen. Grabbing the keys, she waved to Sascha on the way out. "Do you mind if I bring your stuff by *after* the gala event?"

"That would be fine. Besides, I'm dying to know how it all turns out." Sascha punched numbers on the phone then said, "Hello, Damon, honey? I've got a favor to ask of you. Yeah, listen, a cousin of mine needs to get into the gala event this evening. It *is* a matter of life and death." She chuckled. "Her name is Katrina Landry, and she's not after any of the eligible bachelors. She's acting as bodyguard for one of the men."

Katrina paused at the door to hear what Damon's response to that was.

Sascha chuckled. "Camden Worthington. Okay, bye, darling." She coughed, then said, "All set, Katrina. Have a great time."

"What did Damon say about my being the stud's bodyguard?"

"You wouldn't be the first, nor the last. Damon's got a great sense of humor, however."

"So he thinks I *am* after one of Dallas' most eligible bachelors?"

"Most assuredly. You don't think he truly believes you could be there to save Camden's life, do you?"

"You're right. I'm not sure dressed in a gown I'll have much luck, either. See ya later." She prayed this wouldn't be a disaster.

PRESCOTT WORTHINGTON ADJUSTED his bowtie again, smoothed down his dark hair, then hurried out of his bedroom. He hated these gala events, and he hated taking Starla. But his parents were hopeful he'd marry her someday. Still, if he'd had anyone else in mind, he'd have taken her.

Starla had totally annoyed him at the fair earlier. He hadn't realized how clingy she could be when she wasn't in her natural environment—high classed dances or exorbitant malls. It had been his idea to go to the fair in the first place to get away from the pressures of work. And he'd really enjoyed the outrageous food, from the turkey legs to the cotton candy.

The entertainment had been a delight, too, especially Sascha the Sensation's funny predictions for the two of them. Now she acted like the kind of fun-loving girl he wouldn't have minded taking to the dance. She could have really sparked up his evening.

Twins. He shook his head as he smiled. Starla sure had been miffed. Tore into him all the way home about not taking the money back for having a fake reading. What did she expect anyway? Fortune telling predictions were just for fun.

He straightened his tux. In his mind's eye, he could still see Sascha's green eyes sparkle with mischief as she did her reading. And more than once he'd had to control his urge to leer down her blouse, cut nice and low, revealing a good deal of cleavage. Her long nails had mesmerized him as they swayed over the crystal ball, and he'd wished she'd rake them over his back to scratch the itch she'd created. To his surprise, his body reacted to the image of her, his briefs tightening instantly.

Trying to quell the passions running south, he thought of how Starla had irritated Sascha. The fortune teller had fun getting back at her though. He'd fought the urge to laugh out loud when Sascha had called him Starla's brother. He'd never seen her so incensed. And the twins decree, cinched the deal. Starla didn't want children, ever. Twins were worse than anything she probably could have ever imagined, except possibly triplets.

Then too, besides his dealing with Starla, the businesses were getting to him. He needed a vacation. Somewhere away from the glamorous crowds. Some place simple and just plain fun. He felt drained, lacking in any desire to help manage the furniture stores and restaurants he and his family operated in a three-city area. He wanted a break from the pressure of constantly expanding their empire, respite from the headaches he suffered, caused by the constant worry.

He met his older brother in the foyer. "Thanks for letting me use your car earlier, Camden." Prescott pulled his keys out of his pocket. "Yeah, got yours back all right?"

"Delivered while we were at the fair."

Camden shook his head. "I imagine Starla had a fit being taken to a place like that."

"You're right. But then again, she didn't have to come. See you at Lemoyne's." He took a ragged breath, wishing she wouldn't attend the ball either.

"Going kind of early, aren't you?"

"Yeah. I've got to have a word with Damon about Mother's birthday celebration next week."

"See you there. Oh, you are picking up Starla for the event, aren't you? I heard you'd really waited late to even ask her."

"Meeting her there." Prescott knew where his brother was headed with the conversation.

"Well, if you get tired of her, you know me." He waggled his brows.

Yeah, he knew that's what Camden had in mind. But Prescott didn't really care if his studbrother wanted Starla. That was the problem. He just didn't have the kind of feelings of protection or jealousy he should have had with the notion his brother wanted a chance with her. Without responding, he headed outside to his car, figured he'd make his appearance, and leave early.

Anything had to be better than this.

Katrina left Sascha's apartment, then pulled the door shut. She strode across the lawn to her own place. Would the burgundy dress blend in somewhat with the new fashions the other women would wear tonight? She hoped so. A chameleon, that's what she wished she could be.

After walking into her studio apartment, she shut the door closed. Glancing at her watch, she realized she only had another half-hour before she had to arrive at Lemoyne's. She quickly yanked her closet door open. The burgundy gown hung in the farthermost corner of her closet, still scented with lavender. If nothing else, she'd smell good.

She pulled the gown out of the closet and laid it on the bed. Then she considered her pumps. The burgundy ones that matched were a tad high, though they gave her a bit of height. Could she manage to stomp around in them for very long though? And if she had to run to save Camden, could she? She doubted she could. Still, nothing else would do. Her black pumps had lost a heel and her white ones would be gaudy with a burgundy gown. Sighing with vexation, she grabbed the burgundy shoes.

Her gypsy clothes hit the floor, then she slipped into the gown. To her relief, it still fit, only her breasts had filled out a bit since the last time she'd worn it. Yet, she had nothing else half as glamorous.

She tried on her stiletto heels and groaned. They fit, but she hadn't worn anything that high since she'd dressed in the gown two years ago. Hopefully no one would ask her to dance. She'd fall and break her own neck, forget saving Camden's.

Kicking off her shoes, she hurried into the bathroom to freshen her makeup. A light blush to her cheeks, a green shade on her eyelids, and her green eyes sparkled. Well, she might not look like the belle of the ball, but she'd make do.

She stared at her gown and tried to pull the bodice higher. She hadn't remembered it being that low cut. Of course, she hadn't had quite as much cleavage the last time around either.

The extra pounds looked good on her... rounded out the curves nicely. How she could have ever thought being as skinny as the woman at the fair with James Bond earlier would have looked appealing, she couldn't fathom now.

She returned to the living room, grabbed her shoes and beaded purse, and headed for the door. She had no time to lose if she intended to arrive at the gala event early. And she didn't want to louse up her chances at getting a free invitation because of her tardiness.

Her heart fluttered unsteadily as she climbed into Sascha's car. She didn't like to pretend she was someone she wasn't. The notion she might get caught sneaking into the by-invitation-only event nagged at her.

Then again, like it or not, she had an all-important mission... save Camden Worthington, the self-professed Texas stud.

But as she grasped the doorknob on the inside of the car to yank the door shut, a shadow of a man appeared in her window, and he grabbed the handle from the outside and held it firm. Katrina gasped to see the raven-haired man materialize so suddenly, soundlessly out of nowhere. Standing six foot, four and thin as a willow sapling, she assumed she could push him over with a poke of her finger, but his voice was dark and threatening.

"Miss Landry, come with me."

"What do you want?"

"To help you keep your family's secrets."

Heart pounding, she stared at him uncomprehending. Was he threatening her? A blackmailer? No one exposed the family and got away with it. *No one*. If he knew about their abilities, surely he realized that.

Still, she had to find out what he was up to. "I've got an important errand to run. Can I meet you right afterward?"

"*Now*, Miss Landry. There's no time to lose."

Her family came first, always had. Keeping the secret was her ultimate goal. She tapped her fingers on the steering wheel as she considered the image of 007 from the fair... tall, dark, and devastatingly handsome. He needed her help, too.

The question was: who needed her more?

2

P rescott rubbed his temple, infuriated that another one of his headaches had returned. Determined to reduce the stress in his life, he knew his way of living had to change drastically. He'd even seriously considered not attending the ball and asking Camden to handle the affair. Camden enjoyed the crowds and hobnobbing more anyway. But the annual event to promote their businesses was Prescott's task this year, and despite the throbbing in his head, he'd handle it.

A collision in the fast lane on the route to Lemoyne's delayed his progress to his further annoyance. Anything that could go wrong, would. He only hoped Starla would be delayed, too... preferably all night long. Even thinking about her for an instant sent another twinge of pain to his forehead. Tonight, he'd break it off with her for good. He'd tried unsuccessfully twice before. But she'd always managed to worm her way back into his good graces. Not tonight. Not the way he felt about her.

But something else bothered him. He couldn't quite put his finger on it. Something about Sascha the Sensation. Her touch had sent a thrill of interest coursing through his blood, and yet she acted as though he'd burned her with his hand as she withdrew hers so quickly. In that second, her green eyes caught his, and he swore she was concerned about him.

He sighed a ragged breath. He really needed a vacation.

KATRINA GLARED at the dark-haired man as he still held the car door handle. No way was he going to make her do what he wanted her to. "I'll meet you back here in two hours."

Before he had a chance to speak, she jerked the car door from his grasp and slammed it shut. She quickly slapped the door lock down. Twisting the key into the ignition, she turned to see the man mouthing the words, "You'll be sorry."

Then he pulled a phone off his belt loop.

Was she wrong to put the Texas stud ahead of her family? Camden's dark brown eyes willed her to protect him. Her family would just have to understand.

She floored the gas pedal. She was bound to be late to the event now. Would Damon still let her slip in without an invitation?

When she arrived at Lemoyne's, she cut the engine. She'd been here with her family for dinner one evening and knew the layout pretty well. The place, a converted brick warehouse, entertained the locals and surrounding population...a spot of romantic ambience away from the hustle and bustle of big city life. The restaurant served five-star meals while the ballroom provided elegance for weddings and other functions.

She slammed the car door on her gown, cursed, then released it and rushed into Lemoyne's. Though her heels were giving her fits, she hurried through the restaurant, furnished in dark burgundy and forest green. Overhead, soft piano and harp melodies filled the air, none of which soothed her concern.

She continued through the hallway decorated in oil paintings of pastoral scenes that hosted the restrooms and led to the ballroom. Chandeliers washed the room in light. Piped in music from the restaurant added to the tender mood. Another hallway led to the outside for guests using the ballroom exclusively.

All she could do was hope she hadn't messed up her chance to save Camden. Her heart hammered as she found no sign of anyone in charge, just some wait-staff setting up the bar. Katrina tucked a curl of hair behind her ear, attempted to tug her bodice higher, then stepped into the ballroom.

Nobody paid any attention to her, so she walked straight to a table covered in floral decorations. She didn't adjust them but ran her fingers over the soft burgundy rose petals, pretending to inspect them, in case anyone wondered what she was doing in the grand ballroom so early.

Then she spied a man dressed in a tux she assumed to be Damon, the owner of Lemoyne's, and as redheaded as Sascha, crossing the floor to greet her. She'd never met him before as Sascha had seen him on the sly. After Sascha lost her powers due to her involvement with Damon, Katrina had never wanted to meet him. But the man had a disarming manner and a pleasing smile.

"You must be Sascha's cousin." He touched her arm and guided her toward the other end of the ballroom to speak to her in private. "Mr. Worthington just arrived. So if you need to protect him, I thought I'd let you know that his vehicle just pulled into the parking area."

He spoke softly, and she could see why Sascha had been intrigued by the man. His eyes as azure as the sparkling Caribbean waters took in her appearance as if he memorized every detail. Did he know about her special gifts too?

"Thank you, Damon." She tried to keep a cool composure, but her stomach fluttered with apprehension. The stud couldn't see her at Lemoyne's. He'd know at once she played the fortune teller role at Perrytown and wouldn't have an invitation to the ball. Then where would she be?

Damon walked off, and Katrina looked around the expansive room for a place to hide. When the building filled with partygoers, she'd have no trouble keeping out of Camden's sight, though he'd remain in hers. For now, only the wait-staff worked, busily setting up platters of cheeses, shrimp, oysters, crab legs, crackers, olives, and pickles on three white-clothed tables against the wall.

From the hall that led outside to the parking lot, Damon's words echoed off the walls as he spoke, sending a trickle of a chill down Katrina's spine. "Mr. Worthington, we have everything pretty well planned. Did you wish to inspect the food?"

"Thank you, yes."

She hadn't realized the Worthingtons had actually hosted the party at Lemoyne's. Katrina slipped out of her heels and sprinted across the room. She hoped she could make it to the other side before the stud caught sight of her. Then there'd be the police and the reports, and whoever wished him harm would be free to do it because she hadn't been there to stop the villain.

Poor Sascha would have to rescue her from jail with her raspy voice and no car.

Katrina slid into the hallway leading to the restrooms, her nylon-covered feet slipping on the polished marble floors. She would have fallen, if it hadn't been for a man in a tux who grabbed her arm and pulled her close. A man who looked an awfully lot like the stud, only his eyes were hazel, not dark brown.

"A bit early for the party, aren't we, Miss..."

With all her planning she'd never even thought of a name to call herself. She glanced down at her shoes in her hands and looked up to see him smiling at her. She leaned down to set her pumps on the floor. When she wriggled to slip into them, he held her arm to steady her. He was way too close for comfort though, and as soon as she had her shoes on, she stepped back. "Lee Landry."

It wasn't a total fabrication. Lee *was* her middle name, though she never used it.

"Well, Lee, why don't you come with me, and we'll get a drink before the party gets going. I'm Camden Worthington, by the way."

She gulped the next breath. Camden...Worthington...the stud? Who was the other man then? The one who was driving the sports car at the fair? A brother? Had to have been. He looked too similar not to be.

Camden walked her across the floor to the bar. There was no sign of Damon or the man he had been talking to. Then she realized he'd call the man Mr. Worthington. Was it Camden's father he had spoken with?

Damon's face wore a silly grin, undoubtedly amused to see her with Camden when he returned to the ballroom. Camden, the guy Sascha told Damon that Katrina was to safeguard. Only he wasn't the right one. She sighed tentatively.

Damon said to Camden, "Your brother went to make a phone call, Mr. Worthington. He said he'd be right back."

Ah, the other man was Camden's brother all right. The one she must have met at the fair. Unless he had another. The place could be crawling with them. Sheesh. She should have asked Sascha more about the family.

"Fine. Can you open the bar a little early? Miss Landry and I would like a drink."

"Sure thing, sir." Damon motioned to the bartender to serve them.

To her relief, guests flooded into the room at a welcome rate shortly thereafter. Before long, women in their black gowns, some cocktail length, some dipping to their ankles, filled the hall. Their gentlemen companions wore black tuxes, reminding Katrina of a wake. Sascha had been right. Katrina had ended up at a funeral.

Camden greeted several gentlemen and their ladies as they passed by. He finally leaned close to Katrina, warming her neck with his breath and said, "So which family do you belong to?"

She smiled. "The Landry family."

He smiled back. "Of course."

When the music began, to her horror, he led her to the dance floor. He hadn't even asked her, just assumed she'd want to dance with him. She wasn't sure she'd manage in her high heels at all.

As soon as he swirled her across the floor, she caught sight of the other one...the one from the fair. His eyes fixed on her. She knew he was trying to figure out where he'd seen her before from the wrinkle in his brow. He probably wondered who his brother, the stud, had picked up this time.

She'd noticed, too, that not only were all of the women dressed in black, they had their hair up, if long, or cut short in smart, snappy hairdos. Not her. Her mass of brown curls hung over her shoulders, wild and untamed. Even without her costume-like clothes, she resembled a wild gypsy. She really looked out of place.

Luckily, her dance partner never spoke a word, though he held her way too close for not knowing her at all. His hand pressed in the small of her back to guide her, and more than once his fingers moved too low to suit her. Afraid to make a scene, she didn't respond, but when he leaned over to kiss her, she'd had it. She pulled away suddenly. "I see a friend of mine. Thanks for the dance."

Hurrying through the couples swaying to the music, she left the stud behind. When she reached the other side of the room, she glanced back at him, surprised to see his arms folded. He sported a grin from ear to ear as he watched her still as if to say the "chase is on, my dear." Then he walked back to the bar.

She took a deep breath, then turned her attention to where his brother had been but saw no sign of him. The music stopped, then after a few seconds it started up again.

From behind her a dark male voice said over the tune of a waltz, "If you'd prefer, maybe you'd like to dance with me instead of my brother."

The voice sounded familiar, deep and kind. She turned and faced the stud's brother, 007 in the flesh. Did he recognize her? She couldn't tell by the look of admiration on his face. If anything, he looked well pleased to meet her, with a vague sense of recognition tugging at the corners of his lips as they tweaked into a smile.

"I'm really not very good at dancing," she said.

"Nonsense." He took her hand and led her back to the dance floor. "I haven't seen such an extraordinary woman dancing here before. You do seem familiar though. Haven't we met?"

"Possibly."

He held her close, too, but not like his brother, not possessively. To her annoyance, her body warmed to his touch. He was supposed to be her rescue mission, like the cats and dogs she saved. Nothing more. She certainly hadn't planned to dance with him or to feel his body close to hers. His spicy cologne tantalized her, the heat of his skin turned up the heat of hers. She needed to save him, that's all.

Then she considered what he'd said...that he wasn't sure he had met her before. She really thought he knew who she was— that the charade had ended. Or could he just not imagine a gypsy fortune teller attending such a high-classed event?

She stiffened her back. Even if she had a broken-down car

and a studio apartment, it didn't mean she was totally a nobody. She was somebody, just not a rich somebody.

His fingers pressed into the small of her back like his brother's had, but his touch was gentler, guiding her in their dance steps. He danced well, and she loved the way he took control on the dance floor. He kept his fingers from dropping too low on her back like his brother had done, but in his case, she secretly wanted him to press them even lower.

What was wrong with her? No dates for several months—that's what was wrong with her. And her only offer, from a bald-headed guy—not that he wasn't handsome or kind, but she really liked a man with a full head of hair who smelled so much sweeter. Just like 007 did—a spicy scent that made her draw in a second breath and lean a little closer just to get another whiff of him—exquisite heady delight.

She avoided looking at him though. She hoped her nervousness didn't show, and that her hands hadn't grown too sweaty. He was too darn good looking and totally unavailable. When she shifted her gaze to take a peek at him, her breath caught in her throat. His eyes focused on hers, and her cheeks heated with embarrassment.

Was he stud number two? Sure.

Where was his blond bimbo? Probably lurking about somewhere, fuming to see he'd picked up another dame. Jeez, what if his girlfriend caught sight of her? Katrina hadn't considered that. Even if Camden's brother didn't recognize her, the woman at the fair was sure to. Women were usually so much more observant than their male counterparts.

Then she wondered why this Worthington had asked her to dance anyway. He preferred blonds like Sascha said Camden did, if 007's dating the woman at the fair indicated his likes in women. "I'm usually pretty good with names, miss, but I can't seem to place yours."

"I guess we're even. Lee Landry."

"Ahh, our competition."

What? Why would they invite their competition to a party? It must have been a rich folks' thing. "The Landry's have really done some great renovations on their buildings. I didn't realize they had a lovely daughter, though. You must have been away at college."

In her dreams. "And you are?"

His lips turned up in a smile—the same beautiful expression he'd used when she told his girlfriend he was her brother. Ugh. She was losing her self-control. She loved it when he smiled at her like that, as if she were someone truly special. She laughed at herself. He only found her interesting because she was different.

"It's kind of refreshing to get to know someone new. Usually everybody knows everybody at these events. I'm Prescott Worthington, Camden's younger brother."

"Ahh." Yep, the new-girl-on-the-block story.

"I knew we must have known you, or Camden wouldn't have asked you to dance."

Was it only her imagination, or had he pulled her closer at the mention of his brother's name? It was time to make a clean break of things. The notion Prescott would dance with her only because his brother had, really irked her.

Like two little kids, they fought over her. Only Prescott didn't have the nerve to step in and ask her. No, he had to wait until she rejected Camden. Then Prescott thought he'd see if his charms worked any better on her.

Camden raised his glass to her as Prescott turned her on the floor. Yep. They were in some kind of competition all right. A rich man's game. Wouldn't they be surprised to learn she wasn't in their league—not financially anyway—but she was really good at playing games?

She took a deep breath and when she did, he must have figured she was signaling how wonderful he made her feel or some such thing.

He whispered in her ear, "You're really a great dancer, Lee."

For a second, she wondered who he was talking about. *Lee.* Her parents only used her name in conjunction with her first when they were mad at her. Lee by itself sounded foreign.

"Thank you. But the music has stopped."

"If you'd permit me to, I'd like to have the next dance."

Over his shoulder, she spied the blond from the fair. Standing at the edge of the dance floor the woman with her arms folded and her eyes narrowed, looked pissed off to be sure. *Her* Prescott danced with somebody she didn't know.

"It appears someone's waiting for you."

As soon as he released his hold on her to turn to see who she'd nodded her head to, Katrina broke away from him and hurried off the dance floor.

She repeated her mission to herself. *Save Prescott, period.*

She wasn't interested in having anything further to do with the Worthingtons beyond that.

It wasn't that she didn't feel classy enough for them. She knew, though, when they found out who she really was, she'd be in jail for impersonating a rich person for certain.

When she stepped off to the sidelines, Camden worked his way over to her, and led her back to the floor. She chuckled under her breath. Both the brothers were the same in that regard. Neither asked, they just expected she'd wish to dance with them.

"You finished the dance with Prescott, but not with me. Why?"

She'd hurt his ego. Good. He shouldn't have danced with her like she was his.

"I don't even know you and you're too forward."

He smiled the Worthington smile. Both brothers were way too charming.

"He appeared to hold you just as close, but you didn't seem to mind."

Maybe that was because he didn't have stud on his license plates. Come to think of it, she didn't know what Prescott had on his car. It could be something worse.

"I know him better." She smiled slightly as Camden's eyes sparkled in the chandelier light. *Stick that in your pipe and smoke it.* She could see it now, Camden grilling Prescott, and his younger brother denying he knew her at all. Only, he remembered her vaguely. She hadn't lied. She'd met Prescott before, at the fair. Camden, she only knew by his license plates. Camden's lips curved up. "That's why he had a go for you until Starla arrived." *Starla, the blond, who snorted about having twins.*

Okay, well, since the stud wasn't about to release her for this dance, his grip on her assured her of that, she'd play the game a little while longer. "She didn't seem too pleased I danced with Preston."

Camden's eyes widened.

Jeez, Prescott, Katrina. Get the name right.

"Prescott." She chuckled. "Preston is the guy I'm dating." She was dying to laugh out loud. With her luck, she dated someone with the name of Jim Bob or if desperate, Baldy...not some Ivy League Preston, or Prescott or Camden, for that matter.

"Preston...," Camden was fishing for a last name, but she wasn't giving him one.

"Yeah."

"So how do you know my brother?"

"Here and there."

Camden cast her an amused smile. Yeah, she wasn't giving him anything to go on.

"So you've been seeing him secretly then, right under Starla's nose." He laughed.

"*Preston,* is who I've been seeing. Preston, not Prescott."

"Yeah, right. I never thought Prescott had it in him. Shows how little you know people, even when they have the same blood running through their veins." They both glanced at Prescott when he and his date closed in on their location. "I wondered why he'd been so reluctant to ask her to the event."

Yeah, well if Prescott balked at taking Starla to the dance, it certainly had nothing to do with Katrina. She noticed though, he held Starla stiffly away from his body. Her mouth drew down, full of scorn. Why did he even put up with her, if he wasn't inter-ested? Money. That's what made the world go round. She had money and so did he. Katrina's mother always said, "Money marries money."

When the dance ended, Camden still held her hand and moved her off the dance floor. She smiled, trying to think of some way to get him to leave her alone. "I'd heard you like blonds." She didn't know why she said it, only maybe to show she didn't believe for one minute he truly had any interest in her. As soon as the words slipped from her tongue, she realized the mistake she'd made.

He laughed. She figured he hadn't had this much fun in a good long while. "You've been inquiring about me?"

The blood rushed to her cheeks.

He smiled. "Another dance?"

"I'll sit this one out." She wanted desperately to fling her heels across the room. Already her back and the calves of her legs bothered her. Though she'd made a good show of her dancing so far, she was certain she'd soon tumble off her heels if she danced any more.

"A drink then?"

"I already had one."

"They're watered down."

"Thanks, no, Camden."

He folded his arms and looked her over. She turned her attention back to the dance floor, while Prescott spoke to an older couple across the room.

Camden nudged Katrina. "Looks like Prescott's speaking to your family."

Her whole body heated to feverish levels. When Prescott looked her way and smiled broadly, she wanted to melt into the floor like the wax they used to shine it with.

Camden said, "I didn't know the Landrys had any daughters."

Katrina looked back at him. "What?" He'd said something to her, she was certain, but she wasn't sure she'd caught his exact words.

"The Landry family. I didn't know they had any daughters."

That's what she thought he'd said. "Maybe they don't have any."

As soon as Prescott headed across the floor toward her, she grabbed Camden's arm. "I've changed my mind about dancing."

Camden led her to the floor without hesitation.

Not long after to her surprise, Prescott tapped his brother on the shoulder, interrupting them in their dance. "Excuse me, Camden, I want a word with Miss Landry."

"After the dance."

Prescott blocked his path, like a lion claiming a new lioness to add to his pride. Totally amused, Katrina wondered who'd win the male show of prowess. His gaze turned to her briefly as a chuckle escaped her lips. He faced Camden. "She's not who she claims to be."

Camden smiled. "That makes her more interesting then. Move, so I can finish my dance with her." This time Prescott stepped out of the way, but he wasn't finished with her, Katrina could tell. He crossed his arms in apparent irritation. She had one dance with Camden. Then Prescott would return for the kill. What was he thinking under that cap of gorgeous brown hair? Who was she if not a daughter of the Landry's? That's what he wondered.

Camden cleared his throat. "You knew my brother was coming to speak with you already. That's why you asked me to dance, isn't it? You're not a Landry, and you've crashed the party, haven't you?"

He tightened his hold on her as she tried to wriggle free. His smile returned. "We're in kind of a quandary here. The Worthingtons don't like it when Lemoyne's staff let...well, people into the event who haven't been invited. You never know what kind of people might end up here."

"Undesirables, yes, I know. I promise I won't take any doggy bags home with me. You can let me go now, Mr. Worthington."

"Not on your life. Prescott's waiting to pounce on you. It seems I've rescued you for the moment. He's really in charge of the ball this time around, and as long as you stay with me, I won't let him touch you."

"You? You're ready to feed me to the wolves."

"Not if you come home with me, share a nightcap, but I want the whole truth. I mean, women are always trying to meet me, but this wins first prize."

She rolled her eyes. She couldn't help it. Didn't he know how conceited he sounded? *Probably not.* He was good looking and rich. She wasn't surprised women would be after him, but no way did she want him to think she was one of them.

"Sorry, to disappoint you, Camden. I had other business here tonight, and it had nothing to do with you."

He still smiled, not believing a word she said. How could a mere peasant not want anything to do with the Texas stud, after all?

Across the room, Prescott had a heated discussion with Starla from the looks of it. She threw her hands upward and stormed toward the hall leading outside.

"You *couldn't* have been after Prescott," Camden said, his tone of voice indicating how foolish he thought the notion.

"Why not?" Again, the words tumbled out before she could halt them. Camden just annoyed her, but she hadn't any intention of letting him think she desired his younger brother or anyone else...more brothers, cousins, whatever...that belonged to the family.

The music stopped, but he held her to the middle of the dance floor still, waiting for the next dance to begin. "You were afraid he saw you in the ballroom...was that it? That's why you nearly collided with me in the other hall without your shoes on?"

Prescott joined them again as the music started. "Lee, I'd like this dance, if I may."

She wasn't sure what to do. Camden had promised to keep Prescott from probably calling the police on her. On the other hand, she had to save Prescott. Staying with him for the dance was most likely the best move on her part.

"I—"

Camden wrapped his arm around her waist and pulled her close. He certainly had all the right moves to win a girl, but she wasn't buying it. Each time she tried to squirm loose, he tightened his grip. "She promised me the next two dances, Prescott. Sorry, chum. Maybe you should make up with Starla."

He whirled Katrina away from Prescott. "Got you out of that mess, didn't I? You're with me now. You don't need an invitation. My brother can't do anything about it."

Then his face cheered with a smile of impish delight. "So now... what's your *real* name?"

3

P rescott fumed as Camden whisked the Landry imposter away. Who was she really and what business did she have there? Though it'd serve his brother right to get interested in a woman who was a phony, he was still family. Prescott had no intention of letting this woman or any other make a fool out of the Worthingtons. If he couldn't get rid of the woman, Camden was bound to take her home after the dance, given the way he wouldn't keep his hands off her.

Prescott couldn't believe how his brother clung to her, like Starla had done with him earlier in the day. Camden had even acted jealous, like he feared his younger brother would steal the woman away from him. *That* would be the day. He had no interest in Camden's conquests.

Prescott couldn't help thinking he'd seen her somewhere before though. She wasn't one of the Landrys. He'd kind of wondered. He hadn't believed they'd had a daughter. Then he thought she might have been a niece. No nieces, no daughters, according to the Landrys. So then who was the woman who claimed to be one of them? A gold digger is all that came to mind.

Still, when he watched her burgundy satin gown swish with her turns and twists, he wished she danced with him instead of his brother. Everything about her intrigued him... her hair cascading over her shoulders in thick dark curls, the fragrance of lavender that scented her skin and gown, and the design of her dress. The style... the low-cut bodice revealed pearl white breasts of ample proportion and the skirt flounced, giving her a special twirl that captivated his eye. And her eyes, the color of Spanish green olives, sparkled in the crystal lights reminding him of... The gypsy... Sascha the Sensation. *Damn.* She was the gypsy from the Perrytown fair.

Had she followed him to the... no, she'd been with his brother. How had she known about the gala event? He rubbed his temple in annoyance. She must have read about it some-where. She didn't seem to know any of the other guests. And nobody he'd talked to knew her, though several had asked him who the woman was that his brother was making such a fool of himself over... not their words, of course, but his.

When the music ended for the second dance Camden had promised to the imposter, Prescott waited at her elbow again. "All right, my turn."

He didn't pause for any objections, but pulled her away from Camden and hurried her across the floor. The music began again, and Prescott held her close. He would find out who she was, and how she sneaked into the invitation-only event. Then he would kick her out of Lemoyne's.

Instead, he fought the urge to kiss her. The woman drove him insane. Her fragrance, her breasts rising with every quick-ened breath she took, her tantalizing gown, all was enough to distract any man.

He knew she was scared as she tried to wriggle free, but he wouldn't let go... not until he knew all about her.

Hardening his resolve, he proceeded. "I've spoken to the

Landry's. Since they don't know you, I assume you have somehow managed to work your way into the event without an invitation. I want to know who you are, why you're here, and who let you in."

Katrina refused to show her fear and made another attempt to maintain some kind of distance from the man who overwhelmed her with his touch. "If you don't release me, Preston Worthington, I'm going to faint." Whatever hormones she'd stirred up in him, influenced her own and her temple grew fuzzy.

He narrowed his eyes. *"Prescott."*

Katrina had mixed up his name again. Her whole system heated in embarrassment. She couldn't believe she'd called him Preston.

"I'm not holding you that tightly, and if you think you're going to fake a faint—"

"You're crushing me. Let go."

"No. Tell me who you are."

His hand pressured her back possessively this time pressing her against his hard body, and his other held her fingers in a firm grip. If he'd been her boyfriend, she would have enjoyed the intimacy. But instead he overpowered her to her utter annoyance, making her succumb to his will.

She could see he wasn't letting her go, until he knew just who she was.

"I've already told you. Lee Landry."

"How about Sascha the Sensation?"

Her heart pounded way too rapidly. He remembered her. Then her fear turned to annoyance. *Well, high time.*

"You're not a Landry." His voice indicated he was proud of

himself for finding out her secret, almost giddy with delight, but couched in irritation to show he was the one in charge of her destiny. One wrong move and it would be the slammer for her.

"I didn't know the Dallas Landrys had exclusive rights to the name. For your information, I only filled in for Sascha."

The next words from his lips surprised her. "Twins, eh?"

She paused a moment to consider the shift in conversation. "A boy and a girl, if you must know."

"And Starla hooks up with a strawberry blond?"

"All I could see in her future was a week of hair and nail fixings and a teeth cleaning."

His mouth dropped open, and she realized he must have known her schedule... poor man. To think the woman had told him her whole boring schedule. She had to have been some humdrum blond.

"How did you—"

"Know? All women like that do such things. Am I not right?"

He just stared back at her, and she figured he didn't think so. Or horrors, he thought she was stalking the family and their friends. "And me? What do you see for me? You stopped reading so quickly—"

She hadn't much of a choice. Tell him the truth? He wouldn't believe her. Make up something? He wouldn't accept that either. Telling the truth always came easier anyway. Would he think she was crazy?

But keeping the family secret had been drummed into her since she was old enough to understand how different they were from others. How could she tell him the truth without compromising her family?

She took a deep breath. "Okay, look, the truth is, I saw someone trying to hurt you." Before she could say anything more, the music ended, and Camden butted in.

Prescott shook his head. "Sorry, Camden. I still need to talk to Miss Landry."

"I told you I invited her, so lay off, Prescott. The lady's with me."

The musicians took a break, and several of the guests watched the brothers as they looked intent on a fight. Katrina took Camden's arm. "Please, let me speak with Prescott for a moment. Then I'll dance with you when the band returns."

She had no intention of going to the Worthington's home after the event, and every intention of ditching Prescott as soon as she could. The stud would have to find another blond to add to his stables, and Prescott was on his own as far as whatever peril lay ahead for him.

Camden folded his arms. "I'll be waiting."

She nodded, then looped her arm through Prescott's. They walked into the hall, her shoes clicking on the marble floor, echoing off the walls. His body against hers, her arm resting on his, felt comfortable... like she really belonged with him. Until she thought of the beat-up car she owned, and the apartment she lived in. The notion took her right out of her fantasy dream.

"Anyway, as I said, I saw someone try to hurt you, and I had it in mind, I'd, well, watch your back, so to speak."

He raised a brow. "Okay, so the true story? You thought I had money, saw my brother's sports car, somehow found out who I was, and that I was attending this event, then met me here."

"Ahh," she said with appeasement in her voice. "How could I ever fool one as bright as you?

Yes, that's just what I thought."

"Only instead of catching my eye, you caught my brother's."

"Shame, isn't it?"

"You can't have him. When I tell him you're nothing but a gypsy fortune teller he'll have one good laugh—or maybe not. He could be pretty pissed off."

He walked her outside. The stars sparkled against the ebony sky while the lanterns from Lemoyne's cast shadowy fingers of light into the parking lot.

"Need your car, Mr. Worthington?" a valet asked as he hurried to meet them.

"Do we?" Prescott asked Katrina.

"No. May all of your dreams come true, *Preston*." She smiled inwardly. His tan face reddened while his lips thinned. She leaned down and pulled off one shoe, than the other.

"What are you doing?"

"Leaving."

"But..."

She smiled at the change in his demeanor. Had he had a change of heart? Did he want to dance with her further? Or was he afraid Camden would be mad at him for chasing her away?

"What?" she asked, with an irritated edge to her voice.

She intrigued him. That was the matter. He didn't want to lose her for the evening. Not now that Starla had stormed off. Poor baby had nobody to dance with. She imagined that would be the day.

"I want to know the real reason for your being here."

"Will this put you in deep water with Camden if I leave? Do you think he might be a bit angry with you for chasing me off?" She headed across the parking lot. It was time to take care of the other business. The one with the man who threatened her family's anonymity. "Too bad, Mr. Worthington. Deal with it."

He didn't follow her, not at first. Then his footsteps closed in on her, and she turned to face him. She didn't want him to see the old model car she drove to the evening's activity. He'd be sure to think she coveted his money then.

She waved a shoe at him. "I'm gone. Poof. So leave me alone."

"I fouled up your scheming, didn't I?"

"I hear the music beginning. Why don't you find someone else to hassle?"

He hmpfd his annoyance. "You haven't told me—"

He never finished his words as high-beamed headlights blinded them. Before he could react, the vehicle cloaked in blackness appeared. Its deadly beams, the only thing they could see, barreled forward. Katrina shoved Prescott out of the way, falling on top of him in the process.

He hit his head on the pavement hard.

"Mr. Worthington!" the valet shouted, and ran in their direction.

Prescott groaned. Katrina, figuring he'd be all right, rolled off him, then jumped up, and ran for Sascha's car. The SUV disappeared down the road. Katrina had every intention of tracking him down, if she moved quickly enough. She dropped a shoe onto the pavement by accident as she climbed into the driver's seat. Shouting from other guests made her jerk her door closed. She tore out of the parking lot away from the scene of the crime in hot pursuit of the SUV.

Her head spun as her heart pounded sending the blood to her ears. She saved him. She'd accomplished her mission. Now she could forget she'd ever met the Worthingtons. But she still had to ensure the driver of the vehicle hadn't intended foul play. Then she'd take care of the other business... the one with the telephone pole of a man who'd regret he ever threatened her family.

When she pulled onto the highway, the image of Prescott's dark eyes still held her attention, and she nearly collided with a pickup truck. He wasn't going to be that easy to forget.

And the SUV had disappeared. The ebony vehicle just blended into the night and vanished. ***

"What the hell happened?" Camden asked as he reached

Prescott. He dropped to his knees and clasped his hand on his brother's forehead. "Call an ambulance."

"There's one on its way, Mr. Worthington," the valet said, cell phone in hand.

Prescott moaned. For an instant, maybe longer, he dreamed he danced with a dark-haired beauty, and then she was dragged away from him by some unseen force. Barely focusing, he saw a hazy form of a man. His brother? "Camden?"

He tried to get up, but his brother planted his hand on his shoulder and made him stay put. "The ambulance is coming. Just remain still." He turned to the valet. "What happened?"

"Mr. Worthington was walking his girlfriend out to her car. I was busy after that, and the next thing I saw was an SUV with its high beams on barreling across the parking lot full speed ahead. If it wasn't for the young lady shoving Mr. Worthington to the pavement, the vehicle would have struck him."

"Where's the woman?" Camden stood as the ambulance arrived, its colorful rotating lights spilling into the parking lot. "Where'd the woman go?" His voice was agitated, threaded with concern.

The valet dashed across the lot in the direction she had headed earlier for her car.

Prescott rubbed his throbbing temple. "Where is she, Camden? Is she all right?"

The valet shouted from some distance. "I found this!"

He ran back to them as a crowd dressed in evening gowns and tuxes gathered. "She took off her shoes when she stepped outside. This is her shoe, isn't it?"

Prescott held his forehead as he reached for it. Clutching the shoe to his chest, he said, "Yeah, it's hers."

The paramedics helped him onto a gurney.

"I'm all right," Prescott protested.

"He blacked out," Camden told the men.

"We'll take him to the hospital to have him checked out."

Damon hurried outside and apologized. "I've notified the police about the incident. They're on their way now."

Prescott held his head, trying to still the pounding inside, ignoring Damon. "Find the woman, Camden."

"Yeah, right. That'll be about as easy as your making up with Starla is going to be."

Prescott's head thundered with pain. All he could think of was the woman who'd saved his life. But had she really? Or had the whole thing been a theatrical farce? She pretended to see his future, then further faked that his life was in danger.

Sure, she'd had a friend drive the SUV and simulate a mad driver bent on his destruction. Then she'd exit the scene, only leaving her shoe behind for him to find. She'd know he had to find her... to return her shoe to her and thank her for saving his life. What did she think? That he was a moron? Sure. And maybe she even wanted a little money to pay for her heroic efforts, too.

His head hurt more just thinking about the whole sorted mess. Why couldn't she have been a Landry daughter after all?

KATRINA ARRIVED at Sascha's place, totally exhausted. She hadn't realized her mission would be that tiring. Saving cats and dogs proved easier. There was no sign of the long, lanky man who had threatened exposing her family when she returned, but she figured if he wanted money to pay for his silence, he'd show up sooner or later.

She considered the one burgundy shoe as she grabbed the bag of grocery items. If she hadn't been in such a hurry, she wouldn't have been so careless to have lost it in the first place.

Groaning, she approached Sascha's door in her nylon-covered feet.

Sascha still sounded terrible when she answered the door, her eyes soggy from the cold. Stepping into the entryway, Katrina carried the orange juice and tissues to the kitchen. She poured her cousin a fresh glass of juice and handed it to her.

"So how'd it go?" Sascha croaked, following her into the living room.

"Fine." Katrina collapsed on her favorite cushy chair and rested her nylon-covered feet on the coffee table. "I rescued Mr. Worthington. Only my feet will suffer for it for days."

"And I suppose you got nary a dime for your efforts."

"No, and I even lost one of my shoes." She sighed. "Do you want me to man your booth again for you tomorrow?"

"Sure thing. So what did you rescue him from?"

"An out-of-control car. I pushed him down in the parking lot out of harm's way, and he hit his head against the pavement. I didn't hang around after that. Everybody was coming to take care of him. I didn't need to stay any longer." She wasn't really sure what to think about the vehicle. Was it some idiot who'd had too much to drink? She'd really hoped that's all it was.

"He didn't thank you?"

"He hit his head hard and was disoriented, but there were others coming to his aid. Remember,

I hadn't wanted them to really know who I was. My mission was to save him, that's all."

Sascha sipped her orange juice. "He could have at least thanked you."

"Yeah, well, he realized I was the gypsy fortune teller at the fair today and wasn't happy I came to the dance without an invitation."

Sascha's eyes widened. "Oh. He didn't find out how you got in, did he?"

"No. I would never have told anyone, either."

Sascha took a deep breath. "Good. I need favors from Damon every once in a while. Didn't want to mess up my relationship with him. Course, I return the favors."

Katrina reached down and rubbed her aching feet. "There's something else, too."

Sascha studied her with concern. "I can't know what you're thinking until my powers return, but the edge to your voice tells me something's really the matter. What's going on now? Not anything more to do with the Worthingtons, is it?"

"No. A man met me here tonight. He wanted me to go with him so that he'd help me to keep the family's abilities secret."

Sascha's mouth dropped open, then she clamped it shut. "I'll call Aunt Meg."

Nodding, Katrina sighed deeply. Had she said or done something to let the secret out in the first place? Katrina knew she should be the one calling, considering what a strain it was for Sascha to speak, but she waited.

"Hi, Aunt Meg?" Sascha explained to her what had happened. "Yes, just a minute." Sascha covered the mouthpiece. "She wants to speak to you." Could things get any worse?

Katrina took the phone. "Yes, Aunt Meg?"

"Your Uncle Jimmy wants you girls to come home and live."

"But you don't?" She sensed her aunt felt Katrina had to handle the situation on her own. She was like that. She didn't believe in coddling. They had their unusual abilities for a reason.

"He's overly protective. You know what needs to be done."

"But only you and Sascha have the ability to—"

"You must find out who he is. He's targeted you for whatever reason. You have to take it to the next step. Find out who he is, and I'll take it from there."

"Yes, Aunt Meg."

The man would never bother them again once Aunt Meg got hold of him.

Katrina switched the phone off. "Do you need anything else? I really need to soak my feet." "What did Aunt Meg say?"

Smiling, Katrina shook her head. "Sorry, Sascha. You'd think as long as it's been, I'd remember you can't listen in on our phone conversations, not yet anyway. I just need to find out who he is, then Aunt Meg will take care of him."

"Oh, great. That should be easy enough to do." Sascha sighed with exasperation. "I'll help you all I can."

"I know you will, Sascha."

"If you can take care of my booth tomorrow, I'll be forever grateful. I might drop in to relieve you at lunchtime, but I don't know what good I'd do."

"Sounds great."

"Baldy had your car towed to the shop again for you."

"He's a sweetheart."

"He keeps hoping you'll go on a date with him, you know."

"I like a man with some hair, Sascha." Katrina rose from the chair. A full head of dark wavy hair just like Prescott had, the kind she could run her fingers through as she kissed his lips... when they weren't scowling at her. That's what she wanted. "And you know, when Baldy spits from chewing that tobacco of his, well, it just isn't very romantic."

Sascha chuckled. "Yeah, he argues a bit, too."

"Yeah, that also. See you tomorrow."

Katrina locked Sascha's door behind her, then walked to her apartment next door. After entering her place, and without turning on a light, she slinked to her sofa bed. She didn't want to soak her feet. She didn't want to think anymore. Sleep was all she wanted, and to forget the whole day had ever happened.

But as soon as she pulled off her dress, slipped into a flannel nightgown and climbed into bed, she could only think of

Prescott and the way he had held her close. How could she be drawn to a man so different from her? Therein lay the problem. It was the same for him. She served as a novelty to him as he did for her.

She couldn't get the scent of his cologne out of her mind, nor the way he had gripped her hand, like she belonged to him. Though she should have resented it, she felt an odd sort of comfort to know someone wanted her... if only to interrogate her.

AFTER THE ER doctor gave him the green light, Camden drove Prescott to their parents' palatial home where he and his brother had been visiting, to provide a bit of security for the place—despite that it was already wired for security—while their parents were away on their cruise. Preston had suffered no injury, other than a good-sized lump on the back of his head that made even his teeth ache. To think the fortune teller had given him such a headache for no good reason aggravated him even further.

In the den, furnished with the latest suede sofas in hunter's green, the chairs all upholstered in a leafy glade look with greens and burgundies, dark wood paneling on the walls, making the room appear to be a hunter's retreat—showcasing just a bit of their wealth—Prescott fixed himself a gin and tonic before he called it a night.

Camden soon joined him in the den, his look worried as he made himself a drink. "I questioned several of the wait-staff at Lemoyne's, but nobody knew the woman. None of the guests either. And the Landrys said she wasn't related to them, though they mentioned you had already discussed the matter with them. Lee said she knew you though when we were dancing. Was she lying?"

Prescott had no intention of telling his brother anything he knew about the woman. "Listen, it's really late and my head feels like it's ready to split. See you in the morning, Camden." Prescott finished off his drink, then headed out of the parlor.

"Yeah, okay."

At least for now, Prescott had gotten out of explaining where he knew the woman. Hopefully, Camden wouldn't think to ask him about her again. His brother was often that way, one minute interested in a woman, the next, he didn't even remember her name.

Prescott wasn't about to tell his brother he knew Lee as the fortune teller at the fair. Camden had acted so strangely about her, Prescott was afraid his brother might surprise him and attempt to date her. She was a total mystery, and he figured that's what intrigued Camden so much about her. For that matter, that's why he couldn't get his mind off her either. The fragrance she wore, really different, unlike anything any of the women he had ever known wore—more natural and yet a touch exotic— just like she was. The way she'd caught his attention at the fair, a place he normally would never have visited, but he'd thought maybe if he dragged his ex-girlfriend to a few places she would never have been caught dead in, she'd figure it was time to find someone else to hang out with.

He should have left well enough alone, but he couldn't. He would find out who Lee really was and what she was scheming as soon as he could. He had no intention of Camden learning anything about it—or about her.

∽

BUSINESS HAD BEEN SO brisk at the fair all morning, crazy, nutty, from the man's two kids that upset her table, sending her crystal ball to the grassy area at the corner of her booth, to the woman who spilled her cherry coke in a puddle nearly in the same spot, that when Katrina spied her cousin headed for the booth, she gave her a wide smile filled with relief. Sascha returned the gesture, her considering expression saying she knew just how Katrina felt. It was noon, time to grab a quick bite, and a bathroom break. Not in that order.

"How's your voice?" Katrina asked, as she hopped up from her folding chair.

"Not well," Sascha croaked. "If I speak above a whisper, I turn into a frog."

Katrina laughed. "I'll hurry and get a corned beef sandwich so you can return home. I think all the kooks have been here today." All but the one who she hoped would be there... the lanky man, who had threatened exposing her family, if he ever showed up. She planned to give him a special reading, free of charge. "Want anything from the snack bar?"

"Already ate, thanks, Katrina."

"Be right back." Katrina wished she was done for the day. Wasn't that always the way? The more you wanted to leave work, the longer the day seemed?

She realized though, more than anything that she couldn't quit looking to see if HE would come, his girlfriend clinging to his arm—Prescott Worthington—the man who probably would like to strangle her after what she'd done to him. Despite saving his neck.

She kept telling herself she was paranoid. No way would a guy who would never normally come to such a thing, show up again. Only this time if he did, she doubted he'd spend anytime visiting the fair. No. He'd get right down to business and begin interrogating her all over again.

Would he believe her? She shook her head as she made her way through the throngs of people, heading straight for the booth that sold her favorite sandwiches and a well-deserved cup of iced green tea.

THIS TIME when Prescott arrived at the fair, he hadn't brought the ex-girlfriend, nor was he leisurely strolling down the dirt walkways, looking at all the new sights with intrigue. He had one goal and he was stalking toward that goal, trying to get to the fortune teller's booth while maneuvering through the hoard of people with every intention of shaking the truth out of the gypsy fortune teller as quickly as possible, then forget he'd ever laid eyes on her. If she thought he'd thank her for the phony show she put on the day before for him, she had another thing coming.

What made him angriest this morning was that Camden had wanted to learn all there was about her. Totally unexpected, his brother had even questioned Prescott further over a quick breakfast at Prescott's condo. Prescott wasn't telling him what he knew about the woman. Not when his brother found her so captivating. He wasn't jealous of Camden's interest in her or anything. He just didn't want the woman to win at the game she played.

When he finally could get a glimpse of the richly clothed gypsy booth, all he could see was an attractive redhead who looked nothing like the fortune teller he'd met the day before. Well, maybe her green eyes did. And the curve of her lips as she smiled at a potential customer walking by. Was *this woman* Sascha the Sensation?

He stalked to the booth, annoyed he couldn't see the woman who he couldn't quit thinking about. Not last evening as his head had pained him most of the night. Or this morning, with all Camden's grilling. Lee had said she knew Prescott, as if they had been fast friends! "Where's Lee?" he asked of the redhead, his tone demanding and irritated.

Her brows lifted while her orange-colored lips turned up slightly at the corners, her expression amused. "Don't know anyone by that name."

He knew it. The woman had made up an alias. His anger doubled in strength as he clenched his fists. "The woman who took your place here yesterday." He couldn't curb his acid tongue. No matter what, he was going to get to the bottom of this matter.

"Ahhh, Lee."

So what was she trying to pull? Cover up for her friend? She didn't know her by that name, and then all of a sudden, she did?

"Yeah, Lee. I need to speak with her."

"And you are?"

The woman merely whispered hoarsely. He could see why Lee had relieved her of her job the day before. But obviously the woman was still sick. Why wouldn't Lee help her out today? She was in hiding. She knew he'd come looking for her. And she'd make it hard for him to find her.

That was what she'd planned. She was a master game player.

He cleared his throat. "I'm Prescott Worthington."

The redhead's green eyes grew wide, and her mouth dropped open, clearly astonished. Yep, Lee had told her all about him. This woman might have even been in on the whole scheme.

"Surprised?" he asked. He loved to have the upper hand in a situation. The woman squirmed.

She closed her mouth and ran her orange polished nails over the tablecloth. "What did you want to speak to her about?"

"I believe this matter's between Lee and me. Where can I find her?"

He could tell by her hesitation, she meant to protect her friend. He tried another tact. "Listen, she might have told you she had lost her shoe at the dance last night, and I thought I could—"

"I'll pass it along to her."

"The thing is she saved my life." He nearly choked on the words. He believed that as much as he believed his brother planned on vowing celibacy. Groveling further, Prescott said, "I didn't even have a chance to thank her, Sascha. You *are* Sascha, aren't you? The woman who owns this booth?"

"Yes, I am."

She still hesitated to divulge Lee's whereabouts to him. He tried to think of some other way to get her to tell him what he wanted to know.

He considered giving Sascha his private cell phone number, but he was certain Lee wouldn't call him. "Sascha?"

"I'll tell her you stopped by to thank her. Do you have her shoe with you?"

"Seems kind of odd you would work today when you barely have a voice. Where's Lee? From what she told me, you and she are pretty good friends."

Sascha leaned back in her chair. "We are. That's why I'll tell her you came by to thank her." "I'll do it in person."

"Suit yourself."

He wasn't winning his case with Sascha, he could see. She plotted along with Lee on the whole thing. He wasn't leaving the fair just yet. "All right, you can give her my message."

"And her shoe?"

"I'll mail it to her."

"But you don't know her address."

"I will."

Without another word, he stormed off. He would find out where she lived, with or without Sascha's help. His head still hurt where it had met the pavement outside of Lemoyne's. The notion Lee had shoved him down with this faux scheme of hers, infuriated him further.

Then he spied a woman... *the* woman, walking toward him with a slice of pepperoni pizza in one hand and a soda in the other. Her hair curled over her shoulders in waves of dark chocolate shavings and her glossy pink lips smiled at a man who stopped to speak to her... his head as smooth as the tip of a baseball bat. Camden had told him she was seeing some man named Preston. Was this the man? Some old geezer without a speck of hair?

Well, maybe he wasn't that old, but late thirties at least. Perhaps he was in on Lee's scheming, too.

Prescott's gaze focused on her clothes next. His eyes made a dead stop at her blousy shirt. He could see clean through it and that's when he noticed the bald guy looking, too. Underneath, she wore a tank top the same color as her skin. He took a deep breath. *Get a grip, Prescott.* She's not naked under the nearly sheer blouse after all.

His gaze dropped down to the green and blue broomstick skirt she wore. It reached to her ankles, and she crossed her feet, clad in sandals decorated in shimmering glass baubles. Then she nodded to the man and continued on her way.

Would she run away if she saw him? Possibly. Prescott ducked into the crowd. He'd wait until she'd undoubtedly relieve her sick friend, Sascha, at the fortune teller's booth. And then? Well, then he'd get some answers from Lee. No more Mr. Nice Guy.

～

THE LOOK on Sascha's face of sheer panic made Katrina quicken her step. "What's wrong, Sascha?" She joined her cousin in the booth.

"He's here, but he's not the right one. You didn't tell me it was the younger brother you saved last night at Lemoyne's."

"Prescott Worthington? He's here?" Katrina sank into the other lawn chair. The day was half over, and she assumed if the man had entertained the notion of seeing her there, he'd given up on the idea. Now, totally baffled, her blood pressure rose while her hands grew sweaty.

"Yes, he's here. I assumed it was Camden you saved last night, not the younger brother. I've never met him before."

"I thought you said you'd worked at one of their shindigs."

"Yes, Camden and his parents and tons of friends were there. But not Prescott."

"He must have borrowed his brother's car to come to the fair." Katrina took a deep breath. She hadn't figured she'd feel this uptight if she saw him again, her stomach clenched in a knot in uncertainty.

"Well, Prescott's here now, and he's rather ticked off."

"Whatever for? Other than having one free watered-down drink and saving his life, that's all I did." Katrina tried to show bravado as she flipped her curls behind her shoulders, but she was a trifle scared. What if he wanted to press charges against her for trespassing or have her fined for stealing a drink? Nah, that would be too petty.

"Yeah, well, he said he had your shoe, and he wanted to thank you. Only he seemed pretty steamed. Not at all like a person who wanted to thank someone for saving their life."

Katrina didn't believe he wanted to be nice to her one bit. He desired something else for certain.

"Probably annoyed he'd have to feel obligated to anyone.

Debt of gratitude... that sort of thing." She lifted her pizza off the paper plate.

Sascha frowned at her pizza. "I thought you were getting a corned beef sandwich."

"Line was too long and I didn't want to leave you here alone for very long. Why don't you run along home? I'll be there in four more hours with the proceeds from today's sales."

"You don't want me to stick around in case he comes back? I can be a witness or provide moral support."

"I can handle the likes of him. Go home, and give your voice a rest. I'll see you in a bit. I'll even fix dinner for the two of us later this evening. Good old fashioned, homemade chicken soup.

How's that sound?"

Sascha leaned over and gave her a hug. "Sounds great. See you in a little while."

As soon as Sascha headed out the back of the booth, Katrina saw the lanky man watching her from at least thirty feet away at an angle. Before she could stand, a boy ran in front of her booth, chasing a fly-away balloon. Momentarily distracted, she caught sight of Prescott standing not twelve feet from the front side of the curtained table, watching her.

His expression was totally unreadable. Was he angry? Glad or surprised to see her? If she hadn't felt so uncomfortable under his scrutiny, she might have found the notion amusing.

She turned to see where the lanky man was, but he'd vanished. The Indian summer Texas breeze tugged at her hair... the fall day every bit as hot as a mid-summer afternoon. Facing Prescott, she saw his eyes locked on hers, and her whole body heated to fresh heights.

4

Prescott appeared dressed down today...well, as casual as Katrina imagined he could ever be. He wore jeans, but he'd probably just removed the price tag from them when he dressed in them that morning, they were that new. He still wore a button-down collared shirt, probably never dressed in a T-shirt in his life.

Had he ever made mud pies after a spring rain, or built sand-castles on a gray sandy Texas beach? She imagined not. His kind only visited posh white sand beaches on some tropical island and making mud pies was probably as foreign to him as milking cows.

Her brows rose as she considered his leather shoes. They looked like the style a preppy college student would wear, nice and neat loafers, an attempt at casual. And then she wondered why he'd dressed so *casually*. Maybe he'd felt out of place the day before. Returning her gaze to his face, she realized he studied her in return, just as thoroughly.

Okay, they'd had their once over. Now what?

He walked toward the booth.

Stiffening her back, she readied herself to let the showdown begin.

"Did Sascha tell you I came by to see you?" he said, as he stood in front of her booth.

"Sure, what are friends for?" Katrina tried to act nonchalant, but her stomach flip-flopped as if it competed in a gymnastics competition. Her hands grew sweaty again. Twirling the soda in its can, her eyes remained fixed on his. He wouldn't intimidate her.

He seemed at a loss for words, either that or his silence intended to torture her further. Well, if he wasn't going to speak, she would.

She opened her mouth and he pulled out his wallet. She snapped her mouth shut immediately. He cleared his throat. "I want to pay for your services."

Did he know how that sounded to her? Or was she just being paranoid his brother was the stud, and he was number two?

"A reading." She said the words, but she wasn't sure that's what he wanted.

"You didn't finish mine yesterday."

"Then put your money away, and I'll finish it."

He dropped the money on the table. Should she tell him to buy a ticket? Why should Mister Rich Guy not have to do what everyone else did—stand in line and wait at the ticket booth? Then she saw Baldy watching her from the booth across the walk.

She handed the money back to Prescott. "I didn't adequately provide you with your reading yesterday. You don't have to pay me for it again, sir."

"I insist."

Okay, well, she tried to be nice. "I can't take the money. You'll have to exchange it at the ticket booth, and then bring me ten coupons to pay for the reading."

"I didn't have to yesterday."

He could really be difficult. So could she. "Yesterday, Mr. Worthington, I risked losing Sascha's rental space by taking the cash. I had to exchange it for tickets afterward. This place charges the vendors ten percent of their sales. They won't tolerate getting ripped off."

He stared at her for a moment. Was that admiration in his eyes? He turned to look at the ticket booth. The last day of the fair for the weekend and the turnout had really picked up. At least fifteen people lined up to get tickets. She smiled. Would he, or wouldn't he?

Facing her, he smiled, challenge in his eyes. "I'll be right back."

She couldn't believe it. She imagined he never had to wait in line for anything. He'd walk in, and everyone would jump to satisfy his every whim. He strolled over to the end of the line and smiled again at her. Obviously, he intended to show her how determined he was, that he wasn't easily put off.

The business at her booth had been really slow, but all of a sudden things got busy. Soon, she completely lost track of Prescott.

After doing several readings, Prescott stood before her. What was there about him that made her heartbeat quicken? Sure he was handsome, but the way he watched her, like he owned her already when she really was his savior, not his conquest, got to her.

He handed her the ten tickets and held out his hand. "I want a longer reading. Since you know I have twins, tell me who I'll marry."

She didn't bother to even look at his hand as she couldn't see who he'd marry. A gap in her vision plagued her. The dark curly-haired toddlers played in a sandbox, chasing butterflies and six yellow Labrador retriever puppies. Prescott watched them, a grin on his face, one proud father. But the girls' mother never appeared. "Can't. I don't know the reason. I just can't see this for you." He had a look on his face like she faked the whole reading. She hadn't...not about this. He had two children without a wife, as far as she could see. Really bizarre. As she ran her finger over the palm of his hand, she wrinkled her brow. The boy's name was Preston. No wonder she kept getting Prescott's name mixed up. She'd never done that before. How odd. She looked up at him, and his lips still had amusement written all over them.

"Well? You're frowning. Is someone going to attempt to run over me again?"

"Your son's name will be Preston. But I suggest you change it so folks don't get your names mixed up."

"Preston? The same as the fellow you're dating?"

She'd forgotten she'd told Camden that. She guessed he'd informed Prescott later that evening.

Ignoring his comment, she ran her finger along the line in his hand. Touching him sparked a tingling throughout her body. She tried to ignore the sensation and concentrate on the reading. "You have a very long lifeline and should—"

"That's what all of the fortune tellers say. Tell me something that's not common medium gibberish."

She leaned back in her seat. *Medium gibberish.* Since the last time she'd touched his hand for a reading, she'd incurred a mission. What if someone still wished Prescott harm? She didn't want to have to explain herself to him any further or have to find a way to rescue him again. "I've paid twice to have this reading, Madame Lee. You owe me more."

"I saved your life, Prescott." Didn't that count for anything?

He reached for her hand and placed it on his own. "Tell me more."

Like Sascha had said about Camden...saving a Worthington's hide was worth squat.

Katrina widened her eyes, and she tried to pull away, but Prescott wouldn't let her. "Let go of me," she growled. Forced readings were a dangerous business...for her. She could end up in a trance for hours or worse. She'd done it twice before, once to help a friend who had lost a pet, and another, to look for a missing child. After those experiences, she'd never wanted to repeat it.

Finally, she managed to yank her hand away. "You know, Prescott, if you would just ask nicely—"

"You wouldn't do what I asked. So what dangers do you foresee this time? I could tell by the way you trembled, either you foresaw something terrible for me or my compelling personality made you—"

"Try pushy."

"I'm waiting." He folded his arms.

"You won't believe me." She crossed hers. She could be just as stubborn as him. Probably more so.

"Try me."

His dark eyes captivated hers, and she wanted to turn away, but she met his gaze with the same intensity. He wouldn't believe her, but she would tell him the truth anyway. See if he'd pay her to have any more readings after that.

"The same black SUV will make another attempt on your life."

"When?"

"I can't be sure."

She wasn't absolutely certain about the day or the time, but what did it matter? He wouldn't believe her anyway. Then again, she worried...what if someone did make an attempt on him a day or two later, and he had let down his guard?

She laughed at herself. He wouldn't guard against the threat.

He didn't believe her in the least and the notion really irked her. Though it wouldn't have normally. People generally didn't believe in mediums anyway for good reason. Most were fakes. But it bothered her Prescott didn't trust her. Not only that, but she could see she would have to save his rich butt again. "Maybe tonight or a day or two later. I can't be sure."

"How were you so certain about last night then?"

"In my vision, I saw you wearing a tux."

"Ahhh. When the hit-and-run driver makes an attempt again, what do I wear then?" He didn't believe a word she said. He was mocking her in jest.

"I don't know. All I see is the SUV headed straight for you."

"If you see me standing in the way of the vehicle, then you would know what I'm wearing."

"I don't see you."

He smiled. "Oh. So how do you know it's me who he's aiming for and not you?"

What an odd thing to say, but she wasn't really sure of the answer either. "Uhm, this happens to be your reading? Not mine, perhaps? I only see what fate awaits you, not me. If a vehicle attempts to run someone down, it has to be you."

"How come you saw me in the reading yesterday, but not today?"

"These things happen. Maybe because I was there to save you last night, that's why I could see you. Perhaps you won't be so lucky when he makes his attempt again if I'm not there to rescue you."

He chuckled. She was glad he could be so amused. Her skin crawled with goose bumps, however. There wasn't any way she wanted to be put in the position of saving him again. Yet she could see no way out of it.

A man behind him cleared his throat.

Several customers had lined up behind Prescott. Katrina

motioned to them. "Excuse me, Mr. Worthington, but your time is up."

He nodded, then stepped out of line. As a family of four formed in front of her booth, Prescott returned to ticket sales to Katrina's amusement. He was buying some more time with her. Good. Sascha could use the extra cash. So could she. When she worked for Sascha, they split the proceeds after paying for the booth fees and commission to the fair management.

After Katrina finished with the family's readings, a man stood before her who slipped a note into her hand instead of a ticket. Before she could speak, he hurried off.

Opening the note, she sighed heavily. *Meet me tonight, your place, midnight, or else. Lucky*

She glanced up at the next customer waiting patiently to give her the tickets. Drawing her mind back to the business at hand, she had every intention of making Mr. Lucky not feel so fortunate once she finished with him. Before he'd escape his fate, she'd know all there was about him, and then...she'd turn him over to her Aunt Meg.

By the time Katrina managed to get through the next eight customers, Prescott stood before her again. He grinned at her as if he'd won some kind of contest. She waited for the ten tickets.

Instead, he gave her a bundle. "I've paid for the rest of your time here today."

Could he do that? Nobody had ever done such a thing, probably not in the history of the fair.

She stared at him dumbfounded.

"Come on, Lee. You're done for the day. Let's have dinner."

She'd promised Sascha homemade chicken soup, but what she wouldn't give for a dinner with tall, dark, and handsome even if it was a little early in the day. "I have other plans. You've bought three hours of readings, nothing more."

That was telling him. Even if it wasn't what she wanted to say.

His teeth shown this time in a full-fledged smile. "With Preston? Dine with him later. You weren't going to be through here for another three hours anyway."

Well, she supposed that was true enough. Of course, her meal would be shared with Sascha, not some fake Preston. Plus, she didn't have to eat again, just fix the soup for her sick cousin. It could work.

"All right." She grabbed her beaded bag and pulled the fabric over her booth to close it. "So where are we going?"

PRESCOTT HADN'T REALLY EXPECTED her to agree to have dinner with him. He didn't know what was wrong with him. He'd intended to find out who she was and what she was up to...that's all. Instead, he paid a fortune in tickets to have the opportunity to dine with her? He was definitely losing it. Now he knew for certain, he needed a vacation.

"Some place rather casual, the way I'm dressed."

She glanced down at his jeans and smiled. "You look really nice. Do you own any T-shirts?"

As they walked into the parking area, he took her arm. She had no idea where he'd parked his car or what it even looked like...at least that's the reason he told himself that he wanted to hold her close.

Today, she wore another flowery fragrance, just as subtle, just as tantalizing. He had the greatest urge to nuzzle her neck with his face, to draw the scent from her skin with a deep breath. Her lips were still a glossy pink. He imagined she must have touched them up while he bought the last of the tickets. They sure looked lip-smacking good.

Her tank top, obscured by the sheer over-blouse she wore, dipped nice and low, maybe not as much as the burgundy gown she had worn at the ball, but sufficiently enough to interest the viewer's eye. More than once she'd caught him peeking at her blouse.

He'd felt guilty about it as his skin had prickled with heat. Then he straightened his back. It wasn't his fault she'd worn something to make any man take notice.

Now he had to figure out where to go somewhere quiet where they could talk. He had to get her to admit to her involvement with the fake hit man. He couldn't believe she'd continue the tale again today with her new reading.

How could she possibly believe her involvement in such a scheme would endear him to her? He laughed inwardly about her announcement that she would have to save him again. Next time they took a tumble together though, he wanted to be on top. The notion instantly brought an image to mind...his lips against hers, his body heating up with her touch, just like now, without even having her beneath his own. The woman turned him on faster than a match striking a matchbox spun it into a flame.

After thirty minutes, they arrived at a restaurant that appeared closed for business. She balked as he opened her car door for her. "What's going on, Prescott?"

"One of my family's businesses. We'll have a quiet dinner for two. The place doesn't open for another hour so that'll give us time to have a private party."

She squinted her eyes as she read the fine print on the hand-carved oak door. "Okay, it says they're open at four."

He cast her a dark smile. "You don't trust me?" She was the one who couldn't be trusted.

He unlocked the door, then walked her into the building. A

hostess hurried to greet them. "We didn't expect you, Mr. Worthington."

"We'd like a table for two and a bottle of red wine, best in the house."

"Yes, sir." The woman hurried to seat them, then headed into the kitchen.

"So what do you think?"

"It's a lovely place. Kind of Italian baroque."

Pleased she liked the place, he still hadn't any intention of getting sidetracked. Not being able to wait any longer, he began the interrogation. "Okay, let's get down to business. First, what's your *real* name?"

"Katrina Lee Landry. That's the whole thing."

"But you go by Lee?"

"Katrina."

He shook his head. She was some kind of character. That certainly explained why Sascha hadn't recognized the name "Lee" at first. "And you live—"

"Yep."

He leaned back in his chair. "Where?"

"I've given you my name because it doesn't matter any longer that you know it. But you have no need to know where I live or anything else about me."

"We're having a date. That's what people on a date do...they tell things about themselves."

She raised one sculpted brow. "You've paid for three hours of readings. That does not constitute a date."

"Okay, then tell me more about my reading. Why is someone trying to kill me?"

"I don't know if they're really attempting murder or just trying to scare you."

Yeah, just as he suspected. Maybe this guy Preston helped her with the charade. "Why would anyone wish to do either?"

"That, I wouldn't know. Perhaps it has to do with one of your businesses? An old girlfriend? Maybe somebody has a vendetta out for your family, competition, a terminated employee, even a case of mistaken identity. The list could go on forever. Have you made any enemies lately?"

The wine steward brought the wine. Maybe a little drink would make her slip up. Tell him the truth of the matter. He'd definitely delay dinner for a while.

When the waiter arrived to take their orders, Prescott said, "We'll need a few more minutes."

However, Katrina flipped through the menu and pointed at an item. "We'll have the stuffed mushroom appetizers."

Prescott nodded to the waiter who repeated the gesture and hurried away.

Was Katrina on to him? She probably figured he had every intention of softening her up. "Okay, so, Katrina, you said you saw a black SUV attempting to run over me after you had done the first reading. And then you rescued me."

"Yes. I saw you hit your head hard because I'd shoved you out of the way. I wouldn't have hurt you like that, if I'd had time to do anything else."

He longed to tell her what he really thought. See how she would react. He didn't believe her story for an instant. Mediums were all fakes. Nobody could see the future. Instead, he had to patiently extract the truth from her. He clinked his glass against hers. "To fortune telling and the like."

"Here-here, may it always bring you glad tidings."

He swallowed his wine with difficulty. "But so far, it hasn't."

"You can't blame me for that. I have no idea who wants you injured. Besides, doesn't the prospect of having twins cheer you?"

He laughed. "I guess if I consider it means I'll live long enough to father them, it would."

Her cheeks turned rosy, though she didn't seem easily embarrassed, and the notion amused him.

"What I still can't fathom, is why you can't see who my wife is. Is she Starla?" If she continued to play the game, he could too.

Katrina shrugged. "Both children are dark haired. It's possible she could be their mother though."

"You say the boy is named Preston. What about the girl?"

"I don't know. I only get bits and pieces. Like today, you had breakfast with your brother on a deck overlooking a lake. His toast, soaked in honey, dripped three pearls of the sweet, sticky substance onto his trouser leg. Half in jest, you told him he ought to use his napkin on his lap. To which he gave you a look that could have curdled milk, swore, and went inside to the kitchen sink to clean off the honey."

The waitress served the appetizers. Afterward, Katrina lifted a mushroom to her plate with her fork. Then she looked up and smiled at Prescott.

He quickly closed his gaping mouth. How could she have known what had occurred at his condo? His skin grew flushed in trepidation as if a ghostly apparition had sat down to dine with him.

"How did you know?"

"I'm a fortune teller, Prescott. You hired me to tell your fortune."

"No. How did you know about this morning?"

"These mushrooms are very good. Aren't you going to eat any?" She speared another. "All right. You were thinking about it. I don't know why, but the image popped into your mind. I've linked with you...not because I wanted to, but because you forced it on me. You shouldn't have done that, Prescott."

"What do you mean?" He wasn't aware he had forced her to do anything.

"When you wouldn't release my hand—when you forced me

to continue to look into your thoughts. Anyway, now we're linked. It won't last forever. Sometimes it can last for days, sometimes weeks. If I'm lucky only a few hours, but I doubt it—the way things are going for me lately."

She was some great storyteller. Still, he'd test her further. "Okay, what am I thinking now?"

"It doesn't work like that. Something triggered the image in my mind. You can't just have a random thought, then..." She stopped her speech and blushed.

He grinned. Not for one minute did he believe her, and yet when he thought about how much he wanted to bury himself in her, her cheeks reddened, and she stopped her speech. Had she known what he was thinking?

He laughed to himself. He'd have to watch what else he imagined doing with her, if she really could...nah, there was no way she could know what he thought.

She fingered her wine glass.

"What were you going to say?" he asked. "You didn't finish your statement."

"Just that sometimes something triggers the image in my mind. That's all."

He reached across the table and took her hand in his. "If I hold your hand, will this cause difficulties for you? We danced and nothing seemed to happen between us as far as this linking business goes. And what about Camden? Did you link with him also?" Prescott had every intention of unraveling the fairytale she wrapped them up in.

"I have to be doing a reading...most of the time. Sometimes I draw images from a person when we touch, but not always. It depends how much I'm distracted."

"So at Lemoyne's too much noise interrupted your concentration?"

"Something like that."

Yeah, he knew it. She had all of the bases covered. "And now?"

She smiled, he swore, with impish delight. "You're very charming, Prescott Worthington. But you will get no further with me than holding my hand over a dining table."

5

K atrina wondered why their meal orders hadn't been taken. Prescott glanced back at the waitress standing quietly in the wings and nodded. As if on cue, she hurried to the table.

Figuring the entire restaurant staff conspired against her, the notion still amused Katrina. "I'll have whatever you have, Prescott." Before he could speak, she changed her mind. "On second thought, I'll have a nice bloody steak."

He grinned at her. "I'd like the same. Filet mignon, Kat?"

Kat? Did he think she was his...well, he better not. "Filet mignon would be fine, *Scotty*." A muffled chuckle escaped his lips.

They finished ordering, and as the waitress scurried away, he leaned back in his chair, his lips permanently sealed in a smile. "I've never been called Scotty before."

"No one calls me *Kat*, either."

Was he pleased she had called him by a nickname? Guess no one had ever done such a thing to him. Or was he just amused she'd responded so quickly to his calling her Kat?

Only time would tell.

She tucked a curl behind her ear. "Sascha said you still have my shoe." He slid a mushroom onto his plate...the last one left. "It's at home." *Now* what was he pulling?

He must have read her thoughts. She swore his eyes twinkled with mischief when he spoke again. "I couldn't be certain you'd be at the fair today."

"You couldn't have brought it with you? Just in case I happened to be there?"

Katrina glanced at the waitress as she brought their salads. Katrina had never seen the food move so slowly from the kitchen to the table. Only fifteen more minutes, and the place would be open to regular customers. Prescott didn't seem to be in any hurry to have the meal served though.

She dipped her fork into her salad, then looked up to see him watching her. He focused his intense gaze on her, making her nervous. In fact, she'd eaten nearly all of the mushrooms before she realized she'd left him only one. She had to keep doing something to avoid seeing him study her so thoroughly. Hadn't he ever seen a gypsy up close before?

She imagined not. Everyone he had anything to do with dressed so-so, had their hair done just right, fingers and toes perfectly manicured, and knew everyone who was anybody. His circle of friends would never have included anyone like her.

"How would I get you to my place, if I didn't leave the shoe there?" he finally said.

That was her thought exactly. First, his brother wanted to take her to his home, and now Prescott. Was that prerequisite to making it to home base with a girl for them? She imagined it was.

"It's not in my future." She crunched on a garlic-soaked crouton. Leaving the fair to sup with him turned out to be an enjoyable lark, something she hadn't ever envisioned. He barely touched his food though. "You don't like the food?"

He grinned at her. His smile sent a rush of heat spiraling through her. She sure wished he lived in her apartment complex. But, of course, if he did, he couldn't have afforded to buy her meal.

And he definitely wouldn't have owned the classy five-star restaurant they dined at.

After finishing his salad, he sat up straighter. "So you can see your future?"

Only what she made of it. And she had no intention of going to the Worthington's place. Ever.

So sure, she could see her future, as far as that was concerned.

"Yep. I can see my future. Going to your place definitely isn't in it."

The waitress removed their salads, then served their steaks. When she retreated to the kitchen, the doors to the restaurant opened, and the first customers entered the building. Katrina smiled as a couple looked at them, probably trying to figure out who they were to warrant such privileged treatment.

"How do you see how you'll get your shoe back then, if you have a view on what's going to happen?"

"Maybe I'm not going to get it back."

"That makes me sound like I'm somewhat of a cad."

Katrina sliced into her steak, the juices dripping from the meat. "If you say so." He chuckled, making her respond in kind. He really could be cute.

"Okay, so after dinner, Kat, where do we go from here?"

"I have other plans for later on today, *Scotty*. Remember?"

He buttered a slice of brown bread. "I still have two more hours on the clock." He had her there.

"All right, where to next?"

"We'll go for a boat ride."

"I'm not dressed for it."

"We can drop by your place, and you can change. You can grab a bathing suit. Then we could swing by my place, and I can get mine. The day's nice and hot...perfect for an outing."

"Thanks for the invite, but no." She couldn't even vouch for the condition of her one-piece. The last time she'd worn it was too many summers ago to remember.

"What do you suggest?"

"What about a movie?" They wouldn't have any more time for chit chat, and she hadn't been to one in a good long while.

"Rental at my place or yours?"

She smiled as she shook her head. "At the movie theater."

"You can't blame me for trying."

Laughing, she lifted her wine glass to him. "Here's to the effort." He saluted her back.

After sipping her drink, then setting it on the table, she took a deep breath. "Okay, what movie?"

"I haven't any idea what's playing. We can wing it, though."

Prescott pulled a phone from his pocket and punched in some numbers. He never spoke a word, just watched her the whole time, then nodded. She assumed he called the movie theater for an automated listing of shows and their times.

"Spy thriller all right?" he asked.

"Sounds good."

He stuck the phone in his pocket.

"What time?" She sipped her wine.

"In a little while. No hurry to finish dinner."

She would end up giving him more than his three-hour limit, but she'd never had anybody pay so much to spend time with her, and she really enjoyed his company. Besides, like Sascha so aptly reminded her, she didn't often go out in the evening. She deserved to have a little fun.

PRESCOTT WAS HAVING the time of his life. He loved how she called him Scotty, and he knew he was getting close to having that kiss from her wine-flavored lips. The only problem he faced was convincing her to go to the drive-in movie, instead of a regular theater. He figured she wouldn't have minded a drive-in, but it would have put him over his remaining two-hour limit with her. Then, too, she had other plans that night. Did they include Preston?

He'd never been able to convince any of his friends to go with him to the drive-in located at a small town south of the city. Not too many existed anymore, and he really wanted to see one before the place closed its doors like so many before it.

Kat would probably figure something was up when he drove her out of Dallas though. But if he told her his plans, would she balk at going with him? Probably.

He had to handle the situation carefully. She seemed like the perfect date to take to one.

Someone he'd sure like to cuddle up with against his new leather seats, if she'd allow him to.

When they finished their meal, he cleared his throat. "Would you like some dessert?"

"I'm stuffed, thanks. The meal was terrific. Thanks so much for inviting me."

He hesitated. Somehow, he had to keep her occupied for the next two and half hours. It would take a half-hour to drive all the way out to the drive-in after that. But how could they kill two and half more hours?

"The movie's not going to start for a while. Did you want to drop by the Galleria?"

"The Galleria?" Her eyes widened, and he knew at once the mall was probably way too pricey for her. He was used to his dates jumping at the chance to shop there, and he didn't mind keeping them company.

"What time does the movie start?"

Now he was caught. "Later. They don't have an earlier show."

"Is there something else we can see then? Something that starts earlier?"

"I really have my heart set on seeing this movie." He was more interested in the place and company he'd keep than anything else. But he was still reluctant to let her know where he intended to take her.

"I've made other plans for this evening, Prescott. It wouldn't be fair to my friend."

She was back to being formal with him. He knew how to fix that right away. "Can't you get out of them, Kat? I had other plans this evening, too, but I've changed them, just to be with my favorite fortune teller." He hoped she'd not catch him in his tall tale as he'd never called anyone while he was with her to change any plans.

She reached her hand out. "Phone?"

He handed her his phone, totally elated she would cancel her plans to meet Preston that evening, if that's who she intended seeing.

"Hello?" She paused as she watched him, then she took a deep breath. "I've had a change of plans. I'll speak to you later about it, but I'll come to your place, fix you some dinner, then head out again."

She hesitated as Prescott shook his head. No way did he want to lose her for a couple of hours. What if she decided she didn't want to go after all once she'd been at Preston's house for a while? Heck, if she fixed him dinner, who was to say he'd let her back out of his house for the evening at all? And certainly not to go out with another man.

"I know you don't mind my not fixing you dinner, but I promised. I'll see you in a little bit. Bye." She turned off the phone and handed it back to Prescott. "Okay. You can drop me off at the fairgrounds, I'll pick up my car, fix the meal for my friend, and meet you at the movie theater. So which one was it?"

His whole plan fell to pieces right before his eyes. "If I let you go, I'll never see you again." What the hell was wrong with him? He couldn't believe how paranoid he sounded.

Her face brightened in a perfect smile. "Why, Scotty, I already said I'd go to the movie with you. It'll be about the length of time I still owe you."

He hadn't wanted her to consider he'd bought the time to spend with her still. And he knew if he was Preston, he'd have no intention of letting her go out with another man, not ever. Somehow, he had to convince her that she didn't want to fix dinner for the guy.

"Okay, well the thing is, I wanted to take you to a drive-in."

Her lips parted in surprise, and she folded her arms as her green eyes narrowed.

He was in trouble. He just knew it. Backpedaling, he said, "I've never been to a drive-in before. Never to a fair either. Nobody I know would want to go to one. I know, because I've asked. We could go to a regular indoor movie theater, if you'd prefer, but someday, I'm going to a drive-in. I just didn't think going alone would be all that much fun."

She'd closed her mouth at least. And then her lips repeated her smile. "What makes you think I'd want to go to a drive-in with you, Scotty?"

She was still being less formal with him. He assumed he had a chance, if he didn't blow it now.

"I promise I'll be on my best behavior."

She set her napkin on the table. "All right. It's a deal."

He let out his breath. Now somehow, he had to make sure she didn't get hung up at her boyfriend's house. "Are you certain your friend won't be upset with you about leaving after you fix him supper?"

She chuckled. "We respect each other's need to have separate lives." She drained the rest of her wine.

Either the guy she dated was a real jerk, or she had some kind of new relationship he hadn't thought possible. He knew if she was his girl, she'd never want to go out again after she'd come over to share a meal.

"But you've already eaten. Won't he expect you to eat with him?"

"I'll just fix my friend dinner, that's all. So where did you want me to meet you?"

"It's customary for a man to pick up a lady at her home."

"When they're on a date."

Here came the notion he'd bought her time to be with him again. "We can't have two cars at the drive-in. And the fair's in the wrong direction." He finished his wine. "Unless you want to meet me at my house."

KATRINA SHOOK HER HEAD. She really didn't want him to see her crummy apartment. Then again, maybe his interest in her would dwindle when he realized she wasn't in his class at all. Or maybe that's what he liked about her. He thought she'd be some kind of side interest.

She fingered her napkin. Still, she really wanted to go out with him just this once. "All right. You can pick me up at my friend's house."

She had to be there to cook the meal anyway, and that way she didn't have to reveal she lived next door. Plus, it was nice being picked up and dropped off after the evening's activities.

His raised brows made her realize he was surprised to hear her make the offer. Was it because he thought she was seeing a male friend?

"Won't Preston be upset with you when I come to pick you up? I don't intend to honk from curbside, you know."

"I'm not sure why you keep calling Sascha, Preston, but I assure you, she won't mind." His whole body relaxed, tickling her. "Can I join you? I have nothing else to do this afternoon. I could help you make dinner for her. I'm actually pretty handy in the kitchen." He sounded like a forlorn puppy.

"All right. But I'll need your phone again. I have to let Sascha know she's having male company."

He handed her the phone with such enthusiasm, he nearly lost it in her wine glass. She fought the urge to laugh out loud and punched in the numbers.

"Hello?" Sascha croaked.

"Sascha, me again. Do you mind if Prescott Worthington comes to your house to help me make chicken soup for you?"

"You're kidding," she croaked back.

"No, I'm not. Will it be okay? I don't want to put you out or anything, but wanted to make sure—"

"You're going out with him afterward? Jeez, Katrina, what's going on?"

"Uhm, I'm using his phone."

"Oh. He's listening in on the conversation. Sure, bring him on over." She chuckled, then coughed. "Sorry. This is just an interesting development I hadn't expected at all. See you in a little bit?"

"About forty-five minutes to drive out there."

"Did he give you your shoe back?"

"No, he hasn't given me my shoe back." She looked up to see Prescott waggle his brows at her. "I'm sure he'll drop it by your place sometime soon."

"You don't want him to know you live next door?"

"That's right. See you in a few." She hung up the phone, then handed it back to Prescott.

"Okay, Sascha said it's fine with her. Are you ready to go?"

He jumped from his seat and pulled her chair back for her.

Then she saw an image in her mind...in the darkness. Was it at the drive-in theater? Or afterward, when they returned home? She couldn't tell, but it was the black SUV, sitting silent, waiting.

Hopefully her attempt at saving Prescott this time wouldn't hurt him as much. But she did consider whether it was a good idea to go out after all. Still, when she had the visions, they came to pass, and she didn't know when this one would. If she was with him when the SUV made another attempt, she could help Prescott. She was quickly discarding the notion the other incident was just an accident.

"You'll have to drop me off at the fairgrounds to get my car first, and you can follow me to Sascha's home after that."

"What if I take you to the fairgrounds after the show?"

"It'll be too late at night."

"All right, if you promise not to lose me."

She had no intention of losing her date for the evening. Not when she had another mission.

When they arrived at the parking lot of the fair, the crowds had dwindled. She hated to point out her vehicle, never mind the dust collected on its surface. The exterior was duller than a matte finish and in places, the paint peeled off in chunks. But it got her where she wanted to go, most of the time, and that's all that really mattered.

He didn't say a word as he pulled in behind her car. Was he having second thoughts of being with her? Too bad. He'd insisted, and she had to save him again. They had a pact whether he wanted it or not.

He hurried to open her car door for her, and when she climbed out, she pulled her keys from her purse.

"I'll try not to lose you."

She caught him looking at her car again. Yeah, it was in

pretty sad shape, but she hadn't really thought so, until Mr. Luxury Car Owner had a look at it.

She opened the door to her car and cringed when the hinges groaned. Used to the noise, she never paid any attention to it, but with Prescott watching her every move, her blood heated with embarrassment.

"I'll follow you." He hurried back to his car.

They had barely made it to the highway when she glimpsed a black SUV driving behind Prescott. Was she imagining it? Or was she being paranoid? She knew though, whoever she'd seen in her vision, definitely would make another attempt on Prescott's life.

But this time, she wouldn't be there to push him out of the way of danger. Why not? It must occur after he left her home following the movie. She wrinkled her nose. No way would she would spend the night with him. Of course, she'd have to be daft to think he'd be interested in being with her overnight in the first place. What would that make her look like if she told him she had to stay with him the rest of the evening...to ensure his safety? Yeah right. He'd think she was after him for his money.

When they arrived at her apartment complex, she wished she could change clothes. Jeans would have been more suitable at the drive-in, and a sweater for when it cooled down later that night would help.

She parked at the curb, then jumped out of her car. Prescott had been careful not to say a word about the old model she drove, but his unspoken words bothered her more than if he'd told her what was on his mind.

She patted her rooftop as he joined her. "It's nearly old enough to be a classic."

He chuckled, pleasing her to find he had a sense of humor. Then she took his hand and led him to Sascha's front door with every intention of talking to him about the serious business that lay ahead for him. "Prescott—"

"I like the way you call me Scotty," he interrupted.

She smiled at him. "Okay, well, Scotty, I have something really important to tell you, and I'm sure you won't believe me, but someone is out to hurt you." She knocked on Sascha's door.

"Like at Lemoyne's?"

"Yes." She paused as her cousin opened the door. "Look at what I dragged home from the fair."

"Not bad." Sascha grabbed Prescott's arm and pulled him into her apartment. She didn't believe in fancy invites. "You know the cleaning lady only comes on Monday, so I did a bit of a quick job before you arrived."

Seconds later, Katrina banged around among the pots and pans in the kitchen. "I told you we didn't want you to go to any trouble."

"Nonsense. What would Prescott have thought if I hadn't spiffed the place up a bit?"

Katrina looked over at Prescott, who considered the mismatched living room furniture. His family owned four furniture stores, she'd learned, not one of which would carry Sascha's outdated styles.

Katrina pointed to the couch. "The lipstick red, imitation leather couch was imported from Italy last year." She smiled as Sascha's mouth split into a grin. "And that furry footstool? One of the finest faux fur collections all the way from New York City."

"We ought to carry such competitive brands," Prescott said. "You have quite a unique place."

He'd probably never seen such a gaudy mess in his life, but he played along with the game just fine. He crossed the linoleum floor to the stove where Katrina stood. Leaning over her shoulder, he watched as she threw sliced celery into the pot.

"What do you want me to do, Kat?"

He smelled like spicy heaven, and what she really wanted him to do was kiss her good. She turned her head to see his mouth so close to hers. Yeah, that's what she really desired. His body heat warmed her, and her skin prickled with anticipation.

"The cooked chicken is in the fridge, right, Sascha?" Katrina never turned her head from studying his lips. They were good and man-sized, probably well-trained in the pursuit of pleasure.

He overwhelmed her, standing so close, and she grew dizzy.

Sascha pulled the chicken from the fridge. "Ahem, here it is."

Katrina could tell he wanted to kiss her. His mind was filled with the thought from her linking with him. She shifted her gaze to his eyes and found him looking at her mouth with longing.

"I'll put the chicken right here and let you get on with your business." Sascha's words were tinged with amusement. Her flip-flops slapped the floor as she hurried out of the kitchen.

Katrina took a deep breath. "The chicken...could you cut it up?" She motioned to the package sitting on the counter.

His mouth curved up. "I thought you wanted me to do something else."

6

Who was Kat trying to kid? Prescott knew she desired his kiss as much as he wanted to give her one. Still, he had to have her invitation. He hoped she didn't motion to the chicken again, ruining his chance at the moment.

"The soup, Scotty. Business first."

He chuckled. She was willing. He knew it. "Are you certain?"

She hesitated entirely too long to answer him, and he knew she really hadn't wanted to wait. Her fingers pulled at a brass handle, and when the drawer opened, she lifted a knife from it. "Can you cut up the chicken?"

He chuckled. She was certain...business first.

He took the knife and placed the chicken on the cutting board. "Slave driver."

"I don't want to be late for our movie."

He glanced at his watch. It had taken some time to drive out to the fairgrounds and get her car. Then several more minutes passed before they arrived at Sascha's place. To his surprise, an hour had already vanished. He imagined it would probably take at least half an hour to fix the soup. She cleared her throat, and he glanced over at her.

She'd folded her arms, and his gaze drifted back to her breasts, slightly lifted by her pose.

Now what?

"We need to discuss this problem you're having."

"As long as you're going to rescue me all the time, I don't see the difficulty." He continued chopping the chicken. He really enjoyed her company, and he didn't want to get into this make-believe world she created where she pretended to risk her neck to save his life. Why couldn't they just enjoy their time together with no complications?

"I may not always be there to save you. You need to figure out who might want you harmed."

He had every intention of changing the subject—back to the one he wanted to hear more about. "You say you're linked with me. What was I thinking when we stood next to the stove?"

When she didn't speak, he turned to see what caused her delay in answering him. To his amusement, she smiled broadly. "It doesn't take a mind reader to see what you were thinking."

"Would you have objected too much?"

Kat crossed her ankles as she leaned against the counter. "Somehow, I don't think you'd fit into my lifestyle."

He finished carving up the precooked chicken and motioned to the pot. When she nodded, he carried the cutting board over to the soup and poured the meat in. After placing the board back on the counter, he washed and dried his hands. Again, he faced her. "You think you're too good for me, don't you?"

She chuckled under her breath, a deep throaty sound this time that stirred him up all over again. He strode across the floor and stood in front of her. Her defensive posture hadn't changed as she kept her arms locked in place. But her smile told him she wanted what he desired. He took her hands and unfolded her arms. After wrapping them around his waist, he placed his hands on the side of her face. Closing her eyes, she tilted her chin up, encouraging him to continue.

In heaven, he leaned down to press his lips to hers. Then his phone rang. The usually cheerful jingle grated on his nerves.

"Excuse me a moment, Kat." Pulling out the phone, he checked the caller ID. Camden.

"Hello!" He hadn't meant for his voice to be so gruff but of all the times to...

"Prescott, where the hell are you? Starla's been waiting here for you for over an hour. I thought maybe she had her times mixed up so I checked your calendar, but sure enough, you had scribbled in a date with her...for today, an hour ago. What's up?"

Prescott shook his head. "I cancelled the engagement when I broke up with her at the ball." He looked down at Kat's green eyes, sparkling with streaks of amber as she watched him in anticipation. There was no way he wanted to be with anyone other than her right now. Starla wasn't half as much fun, but something else intrigued him about Kat. Something mysterious he couldn't put his finger on. Wanting to know everything he could about her, he didn't care to leave her for a second. He'd never felt like that toward any woman. Now he was the one acting clingy and possessive.

His fingers swept through her silky hair. A natural beauty... every dark brown strand of curl twisting in synchronized rhythm, waited for his touch. He wanted more than anything to kiss her lips, now permanently cemented in a smile of delight.

"Prescott? She's on the deck right now, waiting to hear what's going on. If you've broken up with her—"

"I have, Camden. You know the way she is. She never believes anything you say, unless it's her idea." He knew his brother loved to have a go with her. But he'd be sorry. Under the model-like mold, Starla was totally hollow.

"Well, I'm really not surprised. So where are you?"

"I'm—"

To Prescott's astonishment, Kat reached for the phone. He handed it to her, not sure that it was the right thing to do.

Her voice turned deeper than he'd ever heard it.

"Camden, he said he's busy."

Chuckling, Prescott assumed his brother asked her who she was when she smiled.

"His fortune teller." She hung up on Camden and handed the phone back to Prescott.

He intended to be the one to make the next move after he put his phone away, but she pulled him close and pressed her lips to his instead. Her mouth still tasted of wine, and he savored every drop flavoring her lips and tongue. Her fingers ran through his hair with exuberance as his ran his hands through her long tresses...until a bubbling noise caught their attention.

She hurried to the stove and lowered the heat on the burner. "Hmm, it looks about ready. Do you want a bite to eat?"

He wanted to kiss her further...but he was afraid he'd crave much more if he kissed her any longer.

"I'm ready!" Sascha called out from the living room, her voice dipping and diving in strange croaks.

He took a deep breath of resignation. The women were ganging up on him.

KATRINA SERVED a small portion of the soup for Prescott as he insisted on tasting something homemade. For Sascha, she fixed a bigger bowl. Then she cleaned the kitchen while the two ate. She couldn't handle sitting with them at the kitchen table the way Sascha kept giving her all-knowing looks. Prescott was a dream come true, but not for her.

He might have terminated his relationship with Starla, but there'd be another rich girl around the corner for him. For now, he considered her an interesting diversion.

For the moment, he was that for her also. She had no one of the male persuasion that she found as interesting in her life right now. If nothing else, he could afford to take her to some nice places. She knew it would never go any further than that. She had every intention of being realistic about their relationship.

Sascha rested her spoon in her empty bowl. "So Katrina tells me you're taking her to the drive-in. Are you staying for the late show?"

He looked back at Katrina. She dried off her hands. "If she'll allow me to."

"I'm really not a late-night person, but if I start to snore, you can poke me in the ribs. I wake very easily."

He chuckled. "Do you need a refill, Sascha?"

"Sure, thanks."

He brought the bowls into the kitchen. "The soup is extraordinary, Kat."

"Thanks, Scotty."

Sascha's eyes widened, and Katrina grinned at her. She knew she'd get a thorough grilling the next morning. Katrina spooned another bowl of soup for Sascha, but Prescott declined.

Sascha waved her spoon at Katrina. "What made you decide on a drive-in? I thought the last time you went you said you wouldn't ever go there on a date again."

Katrina would get even. Sascha knew not to bring *that* subject up. She handed the bowl of soup to Prescott as her cheeks must have turned rosy red as hot as they felt.

Prescott set the refilled bowl on Sascha's placemat. All at once he stepped into hero mode with a humorous twist. Katrina was sure the notion a man had upset her at the theater bothered him, but he avoided the issue and addressed her real concern. "This time it's different. She has to protect *me* from someone who wants to harm me."

"Oh?" Sascha nodded. "Don't you think you need to call the police on this one, Katrina?" Her stern look, wrinkled brow, and narrowed eyes, made Katrina realize how serious she was.

"What would I say? The same man in the same black SUV would gun for Prescott...Scotty, again? They would believe me as much as... as..." She looked over at Prescott. They both waited for her to finish her words, but she just shook her head. "You know how it goes, Sascha." Her cousin stirred her soup around and around.

"What's going to happen?"

"I told you."

Sascha looked back at her. "Not all of it."

Katrina bit her lip. She wished she had all of the answers. And she wished she had a gun. "I don't save Prescott the same way." Actually, she worried she wouldn't be able to save him at all. She rinsed out his bowl and stuck it into the dishwasher. "I see the SUV trying to run him down again, after dusk."

"At the drive-in?"

"I'm not certain."

Up until this point, Prescott had listened, his face remaining serious. Then he smiled. "That means you may have to stay with me longer."

Katrina rolled her eyes. "Men are all the same."

Then she had another idea about the threat. She grabbed her purse and pulled the kitchen drawer open. "I guess it's about time for us to go."

She hoped they weren't watching her as she slipped a paring knife into her bag. Sascha's eyes widened. "What are you going to do with that?"

"Maybe I'll get lucky and have a chance at his tires."

"Don't worry." Prescott wrapped his fingers securely around Katrina's. "I'll keep her safe."

"You gave him another reading, didn't you?"

Katrina looked down at the floor. She didn't want to tell Sascha she had linked with Prescott. Sascha would want to know all of the details.

"You didn't..."

Katrina looked up at her. She couldn't help that Prescott had forced it on her. Sascha and she had been warned, repeatedly, not to link with folks. The consequences of doing so had never quite been explained.

"You linked with him." Sascha shook her head. "Why don't we all just stay here and play card games?"

She knew Sascha was concerned for their welfare. "He's going to father twins, a boy and a girl. He'll live through tonight."

Prescott laughed. "That's good to hear."

Sascha frowned at her. "I hope you know what you're doing."

"So do I." Katrina gave her a hug. "Talk to you tomorrow."

"Be sure and bring back my paring knife in one piece. It's the only one I have."

"If I damage it, I'm sure Scotty won't mind buying you a new one."

"Not at all. I'll even pay to get you out of jail if you're caught vandalizing a car," Prescott said, winking at Katrina as he led her to the front door.

TENSION FILLED the air as they got into Prescott's car. Katrina could tell he wanted to ask about the bad-date experience she had, but she didn't want to talk about it. Prescott was a nice guy, she was certain. And she hadn't felt she needed to worry about him at all. There was no sense in dredging up the past.

His hands slid over the steering wheel as they drove to the drive-in. He concentrated on his driving, but his silence made her crazy. Did he want her to tell him what happened on her own, without pressuring her? Or did the threat he had to face, weigh on his mind?

"If the drive-in was a bad idea..."

She took a deep breath. The date incident bothered him. "Sascha shouldn't have brought it up. I'll have a word with her tomorrow about it, for certain."

"There's still time to go to an indoor movie theater. We really don't have to go to a drive-in."

"I haven't gone to the drive-in since the beginning of the season. Don't give Sascha's words another thought. Besides, you said you had your heart set on it."

He tapped his thumbs on the steering wheel. She assumed he still wanted to know what had happened. But she had no desire to discuss it. She leaned back against the cushy leather seats. "It smells so good in here." Besides his whisper of a spicy scent, the leather smelled great. And the seats had a lot more padding than the ones in her car.

She closed her eyes and saw the image of the black SUV idling like a panther getting ready to pounce. But where was it? Its engine rumbled like a cat's motor turned on high. She ran her hand over the leather of her purse. If she found him, and he sat still long enough, she'd fix him good.

"I was surprised Sascha knew we are linked."

"It's only happened a couple of times for me. I wouldn't have seen what would occur with you again unless I had given you another reading...or we linked."

"Why would she assume you had linked with me, and not just given another reading?"

"She guessed."

He chuckled. "So I take it she doesn't have your ability...to read minds."

"Now if I told you she didn't, you wouldn't have her come to your place next week for your party."

"What?"

"I guess your parents hired her. They had her there for a party last year and enjoyed her fortune telling talents, so they hired her again."

"It must have been while I was away on a buying trip. Nobody ever told me."

"She said she hadn't met you before."

"Are you going to be there?"

"She asked me to assist her this time."

"Ahh. I was going to invite you to come otherwise."

Katrina ran her hand over the leather seat. Being in the company of all his family's rich friends didn't appeal to her. "I'll just be part of the nighttime entertainment."

She could tell the way his mouth curved up, and he chuckled seductively, the idea intrigued him.

"I meant, well, I mean..." Her face grew as hot as a baked potato fresh out of the oven. "You know what I mean."

"Yes, well I must admit, you are *most* entertaining."

When they pulled into the drive-in, Katrina studied the cars already parked there. Not one black SUV, but plenty of pickups. Most were turned backward as the occupants set up lawn chairs in the back to watch the movie.

Prescott turned off the engine, then slid over next to her.

She grinned. "No bucket seats."

"That's why I wouldn't have a sporty model."

The overhead lights dimmed as they turned their radio on. Then an animated feature began, and she laughed. "I thought we were seeing a thriller."

"It's after the animated feature. Parents with little kids go home after this."

"You mean we could have come later just to see the adult show?"

"Shhh, not on your life." He wrapped his arm around her and pulled her close.

He was a lot more human than she'd given him credit. She'd imagined Starla would have had no interest at all in seeing an animated film. In fact, his friends probably would have teased him. Why was she even thinking about it? She wasn't a part of his life. Still, she snuggled against his chest. This was one date she would thoroughly enjoy.

Until he said the wrong thing.

"You know you don't have to pretend there's a villain after me. Every second I've spent with you has been truly special, Kat. I just don't want it to end."

She didn't want him to see how angry his words made her. She took a deep breath trying to calm her temper. One wasn't enough, and she breathed the air in twice more trying to settle her irritation. How could he not believe her after the car tried to run him down the first time?

Okay, so he didn't believe she could see the future. That was understandable. But he'd acted like he believed her, and now he didn't. Did he think she pretended to save him? That she hadn't truly rescued him the night before?

She had to get away...have a few minutes alone before her head exploded and she clobbered him. "I'm going to the ladies' room. Be right back."

Hurrying out of the car, she didn't even wait for him to reply. A few steps away from the vehicle, she realized she'd left her purse behind. She strode back to the car and yanked the door open. "Forgot my purse." He handed it to her, and she quickly thanked him, closed the door, and stormed off.

Typical man. He didn't even realize she was mad at him. If he'd thought anything of her actions at all, he probably figured she had bladder problems. Men were so insensitive. If she could have afforded a cell phone, she'd have called Sascha and...well, no, she couldn't call her as she was sick.

Baldy would have been a better choice to call to rescue her. She headed to the bathroom as her thoughts reverted back to Plan A. Rescue Prescott Worthington, end of mission, return to her regular routine, no more dating.

She powdered her shiny nose, reapplied pink gloss to her lips and brushed her hair. Now what? There wasn't any way she wanted to snuggle with him anymore. But she couldn't stay in the restroom all night long.

Cartoon images ran through her mind. He was totally absorbed in the animated feature. She could have walked home, and he'd never have noticed she hadn't returned.

She surveyed the cars in the dark. No black SUV that she could see. A playground in the back of the lot, complete with a swing set, caught her eye. She crossed the parking area to the swings. At least she had a place to sit for a while.

Sitting on one of the swing's narrow leather straps, she rocked back and forth with a gentle rhythm, trying to calm her anger. He wasn't at fault for not believing she could see the danger he was in. But to say she made it up to get close to him? *Please.*

After fifteen minutes, his car interior light turned on as he opened his car door. Wonder of wonders. He'd finally realized she wasn't returning. He walked to the restroom and stood.

She felt remorse when she could see he was worried about her. Okay, so they'd spend a nice evening at the movies together, and then she'd call it quits. He didn't know where she lived, and she didn't have a phone. Keeping her anonymity would be easy.

She walked toward the restroom when a black SUV pulled

into the lot. Its headlights were off as customary when a feature was already being shown.

Was it the same vehicle? She couldn't be certain. The windows were tinted darker than the law allowed. She couldn't see into the SUV at all. Could she turn him in for having illegally tinted windows at least?

When it pulled into a parking spot, she skirted around the back side of several rows of cars. She had every intention of sneaking up on the vehicle, getting his license plate number and...it pulled out of its parking place suddenly, making her heart nearly stop.

Driving back toward the entrance, it headed straight for Prescott. Prescott was oblivious as his mind focused on her whereabouts, she assumed. He crossed the lane in front of the SUV as he headed in the direction of his car.

"Scotty!" Katrina screamed with panic in her voice.

He ran between two parked cars as the SUV zoomed on past. He joined her as she dashed across the parking lot to meet him.

"I grew worried when you didn't return to the car, and then I thought—"

"It was him, Scotty. Didn't you seem him?"

She could tell by the look on his face he hadn't thought he was in any danger. His concern centered strictly on her whereabouts. Didn't he realize her yelling for him caused him to dart through the parked cars, thereby saving his life? Didn't he recognize it was the same black SUV that tried to run him over the night before? "Are you okay, Kat?"

Of course she was okay. Prescott wasn't all right though. Someone played a deadly game with his life, and he couldn't even see it. She wanted to shake him until he acknowledged he stood in harm's way.

"I'm fine," she said with exasperation as she let her breath out in a huff. He'd never recognize it before it was too late, she feared, but she said how she felt anyway. "You are the one in danger, not me."

PRESCOTT JUST COULDN'T GO ALONG with her game any further. He really cared for her, but their relationship could only dead-end with the charade she continued to pull. He'd gotten a glimpse of the black SUV, but he didn't feel for one instant that he was facing a life-threatening danger. "Okay, well, Katrina, I'll drop you off at your place...I mean at Sascha's as that's where we left your car."

She hesitated to answer him. Was she angry that he didn't believe her? He assumed so. But it didn't matter. If she wanted to get honest with him, that was the only kind of game he was interested in playing. He took her arm and led her back to the car, trying to hide his anger that simmered below the surface.

She never spoke a word. He'd secretly hoped she'd say she wanted to stay for the movie. But she remained stubborn. When they returned to the car, she looked straight out the windshield. That was the end of the night's activities.

He closed her door and climbed into the driver's seat. "Do you want to stay for the movie?" She shook her head.

He'd given it a last-ditch effort. Taking a deep breath, he started the ignition. She could be mad all she wanted. He was irritated with her too. The game had gone far enough.

As they drove out of the parking lot, he gripped the steering wheel, trying to release some of the tension from his muscles. He'd expected a lot less tense evening than this.

For fifteen miles, they drove in silence. He hated not having any conversation between them, and yet he wondered if it was for the best. Still, he grew curious as to what she would say if he brought up the silly linking business. "So what do you see now for me?"

For another ten minutes she didn't say a word. Then finally she spoke. "You'll drop me off at my place, and we'll go our separate ways, never to see one another again."

"You don't want me to drop you off at Sascha's place to get your car?"

"I meant Sascha's place."

He rubbed his forehead. Did she live with Sascha? She seemed to know where everything in the kitchen was. Sure, she lived there too. That's why she wanted to leave her car at Sascha's place. Then she'd be home after the show. Only she was careful not to tell him she lived there also.

Was she afraid he would stalk her for heaven's sake? He grunted with annoyance. "You see no more murder attempts in my future?"

She folded her arms.

He chuckled. Since she didn't want to see him socially any further, he would have liked to have cleared the air about her boyfriend driving the pretend hit car. "So who's driving the hit car? Preston?"

"What?" The venom in her voice was deadly.

He frowned. "Preston...the guy you're dating."

"Pull the car to the shoulder of the road."

"Why?" He glanced over at her but couldn't see the expression on her face as dark as it was. "Pull it over now!"

"Give me a reason." He didn't like the demanding tone of voice she used. And he didn't have to be a mind reader to figure out the reason she wanted him to stop the car.

"Please." Her word was couched in hostility, though she'd attempted to make it sound appeasing.

He pulled the car over, and she yanked her car door open, jumped out, then slammed it shut. *Damn it!* He'd considered she might try to walk home, but they were fifteen miles out in the countryside. Miles from anywhere.

He rolled down the windows and shouted to her as he drove the car behind her, "Kat, get back in the car. I'm not letting you walk home in the dark."

She walked for half a mile, and he tried again. "Kat, *please* get in the car." He was irritated. Who wouldn't have been? But her spunkiness was a turn-on too. What he wouldn't have given to turn that anger into some fun good loving.

She finally stopped, then turned to face him. Her eyes narrowed with the headlights shining in them, and she folded her arms. He parked the car, then stepped out of it. "Come on, Kat. Let me drive you home."

"Don't say another word to me."

He nodded. To his relief, she walked back to the car and climbed in. He'd never experienced a date with a woman like her before, and he assumed he'd never do so again. She really baffled him. He loved being with her. She was real and funny and emotionally strong—well stubborn. But he loved the way she was. And yet the business with her accomplice took its toll on their relationship. Couldn't she see she didn't need this ploy of hers to get his interest?

He headed in the direction of Sascha's home. Neither spoke a word.

When he pulled curbside at Sascha's place, Katrina hurried out of the car before he could get out of his side to help her with her door. He didn't want it to end like this. Yet, he could see no way around it.

He waited as she headed to the front door, but the apartment was dark, and he assumed Sascha had retired to bed. Katrina hadn't even said goodbye to him. He really only expected her to unlock the door, walk into the apartment, and shut him out. But instead, she hesitated at the door, then turned and waved goodbye.

Her actions mystified him. What was she up to? He really figured she had no intention of saying goodbye at all—not as mad as she appeared to be.

He wasn't going anywhere until she was safely inside her apartment. Again, she crossed her arms, and he smiled. She couldn't get into the apartment because she didn't live there.

He waited. And so did she. Then she pulled keys from her purse and headed to her car. Totally amused, he leaned back against his car seat. She was truly a character. She pretended to live there. Then again, what if she lived with this Preston? His stomach contents curdled with the notion.

She tried to start her car, but the engine wouldn't turn over, and she hit her steering wheel with her fist. Then she yanked the door open and slammed it shut. This time she headed to an apartment adjacent to Sascha's, unlocked the door, and shoved it open. It shut with a jolt, then lights came on inside, and he took a breath.

Shaking his head, he started his engine and pulled past her car. She lived next door to Sascha.

He had no intention of seeing Katrina ever again. Though there was no way he was making up to Starla either. As far as the party being held at his parents' place later that week that Sascha and her assistant were to attend, he'd make sure he was scarce... like the last time. Another buying trip.

Sure...that would solve the problem of having to see her again.

Or would it? His own thoughts were as insincere as his desire to dismiss her. She'd worked her magic and ensnared him good. But he'd broken the tie that bound him to her. Hadn't he?

7

Katrina had never been so mad in her life...well except for the time she had gone to the drive-in with Darrel Spencer. His hands had been all over her before the movie barely started, and he'd been furious with her when she had made him stop. What did he think he paid for when he bought the drive-in movie tickets after all? Popcorn and dessert?

In the future, she would only go to the drive-in with Sascha. Katrina dropped her purse on the living room floor, missing the coffee table in her anger. She knew nothing could ever come of a relationship with a guy like Prescott. What she would give to know what he thought about her living next door to Sascha's place. She tried to sense what he felt but couldn't tell. Maybe the linking between them had already ended. She could only hope.

She unbuttoned her blouse and tossed it on a chair. The blouse slid to the floor. Then she kicked off her sandals.

He thought she'd put some imaginary boyfriend up to trying to threaten him with an SUV. The notion steamed her. So that she could do what? Catch him for herself?

He had to be nuts.

She slipped out of her skirt and then her tank top. It was time to take a shower and chill out. A good sleep was all she needed.

Stepping into the bathroom, she turned on the light, but the room remained dark. Then she realized the whole place was immersed in blackness. Her heartbeat picked up its pace. She ran to the window and peeked out through the mini blinds. Most of the apartments had a light on or two. And then everything turned dark...the whole world.

She backed into her sofa and collapsed on the velour cushions. The phone was jingling, but she didn't have one. "Hello?" a voice said. It was Prescott's. Damn, she was having a vision. They were still linked.

Closing her eyes, she leaned back on the sofa and watched the movie reel play.

$\sim$

"Hey, Prescott, listen Mom and Dad are arriving on the flight Friday. Are you going to pick them up or did you want me to?"

"You can, Camden."

"So where have you been all of this time?"

"Seeing a movie. I'm on my way home now...nearly there in fact."

"Who did you go with? The fortune teller?" He chuckled.

Prescott's temperature elevated. Camden didn't have any idea who the fortune teller was...unless Starla mentioned he'd met her at the fair. And if Camden had talked to her about it, she might have realized the woman he was dancing with at the ball was the same woman. He rubbed his temple. "Anything going on I should know about?"

"Starla and I took the boat out today. After work tomorrow, we're going to have dinner. Any problem with that?"

"Not in the least bit."

"So how'd your date go?"

"It was different." No way would he admit to Camden it had ended in disaster.

~

DIFFERENT. Katrina rubbed her forehead hard to get the images and sounds out of her head.

Camden chuckled. "Different. Is that good or bad?"

Prescott took a heavy breath. "Listen, I'm almost home, Camden. I just turned down our road in fact. See you in a minute."

"It doesn't sound good. See ya."

No, it wasn't good. A tear rolled down her cheek. Rather, the day with Prescott had been truly wonderful, only he'd thought she'd lied. How could he think that of her?

Then she saw the black SUV. It was parked and waiting, idling, shuddering with unspent energy. But where? When would it attempt to strike again? Who was behind the menace? And why?

~

THAT NIGHT, Prescott lay between his cotton sheets, the 600-count thread like silk against his skin. An owl hooted in an old bur oak, keeping him company. He tried to still his thoughts concerning the time spent with Kat, but all he could think about was her light flowery fragrance and soft curly hair. He'd meant to snuggle with her for the whole time of the thriller. She'd be scared, and he'd keep her safe. Instead, she had to insist on playing her game.

The scowl returned to his face. He took a deep breath in

exasperation. He'd really thought she might have been the spark he needed in his life.

Unable to sleep, he threw his covers aside and headed down the hall to his office. He flipped on the light switch, then crossed the room to his massive oak desk. After pulling a phonebook from his desk drawer, he stared at the residential pages. Katrina Landry. He searched the pages, running his finger down the names. No Katrina Landry or anything close.

Lifting the handset from its base, he dialed the operator. "Hello, operator, can you give me the number for Katrina Landry?"

"City and state?"

"Perrytown, Texas."

"Thank you." There was some hesitation, then the operator came back on. "There is no listing for a Katrina Landry in Perrytown, Texas."

"Is her number unlisted?"

"There is no number listed or unlisted for Katrina Landry in Perrytown, Texas. Can I look up another number for you, sir?"

Sascha the Sensation. But what was her last name? He hadn't a clue.

He rubbed his chin deep in thought. He couldn't imagine anyone not having a phone in this day and age. "No, thank you, operator."

Then he realized Sascha was sitting on the couch when she waited for them to fix supper. She wasn't watching television or anything. Maybe she couldn't afford one. She'd mentioned playing cards. In fact, she didn't even have any music playing in the background. He ran his hand through his hair.

The two women were probably barely making ends meet. Sascha and her sideshows and Katrina and...well come to think of it, he hadn't a clue as to what she did for a living.

His ego shrunk to a tenth of his normal size. For caring so

about Katrina, he certainly hadn't shown it. He was self-centered. That's what he was. Of course, he was used to knowing where the women in his life got their money from...their daddy's wealth. He hadn't ever dated a woman who'd actually worked hard for a living.

He returned to bed. Though he had no intention of taking up where he'd left off with Kat— not with her scheming so. But first thing in the morning, he would find out everything he could about both her and her friend, Sascha. Just for the hell of it.

When he closed his eyes, Katrina's lips pressed against his, soft and willing. He could still taste the red wine flavoring them, and he wished to devour them fully. Her tongue teased his and he smiled.

KATRINA MOANED as Prescott touched his tongue to hers. He tasted like the wine they'd had earlier, and his spicy scent drove her insane. She parted her lips to encourage him further. She wanted all of him. She'd never enjoyed the touch of a man so, and she didn't want to give him up...not right now...not when he tasted so fine.

And then the sensation slipped away. The light in her living room lamp glared at her as she stared back at it. She'd only had a vision. That was all. A vision of...well, she wasn't sure. The past? When she and Prescott shared the kiss in Sascha's kitchen? Or was he thinking of the intimate moment, and it was a linked experience?

She shuddered at the thought. She hadn't ever had anything like that happen to her before. All she knew for certain was that it wasn't in their future.

She walked into the bathroom and turned on the shower.

Once she'd stripped her panties and bra off, she climbed into the tub. As soon as she lathered her hair up with shampoo and soaped her face, the lights went out again.

Was this going to happen all night? No. Soon she'd be in bed and sound asleep. End of visions...unless they turned into her worst nightmares.

In her mind's eye, she saw Prescott driving along the road, his headlights piercing the dark ahead of him. She continued to rinse the soap from her hair and face as she tried to ignore the vision.

Then to her astonishment, his vehicle pulled up behind hers. She grabbed a burgundy towel and made it into a turban over her hair, then another she wrapped over her body. Hurrying to the window, she peeked out through the blinds. Only two cars were parked curbside. Hers and Sascha's.

She took a deep breath. It must have been a vision of what had occurred earlier in the day. There was no way he was returning to her apartment that evening.

After drying herself, she grabbed a flannel long-sleeved nightgown. The nights grew cooler now with the onset of fall, but she refused to turn on the heat until the dead of winter. She just couldn't afford inflated utility bills.

With a yank, she tugged the gown over her head, then walked back to the couch and pulled off the cushions. She only hoped the visions wouldn't continue into nightmarish dreams.

Before long, she'd made her couch into a bed, then climbed between the flannel sheets. Yawning, she knew before she was ready, the day would dawn. Hopefully, Sascha would have a call for a job for her. Substituting at elementary schools didn't pay much, but she enjoyed the job thoroughly. And if she could ever get a scholarship, she intended to get a full-fledged teacher's degree.

She closed her eyes and saw the vision of Prescott's car, long and sleek, prowling her neighborhood. His lights attempted to penetrate the gloom, now foggy from the cool air mixing with the warm. What was he searching for?

She tried to shove the images from her mind. His music played low, a mysterious New Age tune. He hadn't played it when they were driving together. In fact, she hadn't remembered him playing any music at all.

Then her apartment rattled as someone banged on her door. She groaned. The visions were getting way too real. The pounding began again. She turned her head toward the door. It couldn't be real, could it?

Glancing at her time, she saw that it was midnight. All at once she'd realized she'd forgotten about the meeting with Lucky.

In the dark, she jumped out of her sofa bed and dashed to the front door. Peering through the peephole, she saw Prescott standing in the low lamplight on her porch.

Her heart hitched. What in the world was he doing here?

She opened her door with the chain still attached. "Prescott?"

"Can I come in for a moment, Kat? Just for a moment?" His tone was pleading and tugged at her heart.

She took a deep breath. Her mind told her no. He belonged in his high-priced neighborhood...wherever that was. And she lived in a world altogether different. But her heart beat a resounding yes!

Her heart won.

She closed the door, then unchained it. With some reservation, she opened the door.

His eyes took in her appearance from her wet curls to her flannel gown that reached to her ankles where sheep jumped over fluffy white clouds on a lilac background. She imagined the women he'd been with were into slinky satiny, lace-trimmed short teddies. Not flannel granny gowns.

"I wasn't really expecting company." She walked into the kitchen and turned on the light, squinting in the brightness.

His gaze remained focused on her gown, and she walked over to a closet and yanked a velour robe out. Once she pulled it on and tied the belt at the waist, she motioned to the kitchen table.

"Do you want something to drink?"

"What do you have?"

"Milk, orange juice, coffee, tea?"

"Nothing, thank you."

What had he expected? She had a bar? She poured herself a glass of orange juice. "What's this all about, Prescott?"

"Scotty."

She lifted her brows.

He sat down at the table, but she remained standing, leaning against the doorjamb in the kitchen. She didn't have men to her apartment in the middle of the night when she was dressed in her nightgown. There wasn't any way she was getting close to him tonight.

"I can't sleep."

"I'm sure you can afford some medicine for the problem."

"I can't sleep, because I can't get my mind off you, Kat."

She smiled. "Well, I have the same problem, but probably not for the same reason."

"What do you mean?"

She shook her head. She wasn't about to mention the linking business to him again. He wouldn't believe her anyway.

He took a ragged breath. "I saw a black SUV in your complex."

Her brows knit together as she slammed her empty juice glass down on the counter. "Where?"

"Parked a couple of rows of apartments over." She headed for her dresser.

He stood. "What are you doing?"

"Getting dressed. We've got to get the license plate number..."

PRESCOTT KNEW THEN, she wasn't lying about the car. If the person driving it was someone she knew, she wouldn't have been willing to give him the license number. He had the power to find out who the car belonged to—end of game. She undoubtedly knew that.

"The license plates were removed."

She stared back at him, her eyes wide with fear, and her body trembled. She was scared, and he was certain she wasn't acting.

Yet he couldn't believe she could really see the future. No one could do such a thing.

"Was the engine warm? Hell, was he in the car?"

"The windows were too dark. But the car's hood was cold."

"Jeez, Scotty, you risked having him try to run you over again."

He walked over to her, and she acted as though she wanted to run away. He was certain his actions were scaring her now, and he hadn't any intention of doing so, but he was really worried about her. Taking her hand in his, he squeezed it reassuringly.

"Why is he here, Kat? Why is his car sitting in your apartment complex?" "You think it's some guy I've been dating?" Her voice rose in annoyance.

He ran his hands through her wet curls. "What if he was after me because I was seeing you?"

She looked from him to the floor, then to him again. "But I had the visions. I saw him go after you the first time—that's why I had to get into the ball—to try and protect you. I wouldn't have gone if I hadn't had the vision first."

She pulled away from him and retrieved her purse. She yanked the paring knife out. "I'll fix his tires, and he won't be able to—"

"What if the owner of the car hasn't anything to do with what we suspect has happened to me? What if it's just another black SUV?"

"Without license plates?" She set the knife down on her kitchen counter. "And why would a brand-new SUV belong to someone who lived in this place? You've seen what most of us own. Not new top of the line vehicles. That SUV must have cost around $40,000."

"Quite a bit more than that."

"Jeez, the price of a home." He raised his brows, and she quickly added, "Well a good-sized down payment on one."

His thoughts shifted to the owner of the SUV again. "So what do you think? Could it be someone who doesn't like that I'm dating you?"

She folded her arms and gave him a get-real look, chin tilted down, brows raised. "Whoever said we were dating, Scotty?"

But he wasn't giving her up. "Are you free tomorrow night for supper?"

"You think I have a boyfriend trying to run you over and—"

"I thought maybe it was some kind of hoax—an interesting way to get my attention."

Her naked lips pursed, but they were just as enticing as they were when they were glistening with shimmering gloss. "I don't need to get men's attentions in such an extravagant way," she said.

"I don't doubt that, Kat. But you've got mine now, and I'm not giving up on us."

"What would your family think of me living in a place like this?"

"It wouldn't matter to them in the least."

Kat turned her head slightly with her chin down as she considered him. He figured she was thinking, "Yeah, right!"

"My parents want me to be happy, ultimately. That's all."

"How old are you?"

"Twenty-nine."

"And you've never been married?"

"Four times."

She frowned, and he laughed.

"Just teasing. I've never been married. But Camden has been, twice. Neither of us has found the right woman."

"If I invited your family over to dinner, what would they think?"

"I'm the only one you have to please, Kat."

"Somehow, I don't think so."

He shrugged, not about to win this argument. "What about *your* parents?"

"My Uncle Bill would probably ask you for a loan for his chicken farm, Aunt Sally would want some money for her beauty salon built in the basement of their old farmhouse, their kids would want..." She chuckled as he grinned at her. "Just kidding. I don't have any Uncle Bill or Aunt Sally. Mom and Dad would be happy if I found a nice fellow. But they wouldn't be happy at all if they learned he stood in my apartment after midnight while I wore my granny gown."

His gaze raked over her. She looked totally appealing, huggable, but the way she had her arms crossed over her chest, unapproachable. "Looks soft and cuddly."

"It is. So why did you come here to my place tonight, really?"

"I couldn't sleep, Kat. I didn't want there to be any hard feelings between us. And I hadn't asked you for a date for tomorrow night. Then I figured you had an unlisted number as you weren't listed in the phone book. So I couldn't call you either. Only thing left for me to do was run on over here."

He knew she didn't have a phone, but he didn't want to let on.

"Tomorrow, what time?"

"At six? I'll pick you up." He had to anyway as it looked like the car she owned wasn't going anywhere. He wanted to ask where she worked, but because of the lateness of the hour, he decided to ask her the next day. "I guess I ought to let you get to sleep, Kat."

"I'm sorry about the movie. It upset me that you thought I dated some guy who tried to run you over—that it was some kind of scheme of mine."

"Maybe we can make it another time."

"I'd like that."

He looked down at her mouth. More than anything else in the world, he wanted to kiss her.

She tugged at his shirt. "I'll see you tomorrow then."

He couldn't leave without a kiss. The rest of the night, he'd have kicked himself if he'd returned home without giving her a kiss goodnight. He lifted her chin, and she smiled.

Her smile was not all sweetness and innocence. She was one turn on. Touching his lips to hers, he enjoyed the sugar sweet flavor of orange juice lingering there. Her tongue played with his in affectionate sweeps as she tilted her head back to enjoy his attentions though and he knew she was enjoying the kiss as much as he was. He could feel her reluctance to take this any further, the way her hands rested on his hips, not pulling closer, but ready to shove him away. His blood already hot with need, he broke off the kiss before she had to exercise her prerogative.

Looking pleased that he had used some self-restraint, she smiled up at him, tentatively touching only his right hip now, her other hand shoved in the pocket of her robe. "You came all the way here to give me a goodnight kiss?"

"And get another date." He rested his hands on her shoulders clothed in velour. Her whole body was soft where his was hard and getting harder.

And then a knock sounded softly on the door...so subtle, he wasn't certain that's what he heard.

They both stilled and listened. Another knock...louder this time.

Prescott looked down at her, questioning who would be visiting her in the middle of the night—besides himself.

She looked worried and he wondered what the hell was going on.

Prescott released her at once and stormed toward the door. When he yanked it opened, nothing but the mist filled his vision. Without a further moment's hesitation, he ran outside into the dense fog, searching for the man whose footfalls were fading into the night.

KATRINA TOOK a deep breath of the cold foggy air and stared out into the night.

Lucky? Was it him? Had she sacrificed her family's secret because of getting so wrapped up in Prescott, she'd neglected her real concern?

"Prescott!" Katrina couldn't see a thing in the gloom where apartment parking lot lanterns cast an eerie hazy light in the deepening fog. She dashed for the kitchen, grabbed the paring knife off the laminated counter, and headed for the door.

Her porch light illuminated the mist collected around her

doorstep, and the whole area looked like some London Jack the Ripper horror scene. Prescott's shoes pounded the pavement in the distance...at least she assumed it was him.

She stepped onto the porch. No images plagued her now, though she wished she could see what was happening through his eyes.

Her heart thumped at a quickened beat. She gripped the knife tighter. Then a voice from the mist called to her. "Kat!"

Prescott's voice, but she couldn't see him...not yet.

Footsteps ran toward her. She took a step back.

When Prescott appeared from the mist, she breathed in a ragged breath. "Prescott."

"Scotty." He pulled her inside her apartment. "Get dressed and pack a bag. You'll stay at my home tonight."

"But—"

"I didn't see any sign of him. I ran to the area where the black SUV was parked...it was gone. No big surprise. But if he comes back here, I don't want you to be alone. My place has tons of security. It'd be safer for you."

She didn't want to stay, but she didn't want to go to his place either. What would his folks think of her? Of the situation they were in? Somehow, too, she had to meet with Lucky and straighten him out.

"I don't think—"

"Where's your bag?"

She frowned at him. She didn't have a bag—as in a suitcase suitable for fancy excursions. Trips weren't something she took —ever. She went to the closet and rummaged through it until she found her handy-dandy black backpack.

He stared at it, then smiled. "That'll do. What do you want me to fill it up with?"

8

No way did Katrina want Prescott digging through her chest of drawers. She might not have had a slippery chemise to wear at night, but her lace-trimmed satin panties and bras were another story. The next thing she'd know, he'd want to see her wearing them...and then he'd want to see her out of them.

She smiled as she sensed he was wondering what she did wear under her street clothes. "I'm just staying overnight, Scotty. I'll pack my things."

She grabbed a change of clothes, then walked into the bathroom and closed the door.

Did he believe her now about the danger? She hoped so. She could deal with the man easier if Scotty was more aware of what was going on.

She fastened her bra, then pulled her pink sweatshirt over her head. After zipping her jeans closed, she poked her feet into a pair of running shoes. The most expensive shoes she owned.

She threw cosmetics and a flannel nightgown into her bag, then left the bathroom to grab a dress and heels from her closet.

"Okay. I'm ready. I have to call Sascha early in the morning though. Have you got an alarm clock?"

He grabbed her bag, then wrapped his hand securely around her arm. "One or two."

She was certain she was going to have to rescue Prescott again, but for now, his firm touch on her arm warmed her with security.

He walked her quickly to his car, pressing the door locks open. He opened the car door for her and the car's interior lighted. For an instant, she felt exposed, as if someone might be watching them, and she quashed the jittery feeling that crawled up her spine and climbed inside. Unaware of the way she was feeling so unnerved, he closed the door and was soon in the driver's seat and started the car.

"You have a guest bedroom, don't you?"

He chuckled under his breath. "Several."

She figured that. She just didn't want him getting the impression she wished to stay with him in his room.

"Are you sure your parents won't mind?"

"They're out of town until Friday."

She ran her hands over her lap. "You mean your parents let you and your brother stay home alone?"

He laughed out loud.

She loved the sound of his laughter...from the gut...like she'd really tickled him.

He reached over and patted her leg. "You can have the room next to mine. That way if you get scared, you can throw a pillow at the wall, and I'll come running."

"Light sleeper?"

"Very. We have an old hoot owl who keeps me company most nights."

"I envisioned you were pretty citified."

"We have a lot of acreage surrounding the house. Plus, we have two smaller homes on the property."

"Leased out?"

"Years ago someone else owned them, but we bought them out. More privacy for us that way."

"Two good houses not being used by anyone?"

"Yeah, kind of wasteful. We've considered moving them."

"Sure, that would be the way to go. Give them to someone who could use them who doesn't already have a home."

PRESCOTT HADN'T CONSIDERED GIVING the houses away. Selling them would have been the Worthington way. And yet someone like Kat and her friend, Sascha, could have used a place like that to live in. Heck, his parents had a television in every bedroom in the house. Yet, his family rarely watched them. With their busy social schedule, they normally didn't have time. The more he thought of it, the more he realized how much he had that he took for granted, every day.

Kat leaned her head against the seat, and he could tell she barely was able to stay awake. But when they arrived at his place, she sat up straight.

The security gate opened automatically, and he drove onto the brick driveway. Lights illuminated the long drive all the way to the house, though the fog made him drive slower than normal, and he noticed she was taking the whole scene in that she could make out like a kid in a toy store.

She nodded. "This looks just like my Uncle Jimmy's place. Rambling Texas style homestead. Doesn't look too big from the front but keeps extending for miles out back."

He chuckled. Even though she might have felt overwhelmed

by the sheer size of the place, she wasn't about to show it. He admired her for her gumption.

He pulled into a garage with an elevator lift. Her eyes grew round as he parked on the second level of the two-story parking garage. He guessed her Uncle Jimmy didn't have one of those. After grabbing her bag, he hurried around to the other side of the car and helped her out.

"I'll have to tell him about this. He and Aunt Meg have got to get one of these."

This was even better than the Uncle Billy with the chicken farm. He probably wasn't real either.

He walked her inside the house and headed straight for the bedrooms. Her head riveted around like an owl's as she tried to take in all of the sights. "Do you have a pool?"

"Yep."

"I should have brought my bathing suit and skipped work tomorrow."

"We have a loaner you could use. About your size, I'd say."

"A loaner bathing suit?" She laughed. "No, thanks. I'm just kidding. If I have a job tomorrow, I have to work."

She didn't have a regular job even? What did she do that she was on call for?

"One of our furniture stores needs a salesperson. Would you be interested in the job?"

"No. Thanks, Scotty. I wouldn't give up my work for the world."

"But you just said you might not have a job."

"I'm a substitute elementary schoolteacher. I usually have work, but sometimes, I don't."

"Oh." He rubbed his chin already sprouting a whiskery stubble. He must have looked like some kind of ape man. "Maybe you could fill in when you don't have substitute schoolwork to do."

"I'm sure your company would like that. Come in when I could."

"We have a very liberal work policy."

"Because I'm *dating* one of the owners?"

"Doesn't hurt." He smiled to hear her words. She was dating him, and he was truly pleased. "When things get lean, I might check into it."

From what he could tell about her living conditions, things were already way too lean.

"You have a standing invitation to apply for the job." He motioned to a bedroom door. "Your room, Kat." Waving at the next door, he said, "And mine. Don't go down to the next one. An ogre lives there."

"Your brother."

"Yeah, only at this time of morning if we were to wake him, he'd be an ogre for certain."

The door to Camden's room opened, and Prescott fought the urge to shove Kat into the guestroom and lock the door. Wearing a pair of boxers, Camden squinted at them as he rubbed his dark hairy chest. His hair was mussed up, and he sported a fuzzy dark stubble like Prescott. "What's going on?"

Prescott stood in front of Kat, hiding her from Camden's view. "Just rescuing a damsel in distress. Go back to bed, Camden. See you in the morning."

"Who is she?"

"The fortune teller," Kat said, then headed into the room. "Night, Scotty. Thanks, for everything."

She shut the door to the room, and he frowned. Camden had ruined his chance at another goodnight kiss.

"Who is she?" Camden asked again.

Prescott walked to his bedroom. "My date. Goodnight."

"The one you left earlier? The one who hadn't worked out?

You chased her down?" He chuckled. "Must have hooked *you* good. What's her name?"

"Katrina Landry."

Camden's eyes grew big. "Lee Landry? Who the hell is she? She's not related to the Landrys of Dallas. I already checked. What gives?"

"A fortune teller. Listen, if I'm going to make it into work later this morning, I've got to get some sleep, Camden."

"The woman at the ball? The one you threw Starla over for? What did you bring her here for?" Camden stared past him at the guestroom door, then raised his brows. "Why not take her to bed with you?"

"We're not quite there yet. Goodnight, Camden. And don't get any ideas about her."

He grinned. "She danced with me *first*, Prescott." He rubbed his belly. "Did I hear her call you Scotty?"

Prescott walked into his bedroom and shut the door. If his brother tried for her, he'd regret it.

KATRINA SNUGGLED against the down pillows and super soft mattress. The bed was a cushy bit of heaven, and she imagined it couldn't have been made any dreamier unless Prescott snuggled with her under the silky satin-like sheets.

Closing her eyes, she imagined his lips pressed against hers...warm, lingering, reassuring...she groaned. If Camden hadn't interrupted them, she would have had another one of Prescott's toe-tingling kisses.

And why not still? Was he truly a light sleeper? She grabbed the pillow next to her and threw it at the wall adjoining his room with hers.

Then she waited. No response. She wiggled her foot. Then she leaned over the bed to find the decorator pillows she'd dropped onto the floor. She threw a round velvet pillow, a rectangular tapestry, and two satin ones at the wall, one after another. Finding no more pillows to pelt his wall with, she leaned back against the mattress. He must have been in REM sleep.

She reached around the bedside table and touched a tissue box. Hmm, maybe it would make a little louder noise, without denting the wall. Tossing it across the room, it made a slightly louder clunk.

A knock on her door soon followed, and she smiled. "Yes?" she said.

"Is everything all right in there, Kat?"

"No."

Prescott opened the door, and the light in the hallway spilled into the room. He was wearing silk ice blue pajama bottoms and his lightly haired chest was exposed for maximum view. She sighed. Even underneath his garments, he was a perfect specimen of a man. His broad shoulders could have held the world on his back. But now, she just wanted his arms wrapped securely around her.

He raised a glass of milk to her. "I just went to the kitchen for some milk. Would you like some to help you sleep? I know sleeping in a new bed can be kind of difficult sometimes."

Glancing over at the wall, he finally noticed all of the pillows and the tissue box on the floor. Chuckling, he turned back to face Katrina. "Did you get scared? Or were you having a pillow fight?"

She smiled. "I didn't get my goodnight kiss. Camden interrupted us." He pulled the door closed behind him as his teeth shown in a toothy grin.

"Only a kiss, mind you."

"My parents are away."

She chuckled. "Yeah, but Camden will tell on us."

Prescott laughed. His footsteps plodded toward her in the dark. Then he rested his full milk glass on the table with a clunk. "Just a kiss, Scotty." He laughed again.

Did he not believe her? That that's all she could handle for the moment? A kiss? A wonderfully passionate goodnight kiss?

His hands touched her face, his fingers caressing her lips.

She let out her breath, not even aware she'd been holding it. "Your parents won't leave you boys alone again when they find out what you dragged home."

"I brought home the fortune teller we're having for our party, only a few days early."

"I'm only staying the night, Scotty."

"We'll see."

She would have loved staying in the guestroom the rest of the week. The place was as gorgeous as she imagined any high-priced resort might have been. But she knew his folks wouldn't have liked her being there, especially when they found out she was only a substitute schoolteacher.

Then he placed his mouth against hers with the same kind of possessiveness she loved. Was he like that with the rich girls he'd been with? She imagined he was. But it didn't matter for the moment. For now, she loved how he kissed.

She touched her tongue to his just in a playful sweep, but he dove in with fervor, tasting her essence as if his pent-up need was finally unleashed.

She sensed his mind was foggy with desire. She knew she had to stop him before long or she'd be in real trouble. And then he was on top of her, the coverlet, and their clothes keeping them from going too far. But he kissed her with such passion, she was sure if they continued much longer, he'd be joining her under the covers.

As he grabbed the top edge of the blanket, there was a knock at the door. It couldn't have been Camden. Would he have tried to see her when she was in bed like this? When she was seeing his brother?

"Prescott? Are you in there?"

Prescott groaned, then rolled off her. As he strode to the door, he growled, "What do you want, Camden?"

"Your cell phone was ringing."

Prescott jerked the door open. Camden looked around him to catch a glimpse of Katrina. "At two in the morning?"

"Hey, it's not *my* phone ringing. And if you had it turned off, it wouldn't have disturbed my sleep." He winked at Katrina, handed the phone to Prescott, and said, "Night, Lee." Then he sauntered down the hallway.

Prescott said into the phone, "Hello?"

He held his hand over the mouthpiece. "Goodnight, Kat."

"Night, Scotty." As he shut the door behind him, she wondered who would have been calling him at that time in the morning. Then she saw the blue-eyed, blond in a vision. *Starla.*

It appeared things weren't quite over between Prescott and her.

IRRITATED TO THE MAX, Prescott guessed Starla's day with Camden hadn't met with her expectations, or perhaps she got word somehow Prescott was seeing another woman, and Starla was angry about it. Tough, he'd broken up with her. Three times already. Couldn't the woman get it through her head they were through?

Phone in hand, he shut the door to his bedroom, then crossed the floor to his bed. When he climbed under his covers, he ran his tongue over his lips. Kissing Kat was enough to send him over the edge.

Then the shrill whine of Starla's voice brought him to his senses. "Who is she, Prescott?" Kat was someone he wished to spend a whole lot more quality time with. That's who she was. "You wouldn't know her." If Starla learned Kat was staying with him at his place, she'd be more than incensed. "Listen, you know it's been coming to this for months, Starla. I told you a long time ago that I didn't feel things were working out between us. In fact, if you don't recall, we've broken up three times already."

"And I told you how wrong you were. You and I were meant to be together. Not Camden and me."

He was certain she wasn't good for Camden either. And he knew she wasn't meant for him. He'd known he was missing something in his relationship with Starla. She was totally shallow and indifferent. Trying to explain to her how much the businesses were getting him down, hadn't fazed her in the least bit. Her father could handle stuff like that, why couldn't he?

Already his temple filled with pressure. A headache was coming on—maybe because of his lack of sleep—or maybe because of the tension he always felt when he talked with her. "Starla, I'm sorry, but it's over between us."

"Who is she?"

A soft knock at his bedroom door caught his attention. He stared at it for a second. Had he really heard a knocking? Or was it his imagination? "I told you. No one you know."

To his astonishment, the door opened slowly. In the hallway illuminated by the dim glow of a nightlight, Kat stood like an angel silhouetted in her flannel gown. What did she have in mind? He sat up in bed.

She crossed the carpeted floor.

Starla cleared her throat. "Camden will tell me. He didn't know who she was, but he'll find out. He said he would. Then he'll tell me. And then—well, you just tell her—Prescott are you listening to me?" *Barely.*

Kat pulled his covers aside and slipped in beside him. She took the phone from his hand, surprising him even more, though he had to smile at her, wondering just what she was up to.

Kat said to Starla, "You're giving Scotty a headache. Nighty-night."

She turned the phone off, then leaned over him to place the phone on the bedside stand. Her breasts touched his chest, sending a surge of adrenaline through him. "Hmm. Lie back, Scotty, and

relax. You're passing your headache on to me. It hurts something fierce."

He lay back on his pillow and pulled her close.

She smiled. "The headache's going away."

"You're the cure."

Her fingers massaged his temple while he ran his hands over her back. She kissed his forehead. "All gone."

"Yeah, but I have other tensions that need relieving now." No woman could make him as hard as she could in so few seconds flat.

She grinned at him. "Can't help you there. Just don't talk to Starla any more tonight."

When she tried to leave the bed, he shook his head and held her hands hostage. "You can't leave me alone. What if the headache returns?" Her chuckling made him laugh.

She nestled her head against his chest. "All right, but no funny business."

"Jeez, Kat, I can see you're going to be really hard on me."

Running her hand over his bare chest sent a new twinge of need straight to his groin. He groaned and she chuckled. "Sorry, Scotty. With my special powers, I can't sleep around."

He ran his fingers through her silky curls. Her hair smelled like vanilla, and he took a deep breath of the fragrance. "I'm glad to hear you haven't been with too many before me—"

She leaned back from him, and though he couldn't see her clearly in the dark, he was certain she frowned at him. He touched her brow and attempted to smooth away the wrinkle formed there.

"I'm one of those oddities, Scotty—you know—a virgin?" She sighed with exasperation as she rolled onto her back next to him. She still touched the hair on his chest with a gentle caress. "I know you don't believe I have any powers, but the truth of the matter is, I do. And unless I've found my soul mate, I can't...well, consummate the relationship."

A virgin. That was a new one on him. He never would have believed any woman who must be in her mid-twenties—

Her roaming fingers distracted him. He took them in his hand and lifted them to his lips. Still, he liked the notion he could be her first and only true love. His mouth lingered on her fingers. "I like the idea."

She laughed. "Sure you do, Scotty. Like any man would enjoy waiting."

"No really. So if you find your soul mate, you can do it, right?"

"After marriage."

"Oh. How do you know when you've found the right man then?"

"I'll know when the time is right. The problem is he has to realize it too."

Drawing close again, she rested her head on his chest. Her fingers drifted across his chest and touched his nipple.

She was driving him insane with her sensitive contact, and he wanted to touch her back the same way. But when his hand moved from her shoulder to her breast, she pulled away again.

"Time to sleep, Scotty. If I disturb you too much, I'll return to the guestroom."

"Not on your life." He pulled her close. He wanted to feel the warmth of her soft curves against his body. She felt heavenly to the touch, and he wouldn't give her up the whole night through.

She snuggled against him, but his body ached for her. "At least the headache's gone," she teased as if she read his mind.

Did she really sense he was experiencing headaches? Could she truly be linked to him? And if she was, maybe everything else she said was true too.

"What would happen if someone was to make love to you who wasn't your soul mate, Kat?"

That wasn't the question he really wanted answered. What he really wanted to know was...could he be the one?

9

T he notion Kat would have jumped at the chance to marry someone like him, when she had nothing and Prescott had so much, was a given. But what if what she'd said earlier turned out to be true? That she could only marry her soul mate?

It didn't seem possible.

He ran his fingers through her curls. Her breathing grew shallow. He was certain she had fallen asleep and had never heard his question. What would happen if someone took advantage of her? Would they disintegrate due to her abilities? He chuckled under his breath.

She sure had him going. Why didn't she just say she wanted to wait?

He wrapped his arms around her. The night would end way too soon for his liking. He kissed the top of her head, and she snuggled deeper with him, her hand drifting to his thigh.

He moaned.

Maybe the night wouldn't end soon enough.

THE NEXT MORNING, Camden pounded on Prescott's door. "Rise and shine, Sleeping Beauty."

Prescott groaned. Then he sat up quickly in bed. Where was Kat? To his alarm, the woman he had cuddled with all night long had vanished.

He jumped out of bed and strode to the door. Yanking it open, he squinted at Camden. His eyes were scratchy from the lack of sleep, and he blinked a couple of times. Waking up to see Camden at his bedroom door, wearing only a pair of swim trunks, wasn't helping matters either.

"Where's Kat?"

"This woman has more names than—" Prescott shoved past him.

"She's taking a swim. She called a friend this morning. After she hung up the phone, she told me she was free the rest of the day. She asked me for a loaner swimsuit. I thought she was kidding, but then—"

Prescott headed for the swimming pool while Camden kept up with his long stride.

"She's a great swimmer, Prescott, if you're worried about her drowning or something. I gave her a test and certified her for swimming on her own." He glanced down at Prescott's pajama bottoms. "Aren't you going to get ready and go in to work?"

"What about you?"

"I'm taking the day off."

Yeah, because Camden was already making his moves on Kat. The notion infuriated him. How long had Camden been with her? And doing what?

Prescott walked out onto the tile patio, the sun already sparkling on the surface of the water, a slight warm breeze making the live oak leaves dance in the breeze. But mostly all he saw was Kat swimming a final lap underneath the surface of the crystal blue water. Then she surfaced and turned to see him standing there watching her. She smiled.

Her perky expression brightened his morning instantly, waking him better than any caffeine stimulant could.

"She told me to wake you, Prescott. That she should head on home. I offered to take her, but she said she'd wait until you got up."

"Okay, I'll take it from here."

"In your pajamas?"

Camden sure could be irritating. Prescott cursed under his breath, then headed back to his room. He rarely swam any longer. The newness had worn off years earlier. But being in the pool with Kat, now that was a total turn on.

Once in his room, he struggled to get his swim trunks on in a rush, then hurried back to the pool. To his relief, she was still enjoying the water. She clung to the Aztec tile side, her cheek resting on her arm as she had waited for him to arrive. Her eyes sparkled with mischief as she watched him, a small smile curving her lips.

Droplets of water dotted her ivory skin while her drenched curls drifted over her shoulders, floating on the surface of the water.

"Morning, Kat." He dove into the pool.

The warm water felt silky against his skin. Even better was the great pair of legs that grew closer with every stroke he took.

Kat's body wavered slightly as she stood before a water jet. The bathing suit she wore was cut high on her legs and the bodice dipped nice and low.

He swam straight for her, then came up, locking her in place against the blue and terra-cotta-colored Spanish hand-painted tile. "You should have awakened me this morning."

Her green shimmering one-piece enhanced the color of her eyes, making him swear she wore colored contact lenses. Something about her made her appear almost otherworldly—her skin fairly glowed in the soft morning sunlight, and her cheeks were lightly colored—from the sun? Or was it his being so close to her?

Taking a ragged breath, he knew she was too good to be true. He'd soon wake from the dream, and she'd vanish with it.

She touched his face. "You were sleeping so soundly. I didn't want to disturb you."

He kissed away drops of water on her lips, her pink mouth curving up as she sighed deeply.

"Being awakened by you wouldn't have disturbed me, Kat."

To Prescott's irritation, Camden carried a tray of chilled glasses of juice onto the patio. "Here's some orange juice, folks," Camden said.

Get lost, Camden.

"I thought you might need a little get up and go. Prescott can really be difficult in the morning. A little fresh orange juice can sweeten his disposition."

"Really?" Kat's lips nibbled on Prescott's ear, making him groan. "He seems pretty agreeable to me."

"I guess you have all of the right moves then." Camden sat down on a chaise lounge. "Starla called this morning. She asked who the woman was that you were with last night, Prescott. I figured you didn't care if she knew or not."

Prescott barely heard his brother's words as Kat was distracting him way too thoroughly. She'd rested her head on his shoulder while her fingers ran circles over his chest. "What did you want to do today, Kat?" He held her waist, then leaned over and kissed her cheek.

"I really ought to get home."

"Camden said you didn't have any work to do today. So you're free."

"But I don't want to keep *you* from your work."

Camden cleared his throat. "Do you want to give me a reading, Lee?"

Prescott looked up at him. "Don't you have something else to do? I thought you were overseeing having some of our furniture relocated to one of the other stores today, *Camden*." His voice was terse. Would his brother back off on his own or would Prescott have to make it plainer to him first?

"It's already taken care of." Camden leaned back on the lounger. "Starla's on her way over here, by the way."

Prescott could have socked his brother. Had he called her and told her to come over or what?

"She assumed since the lady was with you last night, she might still be here this morning. Of course, she didn't mention anything about it—just asked if she could run on by and spend some time with me. But knowing the way she is, she wanted to see who her competition was."

"And you couldn't tell her you were going to be busy working? As you should have been?"

Kat ran her fingers through Prescott's hair. "Really nice hair," she whispered.

He pressed her close to his body. "Really nice body," he whispered back.

She giggled. "I think I'd better head back to my place, Scotty."

"Want to go for a boat ride?" Prescott asked her, as he had no plan to let her out of his sight for the rest of the day.

The glass patio door slammed shut.

They all turned to face the intrusion.

Starla, red-faced, narrowed eyes, a dragon ready to send them both up into flames.

~

KATRINA'S HEAD HURT. She was certain it was from the lack of sleep. Then she reached over and touched Prescott's temple. "Are you having another headache, Scotty?"

The pain radiated across her temple and even into her teeth. She kissed his cheek, knowing Starla was ready to explode as she stood near the house watching them. Then the tension from Prescott's forehead eased a bit. The pain in her head lessened.

All dolled up in designer clothes, Starla wore a shorter than short miniskirt, not even fashionable as far as Katrina was concerned. An overly tight spandex blouse completed the ensemble.

Starla was trying to win Prescott back.

Starla crossed the patio and practically sat on Camden's lap. He didn't seem to mind as he wrapped his arms around her. But he didn't kiss her. For being a stud, why didn't he? He couldn't think he had a chance with Katrina instead, could he?

"I want a reading, Lee. It seems everyone around here got one but me," Camden said.

"She's...she's the fortune teller at the fair?" Starla screamed. Her cheeks looked sunburned as her nose turned red.

Katrina smiled as she toyed with the ties to Prescott's swimming trunks. "Yes, have you found your strawberry blond boyfriend yet?"

"A strawberry blond, eh?" Camden said. "Hmm, sounds like our gardener."

Starla's claws extended. "So what do you do when you're not picking up men at the fair?"

"I rescue them. It's sort of a hobby of mine."

Prescott's hands slipped around Katrina's waist, and she enjoyed feeling his chest against her back. She was certain he was trying to show he was protecting her from the evil ex-girlfriend. But really, she could handle a woman like Starla.

"Camden wants a reading." Starla ran her fake red fingernail over Camden's bare leg. "You can give me another."

"All right." Katrina hadn't really wanted to give anyone any more readings, not with being linked already with Prescott. She wasn't sure what that could do to her abilities. But the notion she could predict something about Starla that would really happen was just too tempting. Then would Prescott believe her? And what would Starla think? It could be a total hoot. Prescott squeezed her tighter. "I thought we might go out for a bite to eat."

"Maybe we could go out together," Camden said.

"I don't think so," Prescott said, though his tone of voice was more of a definite "no."

The headache returned. Katrina tugged at him. "I'm going to get out of the pool and change. Then we can get something to eat."

He climbed out with her, and they grabbed towels, then headed into the house.

When they were out of earshot of Camden and Starla, Katrina slipped her fingers through Prescott's. "You really shouldn't let her bother you so."

"What do you mean?"

"Your headache, Scotty. I feel it, too. Just ignore her. She's not worth bothering over."

"It's not *her* I'm worried about."

"Oh? What then?"

He pulled her into the guestroom. "Camden."

She chuckled and touched his wet cheek. "I'm not interested in your brother, believe me. And he prefers blonds." She really couldn't believe Prescott would worry about her with Camden.

"He's interested in you. We never had a problem with dating women before, but for whatever reason, he's got his sights set on you."

"He'll have to look elsewhere. So where are we going to eat? Sweatshirt and jeans kind of place or should I wear my dress?"

"Your dress. Not that I want Camden to see you dressed up—"

"But it would irk Starla." Prescott grinned at her.

"You're cute, you know that, Scotty?" She pushed him toward his bedroom door. "I'll be ready in a little while. Do you have a hairdryer I can use?"

"Bathroom down the hall."

He kissed her lips, then his gaze drifted to her bathing suit. "I really had a nice night last night."

She lifted his head so he'd focus on her eyes and not her breasts. "You mean after the drive-in?"

"Yeah, after you joined me last night."

"Yeah, that was pretty nice all right. A lot softer mattress than my couch sofa, and I had a great bed warmer, too."

"You don't have to go home tonight. You could stay here with me."

She shook her head. "Then Starla would stay with Camden and your parents would arrive home early. What would they say then? All these wild parties while they were away?"

He seemed wryly amused. But Katrina was already thinking about the trouble she could cause for Starla, the witch, who didn't know what she had coming if she thought to mince words with her. The reading would come before they went out and ate, served up nice and spicy, enough to give Starla major heartburn. At least that was the plan!

AFTER THEY CHANGED CLOTHES, Prescott thought they were going out to brunch first, but Katrina said she wanted to do the reading for Starla first.

He frowned down at her. "Are you sure? She can really be vicious, Kat."

"I'll be fine, really." Katrina looked so innocent and sweet, yet the hint of the devil shadowed her expression.

He just hoped she knew what she was doing. He led Katrina to the Blue Velvet Parlor, as he thought of the room, where every piece of furniture was covered in robin egg's blue velvet, paintings of blue bonnets all over the walls, and the carpet was even a pale blue.

Starla and Camden were having a discussion about nail polish colors, and Prescott raised his brows a little to see the amused look on his brother's face. Camden wasn't in the least bit shallow, yet he seemed to be truly interested in nail polish. At least on the surface.

"If you still want a reading, Kat said she'd give you one," Prescott said to them, sounding as unenthusiastic as he felt.

Katrina motioned to a card table and seemed determined to see this through. "Shall we?"

They all took seats at the table and Starla lifted her chin and looked down her nose at Katrina and stuck her hand out. Prescott prayed Katrina could deal with Starla, who could be a viper when it came to other women, and not be upset in the process.

Katrina couldn't tell Prescott how she could handle Starla. She'd have to show him that she had everything under control instead.

Taking a deep breath, Katrina took Starla's hand and examined her palm. "Hmm, no strawberry blond in your life."

Her head began to ache, and she closed her eyes. And saw the black SUV. She hadn't expected that and a shiver ran up her spine. Why would she see the vehicle in Starla's future?

She rubbed her temple.

"Well?" Starla snapped.

Katrina's eyes blinked open, and she wanted to slap her. With the interruption, the vision instantly slipped away. She closed her eyes again. "You're going to the Galleria to shop for...a new black lace bra."

Camden chuckled and Katrina opened her eyes.

Starla's cheeks darkened. Katrina was certain it wasn't because the woman was embarrassed about having the Worthingtons know what she wanted to do. Instead, she figured Starla couldn't believe Katrina could have known. Starla didn't speak a word though.

Katrina straightened her back. "Camden?"

Starla grabbed her hand. "What else?"

Katrina yanked her hand away. Linking with two different people, she assumed could be dangerous to her mind, maybe even deadly. She wasn't certain.

"I'll see what else I can see, but you must let me do this my way." She glanced over at Prescott and noticed the worry etched in his brow. Did he believe she could link with others now?

She touched Starla's hand again and concentrated. Again, she saw the black SUV, droplets of water splattered over its waxed surface like a man sweating as he waited to do something evil.

The lights of the mall flashed in its place, shoppers with handled bags sauntering into and out of shops. "You'll meet a man at the Galleria. You'll have an argument."

"What does he look like?"

Katrina closed her eyes and turned her head. "You're... wearing something different—a dress, short, black, low cut on the bodice, high heels." She paused. "You seem to know him. At first, you laugh at something he says. Then you get mad. He's a brunette. Tall, wearing a golfing shirt and slacks. He's got a hat." She squinted her eyes tightly. "Embroidered on the hat are the initials TPJ.

Thomas. You call him Thomas and tell him to leave you alone. He's your...your half-brother."

"I haven't seen him in five years. So much for your fake readings."

Opening her eyes, Katrina ignored Starla's comment and turned to Camden. "Camden?" She didn't really want to do any more readings. Between not having enough sleep and sharing Prescott's headaches, she wasn't in the mood to do much but have lunch and take a nap.

Camden reached out his palm. She touched his hand gingerly, hoping she wouldn't get any kind of a vision at all. But there it was—nightmare of all nightmares—the black SUV. Only dry, not a speck of water marring its dust-free surface.

The car rolled forward. Camden was laughing, oblivious to the hazard behind him. He was its next target. She shook her head. Camden chuckled. "That bad eh?"

"Shhh," Prescott said.

"You...you have a confrontation with Thomas outside of the mall. You're with Starla now. He's really angry about something she's done. I just can't—"

"This is ridiculous," Starla said.

"She's told her parents Thomas embezzled half a million from their accounts, but it was all a lie. She covered for someone else. She didn't like that Thomas got special treatment because he was her father's first child and only son."

Starla snorted. "What are you trying to pull anyway? You're full of lies. Somehow, you've wormed your way into Prescott's arms. Why don't you tell him what you're really all about? How you're some wretched poor person who's after his money?"

Katrina breathed in the air and cleared her mind as she didn't pay any attention to Starla's words. She had more important things to worry about. Starla would have to deal with her half brother on her own, soon, she assumed. But

Camden...that was another story. He was going to need her help.

"Time for lunch." Katrina turned to Prescott. His face was serious, and she worried she'd said too much. But she couldn't help it. The images had cluttered her mind and were struggling to get out. Now that she'd released them, she felt relaxed. But only for a moment.

She stood, placed her hands on her temples, and pressed hard. The engine of the black vehicle roared in her head. The ton of metal lunged forward. She couldn't thwart it this time.

Her hands flew out in an attempt to stop the image. "No!" she cried out.

Instantly, the room grew white, then black. A sprinkling of lights against the blackness...then total darkness.

"KAT!" Prescott caught her before she fell, the color drained from her face. What had she seen this time? His mind told him she couldn't know the future. She just couldn't and yet, there were too many things she had seen. Would her visions come true later that day?

"Kat?" He stroked her cheek with his fingertips.

"Hmpf. She's got all the winning moves, all right," Starla grumbled as she folded her arms.

Camden grabbed the phone.

Kat groaned.

"Wait, Camden, she's coming to." Prescott moved a curl draped over her eye away as her eyelids fluttered open.

She held her head. "I...I—"

"I think you need a little more sleep."

Wanting to know what she'd seen, but not with Camden and

Starla in the same room, he had to remove her to private quarters. He lifted her in his arms and carried her to the guestroom.

Camden trailed close behind him.

Prescott had to get rid of his brother. He didn't want Camden to hear what he had to ask her. "She'll be all right, Camden. I'll take care of her."

"Are you sure we shouldn't take her to see a doctor?" Camden's voice indicated genuine concern.

Certain she didn't need a doctor, he shook his head at Camden. "Maybe you ought to take Starla out for lunch somewhere."

"Yeah, she wanted to go to the Galleria."

"The Galleria?" He looked down at Kat, but she'd closed her eyes again. Had she truly foreseen what would happen at the exclusive mall?

"Maybe you shouldn't—" Prescott said.

Camden laughed. "See you later. Maybe we can all have supper together."

Camden headed down the hall while Prescott touched her cheek. "Kat."

She opened her eyes, then rubbed her forehead. "Scotty? What happened?"

"You fainted." He ran his hand over hers.

She closed her eyes again. "Where's Camden?"

"Taking Starla to the Galleria."

She opened her eyes wide. "We have to go too."

"Not on your life. Besides the fact you fainted on me, I don't want Camden near you."

"This has nothing to do with Camden. I mean, I saw the black SUV, and I have to make sure he'll be okay. But it has nothing to do with anything else."

"What did you see, Kat?" He sat down on the bed next to her.

At first, he'd thought it was the lack of sleep that had made her faint or even maybe the headaches, but now he wasn't certain.

She shook her head.

"I'd love to know what it is you saw."

"I'm not sure. It was confusing. I see bits and pieces. Starla argues with her half brother at the Galleria. I don't know where your brother is. Maybe browsing in a store nearby. Perhaps he's standing with her, but just out of view. I saw her reflection in a mirror-like window. That's why I knew what she wore. It was as though I was seeing everything from her viewpoint. If Camden was there, she wasn't paying any attention to him."

"But you said he has a row with Thomas."

"Outside of the mall, not inside when Thomas first has an argument with Starla. She and your brother must have walked into the parking lot and met him there. Or he was waiting for them. I don't really know."

"And the black SUV?"

"From Starla's viewpoint the vehicle is wet, like it's just been through a shower. When I did your brother's reading, the vehicle was dry."

"Could it have been another day?"

"Possibly."

"What made you faint, Kat? I have to know."

KATRINA COULDN'T TELL Prescott what she saw. Saving Camden's life was foremost in her mind.

Somehow, she had to convince Prescott she wasn't crazy. That she really could see what was going to occur. On the other hand, she couldn't let him know what she had to do. Otherwise, he'd never agree to take her anywhere near his brother.

"Listen, he told me he danced with you first. He has some notion you're attracted to him."

She couldn't believe Prescott's words. How could he think she found his brother at all appealing? Prescott kindled her fire. Camden was a total fizzle.

She took Prescott's hand and kissed it. "I'm not interested in your brother." She rose from the bed, but she was still fuzzy headed. How could she save Camden, feeling as useless as she did?

"Help me to your car, Scotty. I want to go to the Galleria."

"Kat," he said, as he held her arm, "you're shaking, and I don't think you should be going anywhere except back to bed."

"To the Galleria. We'll drive around the parking lot and look for a black SUV. I don't have to walk."

His heavy sigh made her realize he was conceding to her wishes despite his reluctance. "You'll stay in the car."

"Yes." Until Camden needed her, she would. She realized, too, for whatever reason, Prescott wouldn't be there. Somehow, they'd be separated, and she'd have to face the menace...*alone*.

10

Prescott had no intention of letting Kat out of his sight at the Galleria. As far as he was concerned, she wasn't leaving the car in the event she had another fainting spell. Or worse.

He felt all along she was holding back when she told him about her visions. What really happened when she read Camden's palm? Did the SUV hit Camden? Had she seen this and that's why she had fainted? Didn't she trust Prescott enough to tell him what was going to happen?

Why should she? He hadn't believed her all along. Well, and he had to admit he still had difficulty with it. She had no reason to trust him with what she seemed to be able to see about the future.

When she cleared her throat as they climbed into his car, he was certain she had something important to say. He suspected he wouldn't be happy about it either.

"I've changed my mind. Take me home, if you would, Scotty. I'm awfully tired and need to take a nap."

"You can nap at my place." He wasn't about to let her be alone. She wasn't planning on sleeping, he was certain of it. His gut clenched with anxiety. She planned on going to the Galleria on her own. He had every intention of keeping her out of harm's way.

"All right, then, I need to speak with Sascha."

He pulled out his cell phone.

"In private."

He smiled. "I'll step out of the car then."

"I want to talk to her at her home, not like this."

Shaking his head, he motioned to the circular driveway of his parents' home. "You wanted to go to the Galleria. I'll take you there. Besides, if you intended to take your car to the mall, it wasn't working, remember?"

She ran her hand through her hair as her lips turned down in a scowl. He figured she was annoyed with him that he wouldn't let her have her own way. Did she think she was the only one who had a right to save the Worthingtons' necks?

He drove onto the road, then headed for the Galleria. "What did you see, Kat?" He wasn't giving up on finding out what would happen next.

She remained quiet, and he looked over at her. "Watch your driving, Scotty, or we'll never make it there."

He smiled. No woman had ever told him how to drive. "Can you tell where the SUV is parked? Do you see any storefront that would indicate the correct side of the mall?"

"No."

"What about which exit Camden and Starla use? Can you see which store they come out of?"

"No, sorry, nothing, Scotty."

Was she telling the truth? She sounded sincere, but he still felt she hid some of the truth. He rubbed his temple. It was then that he realized he believed her, beyond a doubt. Was he crazy? He took a deep breath. Not in his wildest imagination could he have ever believed such a thing. He had always assumed anything to do with ESP was a total crock. But now, here Katrina was...living proof. He just had to know more about her.

She rubbed her hands on the skirt of her dress. He could see she was anxious. He could feel it, almost as if he was gaining some of her telekinetic vibes. Either that, or he was growing more attuned to her emotions. Her anxiety made him want to show he could protect her in her time of need, instead of the other way around.

He reached over and squeezed her hand. "We'll take care of it together."

She looked over at him, her brow wrinkled with worry. It hit him all of a sudden. Now it was she, who didn't believe him.

If she knew what was going to happen, she wouldn't be so concerned unless somebody wasn't going to be saved this time. He gripped the leather-covered steering wheel with all his might. Her actions made him think he wasn't going to be any help at all.

He took a deep breath. "Can we change the future?"

She didn't say a word as she stared at him. The silence continued. He hated the quiet. "Kat, honey, if you've seen...I'm sorry...when you've seen something in the future, does it always come to pass? Or can the future be altered?"

"I honestly don't know for certain. Sometimes I've felt knowing is a curse. Then I've wondered if perhaps it's a blessing. Maybe because I see these things, I can affect a change. At least I know I have to try."

"Okay, that's what I mean. You don't see what happens...the end result...just that someone is in danger."

"Or something as simple as Starla picking out a black lace bra."

"The size?" He glanced over at her as she raised her brows at him. He chuckled. "I just wondered if you picked up minor details like that."

"I figured you already knew the size."

He grinned broadly as he shook his head. Trying to lighten up the subject matter had worked. Maybe reduced some of the tension in her temple. Her lips curved up, and he knew he'd helped a little, which eased his concern slightly.

When they arrived at the Galleria, he drove slowly around the parking lot. The task was formidable. Fifty percent of Texas vehicles must have been SUVs, many of which were dark colored or black.

They didn't see any without tags, and it looked like there wasn't any way they'd be able to identify the correct one. Not until the driver of the vehicle made his move later.

Maybe she could remember more details though. "What about the sunlight? Was it still light out...the sun way overhead? Or was the light fading?"

She closed her eyes, and he assumed she was trying to recall any further details. "The light was fading. In fact, that's what made it so difficult to see."

"What do you see, Kat?"

"You're not with me. I don't know why, but you're nowhere around. I have to stop it. He's headed straight for your brother, but he doesn't see it. I have to stop the vehicle."

His skin crawled with the notion. There was no way he was letting her out of his sight. "I'm sticking by your side. You're not doing this alone."

He meant to say she wasn't doing anything about it at all. He'd handle it. But for whatever reason, maybe just having the visions made her feel it was solely her mission. Still, she wasn't getting involved in a possible hit on his brother and risking injury herself. He wouldn't allow it.

Then he began to wonder what was going on. If everything was true, who was the madman, and why was he after his family? He pulled into a parking space.

Kat turned to face him. "That's what I've been asking all along."

He stared at her. She knew what he was thinking? He shook his head at himself. She had to have guessed what he was thinking. "Who would want to harm me, and now my brother?"

"Yes. Who do you know who would hold such a grudge?"

No one. He didn't know of any of their competition or ex-girlfriends' family members or their new boyfriends who might have wanted to harm them...not anyone. "No one that I can think of."

"What did you want to do now, Scotty?"

"Have lunch. Are you feeling all right?"

She nodded.

He wasn't certain she was, but maybe lunch would help. After helping her from the car, he walked her into the mall. A steak place was on the other end of the Galleria, his favorite restaurant to dine, other than his own family businesses.

Though he held onto her arm the whole way, her footstep was light and perky. He assumed whatever had made her light-headed was gone now.

She smiled when he walked her inside the restaurant. "Lovely décor."

"Yeah, I sort of borrowed their scheme in decorating one of ours. Kind of an old world feel about it."

She scooted into one of the burgundy leather booths while he sat on the one across from her. Overhead, chandeliers glittered with twinkling lights, softly illuminating the dark interior of the restaurant. "Really nice." She reached across the table, and he extended his fingers to mingle with hers. "Thank you for splurging so much on me. You've been some swell date. And to think I could have been finger-painting with five-year-olds instead."

He grinned at her. "I can see you doing that."

The women he dated always had so much money, nice restaurants never meant anything to them. Kat appreciated everything. Making her happy was all he wanted.

Her fingers touching his warmed him thoroughly. What he wouldn't give to have another night of snuggling with her good and close.

"So about tonight—"

The waiter walked up to their table. "What would you like to drink?"

Prescott ordered a bottle of the finest wine.

As soon the waiter left the table, Kat shook her head. "I can't have anything alcoholic to drink."

He didn't want to get her drunk...well, maybe he did, for her own protection. If she had enough to drink, he hoped she'd give up the notion of trying to rescue Camden.

"Just a glass, Kat, to help relax you."

She tilted her head to the side. "I'm perfectly relaxed."

Grinning, he patted her hand. "Yeah, and I want to keep you that way."

Then they heard a voice neither wished to hear. They turned as Starla whined, "Camden, you could have at least told Thomas he was a liar and defended me or something." Her tone of voice aggravated Prescott, raising his blood pressure.

As soon as Starla caught sight of them, she waved the hostess away. "We'll sit with that couple over there."

Prescott groaned.

Kat patted his hand this time. "Glad you got the bottle of wine. We're both going to need it."

Starla scooted in beside Prescott before he could move to the other booth. Camden grinned at Kat as he sat beside her.

The wine arrived right afterward. "Good thinking, Prescott," Camden said, winking at him.

Prescott figured Camden thought he was trying to get Kat

drunk. Well, he was, but not for the same reasons Camden would have done so.

After the wine was poured, Camden proposed a toast, "To new relationships."

Prescott knew Camden had every intention of trying for Kat. That was the relationship Camden was referring to, not the one he had with Starla now. They'd always had similar tastes in women. Though until now, they'd both only dated blonds... course so many women bleached their hair, it was hard to tell which were the real thing. But Kat...now *she* was totally genuine.

Camden offered to refill everyone's drinks. Starla poked her glass at him. Kat shook her head no, as she nursed her drink. Prescott waved his hand to indicate he didn't want any either. Camden poured himself another. "You sure were right on about Thomas, Lee. Everything happened just like you said."

"I take it you know the scumbag. Are you dating him or something?" Starla asked Kat.

Everyone waited for Kat to respond, but she sat in stony silence. Was she angry at Starla? Or was she having another vision? Prescott couldn't tell. If he'd been sitting beside her, he'd have patted her lap or wrapped his arm around her. As it was now, she rested her hands in her lap, and he couldn't reach her to comfort her at all.

She rubbed her temple. Yeah, he had a blasted headache again, and she felt it. She handed her glass to Camden. He wiggled his brows as he poured another glass for her.

Prescott extended his. The wine would help to ease the tension.

Camden refilled his glass. "We might have to get another bottle before long." Starla giggled. "What have you in mind afterward?"

"What do you think, Prescott?" Camden asked.

Kat motioned for Camden to move. "I need to go to the little girls' room."

"I'll go with you," Prescott said.

"I'll go with her." Starla hopped up from her seat as Camden moved aside for Kat.

Prescott was torn. He didn't want Kat to be out of his sight for even a second. But how would it have looked if he stayed by her side constantly. Possessive? Insecure?

He slid out of the booth. "Be right back, Camden."

"More for me that way."

Camden wasn't a big drinker. Prescott figured Camden's going with Starla was already taking its toll on him.

The ladies were halfway across the room when Prescott charged after them.

"He won't be interested in you for very long, you know," Starla said to Kat. "And when his folks find out who you are... why, they'll have a fit. You better believe they'll have you investigated from your gypsy toes to your uncontrollable coiffure. Then they'll speak to Prescott and that'll be the end of the fun."

Kat was rubbing her temple again, and Prescott wanted to wring Starla's neck. As soon as he closed the gap, he said, "Right behind you, ladies."

Starla's mouth gaped open as she turned to see him behind her, then she abruptly closed it and smiled broadly. She most likely wondered if he'd heard what she'd said to Kat or not. Then she probably decided she was right, whether he heard her words or not.

Either Kat was in so much pain she didn't notice him at all, or she was having another one of her visions. She never acknowledged him and hurried past the bathroom instead. Starla stood before the ladies' room and folded her arms. "You missed it."

Prescott dashed after Kat and pulled her to a stop. "The

ladies' room is back this way." He kissed her cheek as she stared vacantly back at him. "Kat?"

He kissed her lips, which seemed to break the spell. Her eyes widened, and she looked back at the restroom. Starla tapped her foot on the floor. "I thought you had to use the ladies' room."

"No." She took Prescott's hand and walked back to the table with him.

"What's going on, Kat?" He wrapped his arm around her and held her close.

"I don't know."

This, he wasn't buying. "What did you see this time?"

"Haven't you ever had a dream where when you wake, you can't recall what you saw? I have visions like that."

He sighed deeply. He still didn't trust her. Then he grew exasperated with himself. First, he didn't believe her because of what she said she saw, now he didn't think she spoke the truth when she told him she couldn't remember what she saw. "Kat, I want to be there for you." And it wasn't just for the present either. For the long run...that's what he wanted with her.

He couldn't believe he could fall for someone so soon like that. And so hard. Was it only a rebound, from ending his relationship with Starla?

"Where's Starla?" Camden stood up from the booth.

"Still at the ladies' room." Prescott maneuvered Kat into his booth. He'd lock her in, with no way to escape. He'd keep her safe.

Camden grinned at him. "Yeah. Nice maneuver."

"Learned from the best."

When Starla returned, Camden scooted into the booth to sit opposite Kat. "Musical chairs?" Starla took her seat. "What was up back there?"

Prescott reached over and patted Kat's thigh. She was so

quiet he worried she was having another vision. But as long as she couldn't get by him, he assumed she'd be safe.

Camden's ears perked up. "Something I missed?"

Prescott glanced over at her. "Kat changed her mind. You know how women are."

"Yeah," Camden said.

The way Camden said it, Prescott knew his brother figured a lot more had gone on. He probably assumed the women had a catfight.

The waiter took the meal orders, and Camden said, "So about tonight. Do you want to go somewhere, dancing maybe as a foursome?"

Prescott was sure Kat wasn't up to dancing. She needed more rest. "I think we'll have to skip that."

"What? Don't have anything nice to wear?" Starla asked Kat.

She faced her. "What?"

Prescott knew she was way too tired. "We didn't get much sleep last night."

The bitter look on Starla's face, scrunched up with her nose wrinkled like a closed accordion, amused him. She looked as though she'd eaten a really sour pickle. He hadn't meant to say it the way the words sounded. Once Kat and he snuggled together that night, they'd slept soundly. But it hadn't been until close to two in the morning before they'd gotten to that point. Still, he didn't mind Starla thinking he couldn't get enough of Kat.

He glanced over at Camden to see his eyes as round as the base of his wine glass. It didn't hurt for his brother to know how serious he was about Kat either.

Kat's voice was soft, totally at peace. "Yes, I'd like that."

Prescott turned to face her. "I thought you'd be too tired."

"I'd like to dance." Her fingers touched the buttons on his shirt. When her green eyes looked up at him, he swore they danced in the shimmering crystal lights.

"Whatever you'd like, Kat. We'll have the two cars, and if you get too tired, you and I can return home."

He looked over to see his brother and Starla's mouths agape. He lifted his wine glass. "More wine, Camden?"

SHE KNEW NOW, the incident with the SUV didn't occur at the mall. There'd still be the confrontation between Thomas and Camden, she couldn't see much else. But the SUV...it wasn't at the Galleria. It was someplace else. She'd thought the light was fading. It hadn't been. A nightclub's parking lot lights is what gave the appearance of dusk.

The dance club was where he would make his play for Camden. But how did he know their schedule so well? He watched them. That's how he knew their moves. She glanced around at the restaurant patrons. Was he sitting at a nearby table, maybe? Surely, he would be alone. What if it wasn't a man, but a woman? She hadn't considered that before.

Prescott leaned over and kissed her cheek as their salads were placed on the table. She was certain he worried about her as he squeezed her hand to comfort her. She wished he wouldn't be so concerned for her. His headache returned, and she suffered from it too. Besides, she could handle herself.

Camden made her nervous, however. Either he tried to get her attention...to show her he was interested in getting to know her better, or maybe Prescott amused him, he was making such headway with her. She couldn't tell.

Inwardly, she had to laugh about Prescott's ticking off Starla with the remark about their having not slept much that night though. If she'd been a little clearer headed, she might have said the same thing herself.

It wasn't that she didn't want Prescott to make love to her all night long. She'd even considered risking her powers to indulge in the pleasure she was sure he could have given her. But she knew how miserable Sascha had been when she'd lost her abilities.

Sascha joked often enough about it, but she knew her cousin really hadn't felt whole in a long time. Losing one of their senses wasn't an easy thing to live with. Friday, Sascha would be back to her normal self, and they'd celebrate the party of a lifetime at Prescott's family gathering.

When everyone was through with their salads, the waiter served Camden and Prescott steaks dripping with juice and shrimp pasta soaked in white cheese sauce for Katrina. Starla refused to eat another bite. No way, Katrina figured, did the woman want to gain an ounce at the meal.

Probably the extra calories from the wine did her in.

Halfway through their meal, Katrina tugged on Prescott's shirt. "I have to call Sascha." He pulled his phone out of his pocket and handed it to her.

"I have to speak to her in private."

He let her out of the booth. "We'll be back in a moment," he said to Camden and Starla.

Camden shook his head. "I thought she said she had to speak in private."

She'd already started to walk toward the bathroom when Prescott said, "She's been having dizzy spells." He ran to join her and slipped his hand around her arm. "What's up?"

"I have to ask Sascha a personal question."

Prescott walked her to the ladies' room. "Yes?"

"Personal." She grinned at him. "You know...in ladies' business."

"Oh."

"Be out in a moment."

"I'll be right here."

She kissed his lips. "Good, I wouldn't want to lose you."

He gave her a smile that meant he was well pleased with her declaration. "The feeling's mutual, Kat."

She took a deep breath, sure she knew what she was going to do before she did it, and opened the door, then closed it behind her. She punched in the numbers for Sascha. There was no way she was going to wait to find out if she and Prescott were true soul mates. The phone rang four times, then Sascha's voice came on. "Hello?"

"Hi, Sascha?"

"Hello?"

Katrina frowned. She hated Sascha's message machine.

"Hello? Oh, sorry, no one can come to the phone right this minute. Leave a message at the sound of the beep, and one of us will get right back to you as soon as we can."

"Sascha, it's me, Katrina. Listen, I have to know...how can we tell if the man we meet is the right one? I have to know. Can you call Aunt Meg for me? If I ever doubted why you didn't wait with Damon, I realize now how powerful the drive is to be with a man. I'm still with Prescott. We're going dancing, and then I'll be home much later tonight."

"Katrina!"

"Sascha."

"I just walked in the door and heard some of your message. Don't, whatever you do, let yourself get lulled into a situation with Prescott or anyone else."

"I've never even considered such a thing, not until I met him."

"I'll call Aunt Meg, but Katrina, I'm worried with you staying overnight like that with him."

"I had to. He came to see me last night, and the black SUV was parked in our complex." Katrina tucked her curl behind her ear, hoping Prescott wouldn't mind she was keeping him so long.

Then she stared at the door for a moment. He couldn't hear her conversation through the thin walls, could he?

"Why in the world did he come to see you? You went to the drive-in, then—"

"We sort of had a fight. The SUV made another attempt on his life, and he didn't believe I'd saved him. In fact, he thought it was my boyfriend who was driving the car."

"Damn, Katrina. I knew there was more to what was going to happen than you'd let on."

"Yeah, well, he came by to make up, and someone knocked on my door. Prescott worried about my safety, so he took me home with him."

"And?"

"There's going to be another attempt made tonight, only for Camden this time."

"Call the police."

"And say what? A black SUV that doesn't have any license plates is stalking the two brothers? Prescott doesn't have a clue as to who would have a motive to harm them. So we have nothing to go on."

"What are you going to do?"

"Save Camden, what else? I just wanted you to know what was going on—"

"You wanted to know if Prescott was the one."

"I want him to be, Sascha. I want him to love me forever."

"Have you spoken with your mother?"

Katrina took a deep breath. "You know how she is. She doesn't want to discuss the subject of finding a soul mate. I don't think she really believes in it anyway."

"Why don't you ask Aunt Meg yourself?"

Prescott pounded on the door. "Are you okay in there, Kat?"

"Sorry, Scotty. Be out in a moment." She stared at the mirror, but her mind focused on the image of Prescott as he held her hostage against the tile in the swimming pool. "Sascha, I've felt kind of funny about asking Aunt Meg."

"I'm sure she'd be delighted to discuss it with you. You know me, I haven't had any experience...well, helpful experience... with it either. So if she tells you what to expect, be sure and let me in on it."

"The two years is almost up."

Sascha coughed. "Yeah. I won't make the same mistake again." She grew serious. "You were careful, weren't you? I mean, if you stayed with Prescott...you were careful?"

She sensed the anxiety, nearly panic, in her cousin's voice. Katrina figured her going through very nearly the same scenario with Prescott was giving Sascha fits. She was probably reliving the whole nightmarish scene. One moment, Sascha was totally in love with Damon, the next, she'd lost her gift of second sight. And her uncle had been angrier than a bull on a rampage, knowing he hadn't protected the innocence of his niece.

"Believe me, Sascha, the urge to do what you had done was overwhelming. And some part of me wanted to see what would happen. If he were my soul mate...it would prove it, right? I mean, if I didn't lose my powers in the process for two long years."

"Yeah, well, I was so certain Damon was mine. Boy, was I wrong. One fun night that I thought would lead to the rest of our lives together, and my powers just vanished."

Prescott pounded on the door again. "Kat?"

"Got to go, Sascha. If I lose my powers tonight, you'll know I didn't have any more control to fight the urge than you."

11

—————

"Katrina, wait," Sascha said with urgency over the phone as Prescott waited impatiently outside the bathroom at the Galleria steakhouse. "Some guy named Lucky came by looking for you. Said you'd know what it was all about, mentioned something about funding for college. He insisted you meet with him tonight so he could fill you in on the details."

"Lucky. Sascha, he's the one who's threatened to spill the family's secret."

"Jeez, you didn't tell me his name."

Katrina wound a curl around her finger. "When and where was I to meet him?"

"At nine at the diner down the road."

"Nine?" She rubbed her temple. That's when the dance club opened. "Can Uncle Jimmy meet him there instead?"

"If Lucky wants some concession from you, I imagine he'll be watching to see that it's only you who arrives at the diner."

"All right. I'll be there."

"Uncle Jimmy will most likely provide backup. He can wait in the wings. I'll give him a call."

"Aunt Meg needs to be there."

"Yeah, Aunt Meg will fix him good."

"Okay, well, I've really got to go. I'll talk to you later, Sascha."

Now what was she to do? Save Camden's life, or meet with Lucky? Somehow, she had to delay their trip to the dance club.

Katrina left the restroom and handed the phone to Prescott. She raised her brows as he grinned back at her. Had he heard her entire conversation with Sascha? Her whole body heated in embarrassment. What had she said to Sascha exactly? She couldn't remember.

"You really don't have an Aunt Meg, do you?" he asked.

She mockingly frowned at him as she interlocked her fingers with his. "I told you she and my Uncle Jimmy have a house about as big as yours." She smiled as he stared back at her. "What? I was teasing about having an Uncle Billy, but Uncle Jimmy's for real." They sauntered toward their booth.

"And the business about how you love me?"

She knew her cheeks must have been cherry as hot as they felt. "I was supposed to be having a private conversation, remember? Besides, did I say that?"

"What would happen if I made love to you, and I wasn't the one meant for you?"

"Each of us would have to find someone new. The one who was really meant to be our intended."

"Kat," he said, pulling her to a stop halfway across the restaurant, "what would happen?"

"I'd lose my powers for two years."

"How do you know for sure? Maybe it's just an old wives'... gypsies' tale."

"Because a good friend of mine lost her powers that way."

He rubbed his clean-shaven chin as his eyes widened. "Not Sascha."

"Yep." Katrina looked over at their table. Camden studied

them while Starla toyed with her napkin and stared at the table. "I think Camden wonders what we're up to."

"Who had your friend Sascha been with?"

Katrina folded her arms. "I don't believe she'd be happy with me if I told all the sordid facts. Besides, I really don't know all the details. She was pretty secretive about her relationship with...him."

"All right. Sorry. I don't know what came over me. But she thought he was her soul mate and—"

"Yes, and she found out they weren't. By then, it was way too late."

"You said you had to get married first. They hadn't married yet, had they?"

She looped her arm through his and sauntered toward their table. "If you're to be soul mates, why not marry?"

He chuckled. "Okay. I have to agree with you on that point."

As they approached the booth, Starla tapped her red fingernails on the table. "We thought you'd decided to stiff Camden for the bill."

"Hmm." Katrina pulled Prescott close, then kissed his lips with enthusiasm. They were warm and wine-flavored...just like she liked them. "No, Star, we had some private business to take care of."

She grinned when Starla's mouth dropped open. The notion a nobody could call her Star...*heaven forbid*. Starla most likely wondered what kind of private business they had been taking care of. She probably imagined some pretty wild happenings between the gypsy and her ex-boyfriend. Katrina hoped Starla had a good imagination.

Prescott and Katrina retook their seats. He cut another slice of his steak while she twirled her fork into her pasta.

"Once you finish your lunch, what does everyone want to do

next?" Camden asked. "It'll be several hours before we can go to the dance club this evening."

"Take a nap," Katrina said.

Prescott's hand ran over her thigh with interest. She smiled at him as her hormones stirred.

She knew what he was thinking.

Prescott smiled. "Ditto, for me."

Starla glared at them, then pulled a tube of lipstick from her purse. "I'll need to change into something a little dressier. Are you going to wear that quaint old thing you wore at the ball again?" she asked Katrina.

"The fellows seemed to like it, but I believe I might have something else to wear."

Katrina didn't, not really. But she hated for Starla to show her up. On the other hand, who was Katrina trying to impress anyway?

"We'll meet you at the dance club at nine then. Right, Camden?" Starla asked.

"Yeah, I'll pick you up a little before that," Camden said.

Her cheeks darkened.

Katrina smiled. Starla had assumed Camden had wanted to stay with her the rest of the day, but apparently not.

After they paid for their meals, they strolled back through the mall.

Katrina turned to Camden. "Whatever you do, duck to the right after Starla's half-brother calls you an SOB in the parking lot. If you move left, you'll have a shiner for sure. Duck down, and to the right, and he'll miss you. Parking security will take care of Thomas after that."

"Thanks, Lee. You know, you're kind of handy to have around." He stepped close to her and kissed her cheek, then winked. "Save me a dance later tonight."

She knew he did it to aggravate Prescott, and she stiffened

her body in irritation. She should have let him take the chance with Thomas on his own.

Starla grumbled something under her breath afterward, and Prescott tightened his hold on Katrina's hand. He didn't like seeing any of his brother's attentions toward her, nor did he want her dancing with him at all that evening, she was certain.

"See you later," Camden said.

Starla clung to Camden as they walked away. She exaggerated the swing in her hips with her tight skirt swaying suggestively.

Katrina laughed to herself. She might not have the kind of eye-catching latest fashions Starla wore, but she didn't seem to need them, either...not at least around the Worthington brothers. She smoothed down her floral frock. Her schoolteacher's dress would have to suffice for the evening's activities.

Prescott squeezed her hand. "Do you want to do a little shopping, Kat?"

She shook her head. "Fresh out of extra spending money. If you won't be too embarrassed to see me dressed like this tonight—"

"You look great in everything you wear. It's just that Starla's comments about you not having anything new—"

"It doesn't bother me in the least bit." She could tell he really wanted her to wear something else. "Heck, Scotty, if you buy me something else to wear, she'll just say you paid for it."

"Yeah," he said, his face sporting a super-sized grin. "You have no idea how much that'll irritate her and please me."

"Why?"

"Because I never did anything like that for her."

"You hadn't needed to. She probably has millions of dresses and shoes to match."

"Come to think of it, I don't think I've ever seen her wear the same thing twice."

"I could have asked to borrow one of her dresses." Katrina chuckled at her own wit.

He tugged at her hand. "She'll figure you would be too proud to allow me to buy you a dress."

"Should I be?"

He laughed. "So when are you going to call Aunt Meg?"

"What if she says you're not my soul mate?"

"Then we'll know she's a phony."

Katrina shook her head, a smile stretched across her face. The more she got to know Prescott, the more she liked him.

She walked with him down the mall toward the end where their car was parked. "My Aunt Meg has a great sense of humor. She'll like you."

"And your mom?"

"Very serious. And Dad, too. I wouldn't let them know about you at all. They'd have me living at home again in San Antonio with them in the blink of an eye."

He led her into a designer dress store. "They'd think I was a bad influence, eh?"

"I'd say." She ran her fingers over a silky emerald-green dress. "So how come you and your brother still live at home?"

"We don't. Not usually. Camden's just getting over his second divorce. So he moved back in with them for the time being... until he finds a place of his own. I've just been over there helping to manage the place while our parents have been on their world cruise to celebrate their fiftieth wedding anniversary. They're coming back on Friday. We'll have a party, then I'm returning to my place."

"Which is?"

"A condo on the lake."

She fingered a blue cocktail length dress. "Oh."

He pulled a red dress off a rack. "You don't like condos?"

"I thought your parents' place with all the trees and acreage was awfully pretty."

"Lots of mowing."

"Oh."

He laughed. "My parents have gardeners." He held the dress up to her. "What about this, Kat?"

She took it and rested it against herself as she turned to look at herself in a mirror. "Might work." Facing him, she asked, "What about the twins you're going to have? Living in a condo would be kind of hard on a couple of kids, wouldn't it?"

He grinned. "I forgot about the twins. I might have to rethink having a condo."

"I'll try this on. Though…" Her finger ran down the v-cut of the bodice. "It might dip a little low."

"I was worried it wasn't cut low enough."

She ran her hand over the silky material. "Next you'll want me to get something to replace my flannel nightgown."

"I loved the feel of you wrapped in cottony softness. But there's a lingerie shop next door if you'd like something silkier and much shorter."

She tugged at his button. "I think I'll stick to what I have. Much safer."

PRESCOTT CHUCKLED. Was she going to allow him to snuggle with her further? He wanted to make love to her. That's what he really desired more than anything else.

He'd hoped she hadn't seen him clench his fist when Camden kissed her on the cheek. He didn't want her to think he was totally possessive or a jealous person. When it came to her, he couldn't help himself.

Could she see which way Camden needed to duck from getting a shiner from his younger brother? If Camden had pushed it much further, or tried kissing her on the lips, he'd have gotten it.

She walked out of the dressing room. Lipstick red...and pure delight. He grinned. "Looks great. We'll take it."

"Are you sure?" She tugged on the price tag.

Nothing was too much for his girl. "You have to wear that tonight, Kat. It's you. Only thing is I'll have to fight off the other guys who'll want to dance with you."

Her smile cheered him. Her dark curls draped over the spaghetti-straps of the dress. His gaze drifted to the bodice, cut as low as the burgundy gown she wore at Lemoyne's. Yeah, it was just right.

"You were having a headache a moment earlier. It seems it's fading."

He chuckled. One look at her wearing a dress like that, and no more headache. "You're good for me."

She ran her hand over his chest. "What were you worrying about?"

"Nothing."

"Camden?"

"You saw?"

She shook her head. "No...just some vague impressions, but I was busy trying to get dressed. I couldn't focus. But I felt the tension return. Don't worry about your brother with me."

She kissed his lips, and he wanted that nap with her right then and there. "I'll get changed, and we can go home, and get some much-needed sleep, Scotty."

"Did you want to get your own swimsuit? I thought we might pick one up for you so you could swim later this afternoon after we rest."

"You've spent enough on me. Your brother said the loaner swimsuit was his ex-wife's. I can wear it again."

"I can tell you she didn't wear it half as well as you."

"Thanks, Scotty. You know, I might just have to keep you for good."

"I was hoping you'd feel that way."

She waved her fingers at him, then headed back into the changing room.

Then his focus shifted to the danger that lay ahead. What he couldn't understand was what had happened? They weren't staying at the Galleria until dusk. Maybe they were at the dance club instead. But it would be dark by the time they arrived there. Had it been a different day than she had envisioned?

She walked out of the booth, the red dress back on its hanger. He could hardly wait to pull her close in the dance steps tonight.

He walked her to the checkout. "About the SUV—"

"Yeah, sorry about that. I think it's going to be tonight at the dance club. The lights are dim in the parking area, and I believe I thought it was turning dusk, when it really was night already. I'm still not certain. The fight between Thomas and Starla kept distracting me."

Prescott paid for the dress. Once the clerk had it bagged on its hanger, he carried it for her.

"Are you sure you don't want to model swimsuits for me?"

"I thought you said you liked the one I wore this morning."

"I wouldn't mind seeing you in some other kinds...a bikini maybe?"

"String?"

Yeah, a string bikini. That'd really be something on that curvy body of hers. "Then the lingerie shop after that." If he saw her in a string bikini, he'd have to marry her. No doubt about it.

"Strings are for wrapping packages."

"Around you, that'd be the best-looking package I'd ever seen."

"One of the things I hate most is shopping for bathing suits."

Still, he was determined to get her one. And anything else her heart desired. Somehow, he had to get her to talk to her Aunt Meg...soon.

He rubbed his temple. Was he crazy? He was talking marriage already...that's what he wanted. But could she be his? He had to know. And what about the twins? Were they hers? Or did he marry someone else in the interim? She had to be the one. He'd lost his heart to her for good.

But what if she wasn't considered his true soul mate? Would she give them a chance anyway? Give up her powers for him? He sighed deeply. He couldn't ask it of her.

She touched his temple. "You are such a worry wart. I'll talk to Aunt Meg...later. We have to resolve this situation with the black SUV first."

"When do we become unlinked? I'm not certain I want you to know what I'm thinking all of the time."

She grinned at him. "Women don't need to have special powers to know what men have on their minds when it comes to them. All they have to do is see the guy's tongue hanging out of his mouth to know what's up." She glanced down at his trousers.

He chuckled and pulled her into the swimwear section of one of the larger department stores. "I thought I'd retracted my tongue soon enough that you hadn't caught sight of it when you wore the red dress." However, the bulge in his trousers was another story. That, he couldn't hide. "Nope."

She poked around at swimsuit after swimsuit.

He pulled out a nice skimpy design.

"Only toothpicks can wear something like that."

Pulling at the top, he said, "It looks to me like someone bigger than toothpick-sized would have to fill the top." He glanced over at her bodice. "Someone shaped more like you."

She grabbed the bathing suit and shoved it back on the rack.

"Too skimpy. I mean, if I wore that...well, for heaven's sakes, for one, it doesn't leave much to the imagination."

"That's what I like about it." He pulled it out again.

Her cheeks reddened, and he figured she could see he was trying to visualize her curves tucked into the scanty swimsuit.

She unhooked a shimmering aqua one-piece from the clothes rack. "Now this is more like it." He wrinkled his nose.

She laughed. "It doesn't have a skirt to it. What more do you want?"

"Less...is what I want." He untangled another string bikini and held it up to himself. "What about this."

She glanced down at his trousers...still bulging with interest. "I don't think it would hide enough."

"Come on, Kat. Just try one on."

"You can't swim in those things, Scotty. They're just for show. Try diving in them, and a gal would lose them, like that." She snapped her fingers.

He waggled his brows. "The notion is getting better and better all of the time."

"Yeah, I can see it is." She fingered the size tag on the suit. "Too small."

She turned her attention to the one-pieces again. A leopard suit...she practically purred over it.

He had to admit the blended colors did look great with her coloring. "Okay, we'll get two of them. One for looks and one for action. Though I have to admit, you'll stir up some action in the one just for looks."

She laughed and shook her head. "I can see you've got your mind set on this." She disappeared with the two swimsuits into the dressing room.

He tapped his foot on the floor as he waited. "Remember to show them to me!" he finally hollered. He didn't want her telling him how the bikini didn't fit when he knew it matched her body perfectly.

A couple of women customers laughed.

His face warmed with chagrin. Then he straightened as Kat stepped out of the dressing room wearing the leopard suit. Like the one she'd worn earlier in the pool, it was cut high on the leg and low on the bodice. He motioned for her to twirl around for him. She did.

"Yeah. That looks pretty fine."

She walked over to him and kissed his cheek. "You're drooling again."

"Sure am. Hurry and put the other one on now."

"I only need one."

"Relationships require compromise."

She smiled at him. "I only wanted to save you some money." She turned and headed back into the changing room.

At that moment, he noticed some men admiring Kat. He chuckled under his breath. Even if the women they tagged along with were done with shopping in the swimsuit section, the men hung around to find out what happened next.

As soon as Katrina walked out of the dressing room, a couple of them clapped. Her cheeks grew flaming red, and she turned around and ducked back into the safety of her cubicle.

He hadn't even had a chance to tell her how much he liked the swimsuit on her. The other fellows still hung around, hoping the show wouldn't end. Prescott wanted Kat to wear something like that just in private with him.

Her cheeks were still lightly flushed as she carried the swimsuits out of the dressing room. He took them from her and walked her toward the checkout counter.

The other fellows smiled at her, and he was certain they were disappointed the show had ended.

"To the lingerie shop next?"

"No." She twisted her mouth as she considered the two-piece. "I'll never wear it."

"Just for me." He rested the suits on the clerk's checkout stand. "This afternoon after we have our nap, we can take a swim."

"And Camden? Won't he be hanging around the house? I thought he was going to spend the rest of the day with Starla, but I guess not."

"He's not interested in her."

"And she's truly not interested in him."

Prescott lifted the sack off the counter and headed for the mall entrance. "You're right."

"She's still carrying a torch for you."

"She didn't care about us...not really. Not until I told her it was over between the two of us. Now she doesn't want to let go."

"What about the thing she said concerning your parents? Will they investigate me like she said, and that'll be the end of us?"

He grinned at her. "Why? Would they find something out about you? A deep, dark mystery?"

"Most assuredly." She tucked a dark curl behind her ear. Every time she did it, he wanted to run his hands through her hair and nibble on her exposed earlobe. A glass bauble dangled from her ear...a gypsy's miniature crystal ball catching his eye again.

Walking through the mall, he pointed to another lingerie shop, the third one he'd signaled to. She shook her head. He was dying to see her dressed in a translucent nightgown. He wanted to see the color of the nubs of her breasts poking so prominently against her swimsuit that morning as he stood close to her in the pool.

With regret for not having talked her into the new negligee, he led her outside to his car.

Maybe another time.

"Only if we're meant for each other," Kat said, her smile warming his heart.

"How long did you say we'd be linked?" He couldn't get used to the notion she could know what he was thinking...not all of the time, but enough to make him worry about what came to mind. Though in truth, he wasn't certain he could curb his thoughts when they came to seeing her in string bikinis and sensuous red dresses.

She fiddled with her curls again as the Texas wind blew them in her eyes. "Not certain." He opened the car door for her.

"I've had this only happen twice and for one, it lasted a whole day, the other for a few hours. I've heard it can last several days, depending on the circumstances. That's okay. Just keep thinking those thoughts. It let's me know what you're up to."

He laughed. "I like to believe some of my thoughts were private."

"I won't tell anyone."

He chuckled again as he climbed into his car. "I thought I had a pretty good poker face. With you around, nothing's sacred."

The idea she knew what he was thinking got him all worked up again though. She didn't seem to mind he had such thoughts about her. Now if he could only convince her she was the one and only one for him, he'd be all set. He relaxed. Naptime next. Swimming later.

As soon as he started the engine, she grew serious, her face externalizing her worry. Her eyes narrowed as she stared at the windshield.

He looked out but saw nothing to disturb her. She was having another one of her visions. What did she see this time?

12

Prescott waited until Katrina took a deep breath and turned to face him. He hadn't wanted to disturb her vision, but when he saw how colorless her face was, he knew it couldn't be good news. "I have to go home now, Scotty."

It wasn't what he wanted to hear either. The muscles in his stomach and neck tightened with concern. "What's wrong?"

"My Aunt Meg's in the hospital. I need to inform Sascha. My Uncle Jimmy tells me he can't get through to her on her phone."

"I'm going with you."

Without waiting for any concession on Katrina's part, he drove out of the parking area and headed down the highway toward Perrytown. No way was he leaving Kat alone. The threat of the black SUV plagued them. Somehow Kat had to be tied to the whole thing. He was certain.

Then, too, he wanted to know what would happen to Camden if they weren't there to protect him later that night. Why wasn't anything going as she envisioned? She must have had the wrong day. She'd already been incorrect about the time of day. Maybe she wasn't right about losing her powers if he made love to her. That would be good news.

"What's happened to your aunt, Kat?"

"She's been the victim of a mugging."

"Where?"

"South side of Perrytown."

"I don't know the town all that well. Is that where she lives?"

"She and my Uncle Jimmy own a mansion on the north side...similar to your place. Several antique stores are located on the south side. Apparently, she was shopping there when someone attacked her."

"Is she going to be okay?"

Kat wiped a tear away. "Yes."

He reached over and took her hand in his. "Are you going to be all right?" His stomach knotted to see her tears, making him feel impotent all at once. He could see she was restraining her emotions, trying to keep a positive outlook. The lack of sleep probably made it more difficult for her to keep her composure.

She nodded. "She never saw him or her. Just heard the culprit's footsteps. In broad daylight, Scotty. The maniac hit her in the back of the head and stole her purse. How could anyone do such a thing?"

"Probably a drug addict looking for money to buy another fix. How's your Uncle Jimmy taking it?"

"He's going to kill the mugger."

Prescott glanced at Kat. Was she serious? Her mouth was grimly set. Yeah, she was. And if someone had done the same thing to Katrina, he'd have felt the same way. "Does he have a clue as to who the mugger was?"

"Nobody saw anything, but you know, that's the problem. Folks can see a whole lot of things, but don't see anything at all. Do you know what I mean? Uncle Jimmy's doing some investigating on his own. Sometimes he's able to pick up things where the police fail. It's not their fault, but Uncle Jimmy has a knack at helping folks to remember details more clearly."

"So Uncle Jimmy is your blood relative? He reads minds, too, I take it."

"No, I mean, yes, he reads minds, too, but Meg is my blood relative."

"Am I the only one you know who doesn't have any physic abilities?"

She smiled and patted his hand with her free hand. "I know several who can't. You, your brother, and Starla."

"That's it? No one else?"

She cast him a small smile.

"What about the fellow Sascha was seeing? The one she lost her powers over?"

"No, he had no powers."

"So your soul mate doesn't have to have them?"

"No."

He took a deep breath to slow down his heart rate. "That had me worried there for a moment."

She squeezed his hand firmly. "My parents don't have any powers either. To them, you'd be perfectly normal."

"And to you?"

"Better than perfect."

"Unless I'm not your true soul mate."

"That would present a problem."

His heart sank with the concept. He didn't want it to be a problem. He wanted to be the solution to all of her problems... not add to them.

When they arrived at Sascha's place, she bolted out of the door. Her outfit would have been a dazzling spectacle in any crowd, surreal purple splashed with orange rays of sunshine and golden moons and stars. She was as well-built as Kat, curving generously in just the right places, but definitely more flamboyant.

"I take it you're driving us to the hospital," she said, as she jumped into the back seat before Prescott could get the door for her.

"Uncle Jimmy said he couldn't get through to you."

"The phone's been acting strange. It's been out all morning. I called the phone company from a neighbor's phone, and they said there wasn't a problem."

"Where's your car, Sascha?" Kat asked, her voice rising with incredulity.

"Stolen. Someone stole it before I woke this morning."

"Great and mine's on the blink again. So what have the police said about your car?"

"Probably joy riders. Nobody would want it for its intrinsic value."

"I'll send a loaner over for you, ladies. Where's the hospital?" Prescott asked.

"You've got yourself a knight in shining armor, Katrina."

"Yeah. Great in and out of his suit of armor."

Sascha cleared her throat, and Katrina laughed.

"In a bathing suit, I mean."

Prescott chuckled. "So are you related to Kat, Sascha?"

"She often hides the fact. She tells everyone we're good friends. But the truth is we're first cousins."

"And good friends," Katrina said.

"Ahh. Is Aunt Meg your mother then?"

"No. My mother is her Aunt Susan." Her seatbelt clicked closed. "To go to the hospital, head south on the main road, then it's two miles from there."

Being married to Kat would add some lively relatives to his family mix. Something he totally approved of.

When they arrived at the hospital, Prescott had no intention of being left behind in the waiting area. He hoped if he could meet this Aunt Meg himself, she might be able to see if he was the right one for Kat. If it worked that way.

Sascha immediately put up a roadblock as they headed for the private hospital room. "Don't you think Prescott should wait outside of the room? Family only kind of thing?"

The decision was made for them. A notice on the outside of the door stated only family could visit. Prescott sighed deeply. He kissed Kat's cheek. "I'll wait for you outside of the room." He secretly hoped she would talk to her aunt about him. But he realized at once how selfish he was being.

"Sorry, Scotty." She kissed his cheek. "I'll try not to take too long."

"Take all of the time you need, Kat. I'm not in any hurry."

Though he still worried about the evening activities and his brother. Would Kat even want to return with him to Dallas to dance? Or would she want to stay with her aunt instead? Then what would happen?

Katrina walked into the room with Sascha and frowned when her aunt touched her bandaged head. She was a petite woman with the courage of Hercules. But in the bed, she seemed fragile for the first time in her life. Katrina wondered at once if it had to do with her powers. Had she lost them due to the concussion she had suffered?

"Hi, girls," their aunt said. Her dark brown curls rested over a padded silk bed jacket. Her petite frame looked smaller than usual in the metal hospital bed.

"Aunt Meg," they both said in unison.

"Are you going to be all right?" Katrina asked, as she and Sascha pulled chairs up on either side of the bed.

"Your young man can come in, Katrina. Kat, does he call you?" She smiled weakly.

"The sign says no one but family—"

"No sense in him waiting outside the door. Poor thing's trying to hear our conversation...the strain on him is something awful."

Katrina chuckled as she hopped up from her chair. When she pulled the door to the room open,

Prescott jumped back, visibly startled. She smiled at him. "Aunt Meg said you can come in."

"Are you certain? I won't be any bother?"

"Come on in," Sascha hollered.

He and Katrina walked into the room.

"Sit," Aunt Meg said. He grabbed the last chair in the room and situated it next to Katrina's. When they were both seated, Aunt Meg cleared her throat. "Now what is this all about?"

Katrina was getting mixed messages. Her aunt was probing her mind, but Katrina was linked with Prescott and his concern gave her another shared headache. And...she looked over at Sascha, who grinned back at her, Sascha's powers were returning. She was trying to find out what everyone was thinking too.

Katrina faced her Aunt Meg. Her normally cheerful ivory skin was dulled by the injury and fright she'd experienced. Her green eyes no longer sparkled.

"What do you mean, Aunt Meg?" Katrina had to have clarification of her question. She wasn't certain her aunt was referring to Prescott and her. Though that's what she wanted addressed. And certainly, that's all Prescott had on his mind. She could sense Sascha was dying to know, too... what was the secret to finding their soul mates?

"The vehicle that haunts your visions."

Katrina's mouth dropped open. She quickly clamped it shut as she frowned at her aunt. "What do you mean?" Had her aunt only read her mind? Sure, and she wanted to know what it was all about. "The black SUV that nearly ran Prescott over at Lemoyne's?" Aunt Meg took in a heavy breath.

"What do you know about it, Aunt Meg?" Katrina asked.

"You have to stop it, Katrina."

"Yes." She knew she had to. She'd known it all along. The sensation was like a task undone, plaguing her to finish what the menace had started.

Prescott squirmed in his chair. "The police need to handle the matter."

Aunt Meg pulled her covers higher as she grunted her annoyance at hearing his words. "What do they know? Nothing. They'll never stop it."

"Kat can't go up against this madman alone," Prescott warned.

"She's been successful so far, hasn't she?"

"What about tonight?" he asked.

"She'll have to be awfully careful tonight."

He reached over and locked his fingers around Katrina's hand. "We're staying at my folks' place tonight."

Aunt Meg nodded.

But Katrina knew she would attend the dance. Somehow, she had to save Camden's life. Maybe that's why Prescott wasn't around. She had to do it on her own. She'd find a way.

Aunt Meg closed her eyes. "Yes, dear." She motioned to Sascha. "You'll stay with me here. Your Uncle Jimmy will take you home with him. He needs someone to fix his meals so he doesn't starve to death."

Sascha laughed. "You ought to have taught him better, Aunt Meg."

"You know him. He still thinks it's women's work."

"Do you know who attacked you?" Katrina asked.

Aunt Meg's eyes fluttered open. "Your Uncle Jimmy has his suspicions."

"A drug addict?" Katrina's head grew fuzzy with information. Her aunt hid valuable clues from her, she was certain. A semitransparent cloak fluttered in the breeze, hiding the elusive details. Why wouldn't she tell what she knew?

"I'm weary, Katrina. I can see you're very tired as well. Get your rest, dear. Everything will be clearer later."

Was that the problem? The reason she couldn't see what Aunt Meg was thinking? Because she was so tired? Sure, it had happened to her before. She'd wished now she hadn't risen so early after having hardly any sleep. Once she woke, she couldn't fall back to sleep any longer. And the lure of the pool had beckoned her to swim.

Katrina ran her fingers over the arm of the chair. "And Lucky?"

Everyone watched her, and she knew Prescott worried about her more than ever.

Her Aunt Meg shook her head. "He's a distraction. Go after the SUV."

"A distraction? He's trying to make me miss saving..." She choked on the words. At nine, Lucky had said to meet him at the diner. The same time that she'd be at the dance club. And before this, the party at Lemoyne's. He'd attempted to thwart her from appearing there to save Prescott.

"Yes, dear."

"He's involved with the hit man."

"Yes."

"I have to report him to the police."

"Do, but they won't listen. You have no evidence."

"But what about you, Aunt Meg? Will you be all right?"

"Yes. Sascha and your Uncle Jimmy will take care of me. You take care of yourself." The door to the private hospital room slammed open making everyone in the room jump.

Katrina wrinkled her nose at her uncle in annoyance. "Uncle Jimmy, you nearly gave us a heart attack."

His six-foot-four height loomed in the doorway as his dark eyes took in the stranger. Prescott had already stood to greet him, his own six-foot height dwarfed by Katrina's uncle.

"This is Prescott Worthington, Uncle Jimmy. And Prescott this is—"

"I'll be having a word with you," her uncle said to Prescott, as he shook his hand.

Katrina groaned inwardly. Her uncle was taking on the role of her father, since her father wasn't there to protect her against Prescott. She didn't *need* protecting from him!

"IN THE HALL," Katrina's uncle said to Prescott.

Prescott would get a lecture big time now. Forget any further thoughts of cuddling with Katrina in his bed...or even looking at her again in that scrumptious bikini.

He crossed the floor behind Jimmy and walked into the hall, then shut the door. He assumed they'd just talk outside the room, but Jimmy kept walking.

They took the elevator to the first floor, crossed through a waiting area, then stepped outside the hospital.

"I don't want Katrina to know what I talked with you about." Jimmy rubbed his clean-shaven face. "Come to think of it, you're linked with her. She'll know anyway." He cleared his throat. "All right, well here's the deal. She thinks you're the one for her, but I believe you're not good enough."

Prescott couldn't believe what he was hearing. He could give her anything her heart desired. And he would, too. Anything.

Her uncle nodded. "Sure, you can buy her everything she wants, but that's not what counts."

Prescott hated that everyone could read his mind.

"And that's part of it too...that you're uncomfortable with the way we are," Jimmy said. "You don't know what you're getting yourself into with a girl like that. Frankly, I don't think you can handle it. She needs someone who has our abilities. Someone who can be sympathetic to her needs like we can."

"Are you saying I'm not suitable to be her soul mate?" He hoped his words didn't sound as caustic as he felt about Jimmy's accusations.

"If I knew about such a thing, I could make a lot of money off it, matching up only those who should be with one another. Hmpf. Put a lot of divorce lawyers out of business, I can tell you. No, it would be nice to be able to play Cupid and get it right, but it's not possible. All I'm saying is I don't want you getting any ideas where Katrina is concerned. Sascha's had her bout of bad luck and learned her lesson the hard way. My nieces are my responsibility, and I failed where Sascha was concerned. I won't fail again, mind you."

Why would they be his responsibility, not their parents'? Heck, weren't the women old enough to be on their own?

"When a child is born to parents who haven't the ability, a relative takes them in who has the wherewithal to handle them. And as to your second concern, they're not completely on their own, frankly, until they're married." He paused his lecture, then added, "I guess Katrina hasn't told you. Aunt Meg and I raised the two girls."

"No, Kat didn't tell me. She just said her parents live in San Antonio."

"Yeah. They visit her when they can. But you see, neither of my nieces' parents is comfortable with their abilities. That's why it's best that they were raised by their own kind. And both girls would be better off with husbands who have their...talents."

"Someone of your choosing, possibly?"

Jimmy smiled. "You're pretty good at figuring this stuff out, even if you don't have our abilities."

They turned as Katrina walked outside of the hospital. "Are you done with Prescott?" she asked her uncle. "Aunt Meg wanted to sleep."

He looked over at Prescott.

"Were done, Kat." Prescott extended his hand to Jimmy. "Pleasure meeting you, sir."

"Remember what I said." Jimmy shook Prescott's hand with a gorilla grip as an added warning.

Katrina gave her uncle a hug. "Take care of Aunt Meg."

"Be careful yourself."

She reached for Prescott's hand and slid her fingers between his, instantly making the tension in his muscles ease.

They walked to his car in silence. When they climbed inside, Prescott noticed her uncle still watching them, his arms folded in determination.

"That went well." Prescott pulled out of the parking lot.

"Don't mind my Uncle Jimmy. He lectures all the guys we go out with."

"Except for the one who stole away with Sascha."

"Yeah, well, she remained secretive about him. None of us knew of her involvement with him."

"Who was he, Kat?"

"Damon."

Damon...he'd have never thought... "I'm surprised your uncle let him live."

"He'll pay a price."

"Oh?"

Katrina shook her head.

That looked like a closed topic for the moment. He still wondered how Kat had been able to get into the ball without an invitation. "Damon's the one who let you into the dance then?"

"You won't get mad at him, will you?"

He took a deep breath. How could he be mad at Damon when he allowed such an intriguing woman into his life? "I'll have to thank him."

Out of the corner of his vision, he noticed she studied him. Finally, she spoke up. "I see you're thinking about tonight. But what I want to know is what Uncle Jimmy said to you."

"The usual kinds of things an uncle would say who's acting on his niece's father's behalf and concerned for her welfare."

"He told you to keep your hands off me?"

Prescott's lips turned up as his stomach warmed. Any notion of having his hands on Kat instantly perked up his instincts. He envisioned curling up with her for a nap first. Her body enveloped in his like the green petal-like leaves tightly wrapped around the colorful petals of a flower.

Afterward a swim... He wished he could be the strings on that bikini, hiding all of the treasures she possessed. Rubbing against them, bringing them to life.

She chuckled. "Really, Scotty, you must keep your mind on your driving."

He laughed. "I'll never get used to this. When does the linking end?"

"I haven't the foggiest. Maybe any moment...perhaps days." Leaning her head against the seat, she closed her eyes.

He thought about the dance, moving her across the dance floor in synchronized paces, her red silky skirt twirling with their step. As much as he desired to dance close with her, he had no choice. They'd have to cancel. He hadn't any intention of letting her get near danger of any kind, despite what her Aunt Meg had said about Katrina handling it.

"Yeah, I agree about the nap, Scotty. Even Aunt Meg said I needed to take one."

"With me?" He was surprised when she spoke. He'd thought

she had drifted off to sleep. Had she known he hadn't any intention of letting her go to the club?

"She didn't say anything about where I was going to take my peaceful repose."

"What does she see for our future?"

Katrina stretched her legs. "I couldn't ask her. I could barely concentrate on what she had to say to me. My mind had rather wandered."

"Because?"

She tucked her hair behind her ear. "You were my only concern at the moment. I wanted to know what Uncle Jimmy was saying to you. I worried he might frighten you off."

"I'm not one to be easily scared away." He reached over and ran his hand over her floral skirted leg, the satiny fabric sliding over her skin.

She touched her fingertip to his hand and traced the bones, sending sparks of interest to his groin. "Yeah, well she finally told me if I ignored her advice while I concentrated so hard on my uncle's conversation with you, to go save you from Uncle Jimmy. So I did. You know it's almost impossible to listen to two conversations at once. In the end, I could barely make out anything anyone said."

He knew how that was. The warmth and softness of her made it difficult for him to think about his driving.

"Aunt Meg liked you, by the way."

He smiled. "Well, that's one down."

"Uncle Jimmy's all right. He has to act tough, especially after what happened with Sascha."

"He thinks you should only marry someone who has your same abilities. He said I wasn't good enough for you."

Kat nodded. "He's probably right." He squeezed her knee, making her giggle.

"Quit it, Scotty. That tickles. Watch your driving."

He chuckled. Then he grew serious as he considered a notion that had been bothering him. "You say your uncle and aunt are pretty well off. Why don't you have a phone or television?"

"I distinctly remember you saying you thought I had an unlisted number."

Now, he was in trouble. "I have to admit I called information to get your number."

"Ah. Well, truthfully, my uncle expects us to make it on our own. But he'd help us out all we wanted. As for phones, I hate them. I was so sick of unwanted sales people calling, I finally had them stop my service. I just borrow Sascha's whenever I need to."

"And the television?"

"What's to watch? Nothing interesting. I finally decided, why have one if I wasn't ever going to watch it anyway?"

"So in reality, you're just very frugal with your money."

"I don't have a lot to spend on nonsense, if that's what you mean. And I do take pride in earning my own way. Sure, my uncle could give me more than enough money to have all the little niceties in life. But I'd feel obligated to him. I really don't like feeling that way."

There was a lot more to Kat than he'd ever thought. She certainly made him rethink his values of what was important to him in life. The better he got to know her, the more he knew she was good for him. He just had to show her how much he needed her in his life.

Then he thought about the discussion that took place in her aunt's hospital room. He took a deep breath. "What's with this Lucky?"

"He approached me the night of the ball. He wanted me to go with him and talk about keeping my family's abilities secret."

"And?"

"I rescued you instead."

He could have kicked himself for having ever doubted her. She had put her own family at risk when all he did was ostracized her for it.

"It's all right, Scotty. Anyone would have felt as you did under the circumstances. At least you don't doubt me any longer, and that's the first big step."

"To?"

"Being a proper soul mate." She smiled at him, and he squeezed her hand tightly.

When they pulled onto his parents' gated property, Kat shook her head. "I meant to tell Aunt Meg about that garage of yours."

He was going to ask what her aunt and uncle did for a living, but when he spied Camden's sports car in the garage, his thoughts turned to his brother. His jaw clenched in annoyance. Secretly, he'd wished his brother hadn't returned to the house. Prescott had hoped to spend the time alone with Kat. Then he had another thought. "Want to go to my house instead?"

She smiled at him.

Yeah, he wasn't being very subtle. He couldn't help himself when it came to her. He wanted exclusivity.

"I'm too tired, Scotty. Don't worry about your brother being here."

"You won't wear the bikini for me later."

"I won't?"

She would. His heart thumped harder with the notion he could get his hands on those tiny strings. But he didn't want Camden to see her dressed like that. He'd try for her, Prescott was certain.

Prescott opened her door for her, then lifted her packages

from the backseat. She grabbed at his shirt and pulled him with her to the house.

"Honestly, Scotty, he has no chance with me. I keep telling you that."

"Sorry, you just don't know my brother with women."

"Sure I do. He's a Texas stud."

"You noticed."

"His license plates."

"Oh."

She laughed. "I'll be dancing with you tonight, not him."

"You see that? In your visions, I mean? You'll be dancing tonight?" He wasn't going to allow her to leave his parents' house. How could she see she'd be dancing with him at the club?

"I thought that's what we had planned for this evening. I'll wear the lovely red dress you bought for me. We'll have a good time. And Starla will dance with Camden."

They entered the house. To Prescott's relief there was no sign of Camden. "Which room,

Kat?"

"You want me to use a different room this time?"

He tugged her to his bedroom. "It worked before."

After he closed the door to his room, he waited. She folded her arms. He motioned to the bed. "Now this is exactly what my uncle would object to." "But not you." He unfastened the buttons on his shirt.

"Don't remove too much." She pulled her dress over her head and when she laid it on a chair, he stilled his hands midway down his shirt.

Her lace trimmed lilac slip was nearly as good as a slinky teddy. He would enjoy wrapping his arms around her while they rested. Flannel was soft and cuddly, but this... totally tantalizing.

She pulled off her shoes and slipped under the covers.

Patting the mattress, she said, "Coming?"

Easily. Just by getting an eyeful of Kat in the bikini earlier. And by thinking of her dressed liked that, he was hard all over again.

"Yeah... but we won't discuss it any further."

13

Katrina loved the way Prescott wrapped his arms around her in a loving embrace. She had nothing to fear concerning his intentions toward her. She knew he wanted her, but she knew he'd wait. Her abilities to read his mind told her all she needed to know.

Soon his breathing grew shallow, then she fell asleep.

When she woke, the room appeared way too dark for only a couple of hours to have passed. She pulled herself out of Prescott's warm arms, not really wishing to leave him. But she knew she had to. It was time to save his brother's life.

She picked up the bag with her dress in it. She couldn't believe they'd slept so long. It was nearly time to meet Camden at the dance club, but as she walked into the hall headed for the guestroom, she met Camden face to face.

His eyes roamed over her slip, then he smiled. "Not quite ready for the dance, Lee?"

"Katrina." She hurried to her guestroom. Then she stopped and turned. He still watched her with interest, and she took a deep breath. The next words out of her mouth would hurt

Prescott's feelings, but she had to do it. "Can you take me to the dance?"

Camden's eyes widened in surprise.

"Prescott's plum tuckered out. Can you take me, and he can meet us there in a little while?"

"Of course." His amber eyes studied hers as if he was trying to figure something out...like maybe he thought she was really after him and not his brother. The smile returned to his lips.

"I'm Prescott's date, Camden. You have Starla, remember that."

"But you want me to take you."

"Of course, so that Prescott can sleep a little longer, that's all." She entered the guestroom. Her heartbeat pounded with anxiety. She knew Prescott would be angry with her. How could she tell him she had to do this on her own? She couldn't. He wouldn't believe her. Nope, he would not allow her to go if he could help it. She knew because she'd already read his thoughts on the matter.

As she slipped into the red dress, she sighed. She could see in his dreams he was thinking of holding her close in the pool. His fingers worked on untying her bikini strings. She shook loose of the image. If she didn't hurry to the dance with Camden, Prescott would find she wasn't in bed with him and most likely waken. When he awoke, he'd stop her.

She shoved her feet into her pumps and hurried out the door, nearly colliding with Camden, waiting for her there. "Let me write a note for him first."

He led her to his office. "I guess this means I get the first dance." He pointed to a pad of paper and pen.

"Starla is your date, and she gets the first dance and every-thing after that." She scribbled a note. "Where can I leave this so he'll see it?"

"Tape it to your door. He'll come looking for you there first, undoubtedly."

After she attached the note to the door, she grabbed his arm and hastened to the garage.

He grinned at her as they climbed into his car. "You sure are different. You do realize Prescott is going to throw a fit?"

"It can't be helped."

"You haven't had an argument with him, have you?"

She figured he knew the answer to that. She'd just come from Prescott's bed for heaven's sake. "I told you, he needed to sleep longer."

She could tell from the way he furrowed his brow at her, he wasn't buying it.

When he pulled out of the garage and headed down the driveway, she was certain she'd seen Prescott open the front door. She rubbed her temple as the pain began to radiate across her forehead. He was fit to be tied, and she knew there'd be more trouble at the club than she'd ever bargained for.

"Is something wrong, Lee?"

She narrowed her eyes at him. "Katrina."

He chuckled. "Sorry, you told me it was Lee. I can't get used to you changing your name so often. So what's your story exactly?"

"What do you mean?"

"How did you get into the ball without an invitation, for one thing?"

"I didn't need one. I was with you, remember?"

He laughed out loud. "Yeah. Now you're with me again."

"You have Starla to keep you company tonight."

"She hadn't planned on going. She called me and said she couldn't go."

"Turn the car around."

"Why?"

"I've made a mistake."

She wasn't sure what was going on in her head. Was she creating the scenarios? Or what? She was supposed to see things that would occur, not what she made of them. If Camden hadn't planned to go to the dance after all and Prescott hadn't either, she'd made a real mess of things. She had to return home at once.

"We've already told Prescott we're going to the dance. If we turn around now, he'll miss us."

She folded her arms. "Why did Starla cancel going to the dance club?" What else could go wrong?

Camden glanced down at her dress. "Maybe she didn't have anything else half as nice to wear as you have. Did Prescott buy it for you?"

"Sweet of him, wasn't it?"

"You still haven't told me what you're all about."

"You're right."

"But you've talked to Prescott. I know he knows all about you, but he won't tell me a thing. How did you know Thomas was going to try and punch me in the parking lot anyway? I ducked like you told me to, missed a fist in my eye for certain. And mall security picked him up. Just like you said they would."

"You know how some people are double jointed? Or some folks have photographic memory? Well, I have a higher sense of intuition."

"A fortune teller."

"Only for fun. It's not my chosen profession."

"Which is?"

"Elementary school teacher."

"But you didn't work today. Was school out?"

"Substitute teacher. No work for me today."

"Ah."

"Can you drive a little faster, Camden?"

"No, they really watch the speed around here. Why? Are you in a hurry? The club only just opened."

She tugged on a curl. "Prescott's trying to catch up to us."

"Well, if he's speeding, he'll get stopped. He ought to know that."

She smiled as swirling, colored police lights filled Prescott's vision. "He did."

"Are you sure you didn't have a fight with him?"

"Nope. No fight. I don't understand why Starla called off your date with you, though. Are you sure you didn't have words?"

Camden hesitated in answering her. And his voice seemed deeper, like he was really bothered, when he finally spoke. "She's still hung up on Prescott. I've never dated a woman who was more interested in my brother than in me."

How humbling. Katrina nodded. Still she was surprised Starla wouldn't have shown up to make a play for Prescott. Starla must have figured she had a better dress to wear than Katrina. For her to cancel all of a sudden, didn't make any sense.

Then she had a notion. "Take me to Dean's Diner first. It's just around the block."

"Are you hungry?"

"I have some business to attend to there."

"Whatever your heart desires."

She had no desire to meet the slime who called himself Lucky anytime soon, but she'd make an attempt to stop him in his game. She only wished she had her Aunt Meg's special ability.

A couple of minutes later, they pulled into the diner. "You wait here. I'll be just a minute."

"But—"

"Wait, please."

Katrina hopped out of the car and hurried into the brightly

lit restaurant. In one corner of the room sat the man who'd plagued her for several days. Now was the time to end this business.

He smiled as she stormed toward him.

No reason to smile, mister. She reached his table and shoved it against him, pushing him against the wall. His mouth dropped open as his eyes turned into saucers.

"I don't know what you know about my family, but surely you know how dangerous we can be."

She reached for his hand, but he quickly stuck it in his pocket. He must have known she could read his mind, maybe even learn who he really was. He'd been warned. So he must have known about their abilities, but not all of them. Unless that's why Aunt Meg was injured.

Her stomach grew queasy. Sure, that's why she'd been attacked. Was this worm the one who'd done the deed?

"What do you know about a mugging that occurred in the antique district of Perrytown today?" she growled.

"Listen, I don't know anything about—"

"My Uncle Jimmy will believe you do. When he gets through with you, there won't be enough left to—"

"Lee?"

Katrina turned as Camden crossed the diner.

As soon as he distracted her, Lucky cleared out of the place.

She scowled at Camden, then hurried back to his vehicle. "You were supposed to stay in the car."

"Was that Preston?"

"Who?"

"The guy you were dating."

"I wasn't dating any Preston."

Camden pulled the car door open for her. "I knew it. You were seeing Prescott on the sly. So who was that bean pole you were talking to?"

"Somebody who's going to be in a lot of trouble soon." Sooner, if it hadn't been for Camden's interruption, but she noted he had looked more worried about her than anything. She sighed.

When they arrived at the popular dance club, the colorful chaotic lights flashed in blues, greens, yellows and reds while the music beat thunderous tunes all the way into the parking area.

As soon as they stepped into the club, darkness enveloped them relieved only by the swirling lights on the dance floor. Katrina immediately lost her ability to monitor Prescott's thoughts. Too many distractions filled her mind.

First, he fumed about getting a traffic ticket, then he disappeared from her vision like a puff of mist evaporating in the sun. Her stomach fluttered with nervousness. All at once she felt handicapped. This was how Sascha had to cope day after day... until today. She could tell her cousin was ecstatic to regain her powers, if only in part.

Camden took hold of her arm and led her to a table. "What would you like to drink?"

"A Tom Collins."

"I'll be right back."

The place was already partially packed with dancers, and the only thing she regretted was she couldn't dance with Prescott.

Then across the room a tall blond-haired man caught her eye and he, hers. Had he seen her with Camden? She'd hoped he had. Darrel Spencer. The man who had groped her at the drive-in theater. She still couldn't believe she'd met him at an elementary school Easter egg hunt. He'd seemed nice enough, divorced, no children, a teacher too. But he'd wanted to go a lot further than she was willing to...and on their first date.

What made her the maddest was that he'd been so angry

she'd rejected him, he'd left her stranded at the drive-in. Sascha and her aunt and uncle had been out of town, and poor Baldy had to come to her rescue. He hadn't seemed to mind, but she felt bad she'd never gone on a date with him, and then had to ask him to save her from her date with someone else.

Darrel moved toward her, negotiating between the spectators nursing their drinks. She looked back at the bar. *Hurry up, Camden.*

"Are you with someone?" Darrel's voice grated on her as she turned to see him behind her. She'd seen him at the school twice this year already when she'd substituted. But they hadn't spoken a word. He wouldn't apologize, and she wasn't about to have anything more to do with him.

The anger still festered, and she meant to say something a little less venomous, but the words slipped out anyway. "Get lost."

Camden stepped up beside her seat with their drinks. He eyed Darrel with suspicion. Still waiting for an introduction, he set the cocktails on the table, but she didn't give any.

Darrel finally extended his hand to Camden. "I'm—"

"Out of here," Katrina said, finishing his statement for him. "I already told you to get lost." She lifted her drink and took a sip.

He smiled at her. "Yeah, right." He looked over at Camden, who'd taken his seat next to her. "She's something sweet." Then he sauntered off.

"Who is he?"

"A fellow teacher. I went out with him once. He had octopus tentacles and thought I was easy. Which I am not."

Camden smiled.

"What?" His smile irritated her as her skin prickled.

"Nothing."

"No, what?" He was really making her mad. What did he think about her anyway?

He took a swig of his cocktail. "You came out of Prescott's room, twice today already."

"Yes, well, nothing happened."

"I believe you."

The way a silly smirk rested on his mouth, she knew he didn't believe her at all. "Yeah, right." She swallowed another sip of her drink.

"No, really. Now with me, you would have wanted something more to happen."

"In your dreams."

"Hmm-hmm."

Her eyes widened as Starla appeared on the other side of the dance floor. "What's Starla doing here?"

"Let's dance." Camden yanked Katrina from her seat and pulled her to the dance floor.

"Camden, what's going on?" Her voice elevated with annoyance. She knew there was more to the situation with Starla than he had let on. Then she realized what had happened. When she'd asked Camden to take her, he decided to forget taking Starla. "Did you stand Starla up?"

"She only wants to see Prescott. She didn't want to go to the dance with me. I'm certain she's here looking for her former lover boy already."

The notion Prescott had been Starla's lover made Katrina's blood turn green with envy. She'd never been jealous over anyone in her life. If he was her soul mate, she shouldn't have such feelings, should she?

She blinked hard as Prescott came into view, his head twisting back and forth as he searched the crowds for her. "Prescott," she said under her breath. "Here comes real trouble."

Prescott's face was dark with anger. He didn't look like

anyone to be trifled with. She hadn't wanted the brothers to fight over her, but she knew she had to protect Camden that night. What else could she have done? She'd made a royal mess of things.

Camden turned to face his brother. The way he gripped her arm, she knew he didn't want to give her up to Prescott.

Then Prescott spied her. His gaze shifted to Camden, then he stormed across the dance floor.

When he reached them, he pulled Katrina away from Camden. "I'll have this dance, thank you, Camden."

As if she was a rag doll, they fought over her like two little kids. "Listen, Scotty, you know what my Aunt Meg said. I've got to handle this myself."

"Not on your life, you're not."

Before Camden could object to Prescott's stealing Katrina away from him, Starla hit him in the shoulder. "Hey, I thought we had a date tonight."

"Yeah, but I thought we were supposed to meet here," Camden fibbed. Starla turned to Prescott. "Didn't he say he would pick me up at my place?"

Prescott shrugged.

Katrina laughed to herself. She considered the spandex dress Starla wore. She was a tall slim woman, and could get away with wearing such an outfit, but the guys didn't seem impressed.

Prescott pulled Katrina away from them on the dance floor to her surprise. "I'm not letting you out of my sight, Kat, for the rest of the evening."

"What if I have to visit the little girls' room?"

"I'm going with you. I'm serious about this. You're not going to be alone for a second without my being there with you."

She smiled. "I love it when you're my knight."

He shook his head, his brow wrinkling. "What happened to our swim time?"

"We sort of slept through it."

His lips turned up in a smile. "I was so sure I had you in my grasp in the pool, then all of a sudden, you vanished."

Her cheeks warmed. She'd remembered exactly what he thought of when he had her in his hands, his fingers working to undo the wet ties to her bikini.

He laughed. "You saw what I had in mind to do?"

"Yeah, well you're pretty transparent, even without my abilities."

Leaning over, he kissed her lips, their hips still swaying to the music. Her whole body warmed, and she wasn't sure if she could wait. Could she live without her powers forever, if she chose Prescott to be her one and only? What did it matter if he wasn't her perfect soul mate anyway?

"What are you thinking, Kat? Are you having a vision? You get so quiet and have that faraway look."

His hands moved down her bare back, and she wanted him to pull her even closer. Already she knew his appetite for her had grown to such an extent his trousers had to have been cutting off the circulation. He was harder than hard as his legs straddled hers while they rocked to the music. Even when the tempo built to a fast dance, he wasn't letting her go.

Her hands wrapped around his body, and she pulled him closer, encouraging their intimate dance. Her whole body ached for him to fill her with his love. Was she nuts?

Yes. She had to finish the business with the evil lurking just outside the building. There wasn't any way she could sense anything with all of the noise inside, Prescott's warm body sending thrills of passion twisting through her system, and the colorful lights that filled her sight.

Was he in as much agony as she was? He grinned at her as he lifted her chin and touched his lips to hers. Yeah. He was.

PRESCOTT CARED ABOUT HIS BROTHER...USUALLY. But not when Camden took Katrina to the dance right out from under Prescott's nose. He'd been furious, his muscles constricting in fervor when he'd seen the two of them drive off in Camden's stud car. He knew why she'd done it. She had some notion she was the only one who could save the Worthingtons from harm. But she was wrong. And he would prove it to her.

Camden. He was another story. Camden wanted Katrina. Prescott wasn't about to let him have a chance with her. His older brother knew just what he was doing. There was no way Camden had thought he was supposed to meet Starla at the club. What a crock of Texas Longhorn bull.

Still, Prescott hadn't wanted a bigger scene than they already had made so he'd let the lie go. Starla's interruption couldn't have been better timed. Now it was time to get back to important business, making Kat his.

All he had to do was take hold of her arm as he moved her across the dance floor, and she'd already made him hard. Dancing with Starla had never given him such urges. Kat had to be his soul mate, hadn't she?

He'd tried to curb his thoughts, his hands touching her soft skin, her breasts swaying to the music, her legs swishing around his. Then to his surprise she pulled him even closer.

Trying to maintain control of his own desires, he hadn't expected her last maneuver. She wanted to feel his hardness against her thigh. Her touch nearly sent him over the edge as she rubbed up against him. And her fragrance, like orange blossoms, gave him a heady delight.

He kissed her lips softly, trying not to work them up any more than they already were. But she wasn't stopping there. She parted her lips for him, willing him in. He groaned.

Turning his head slightly, he whispered in her ear, "You're going to have to be Mrs. Worthington, if you do much more to me."

She had the look of a vixen, her green eyes oddly colored with the florescent lights flashing overhead. Her skin was moist with perspiration from the heat of their bodies. And her heart beat way out of bounds.

Did she know what he was thinking? How he wanted to take her right there? In the middle of the dance floor with all of the dancers shaking their booties all around them?

Her lips curved up suggestively as she moved her hands down to his buttocks and pressed him against her tighter. Didn't she know what she was doing to him?

Maybe the music and lights worked her into such a frenzy, made her lose control of her inhibitions. He'd have to add the special lighting and effects of the music to his condo if such a thing turned her into a bundle of raw love. "Do you know what I'm thinking, Kat?"

She shook her head. Then she laughed. "Of course I know what you're thinking. You're a man, after all. But if you mean, can I read your mind? No. Too many distractions."

"I'm going to have to tell your Uncle Jimmy there's not going to be any other man in your life even though he has some notion that some guy who's got your abilities has to be the one."

She chuckled. "Maybe he has something there."

"Nope, I'm not going along with it."

She kissed his neck, sparking further desire.

"We've got to go home, Kat."

"No, we're perfectly safe here."

He laughed. "You are a vixen, as I suspected. You can't get me this hot and bothered without paying the consequences."

"You'll have to drop me off at my place after the dance."

He shook his head. "Nothing doing. We're swimming after the dance."

"If I wear the bikini, there's bound to be trouble."

"I'll try to behave myself. Camden will be around anyway, putting a damper on things."

"Good thing."

He groaned. "Kat, we've got to get married."

Her eyes grew big. "You really shouldn't joke about a thing like that."

The music had stopped, but he still held her close. "I want to marry you, Kat. I can't think of anything else when you're not with me. When we're together...well, I want you for my own."

She tugged at his belt loop. "I don't know if you're the one. That's the problem. I don't know if I can live without my powers if you're not."

The music started again, and they danced close. She waved her hand at the room. "Even in here, I have no powers. There's part of me that enjoys not knowing what's going to happen, a sense of peacefulness. On the other hand, I feel a panic worming its way into the pit of my stomach. I want to know what you're thinking and what's about to happen. It's just something I'm used to. I can handle a few hours without it, but I'm not sure I could stand not having them for a lifetime."

In his heart, he knew he had no right to ask her to give up her powers for him. Her uncle was correct in his assessment of the situation. Prescott really didn't know how to deal with a woman who had such abilities. He was being totally selfish again.

"Let's have a drink and cool down a bit, Kat." He hadn't been that hot since he'd gotten sunburned in the Fiji Islands.

"Kind of sweltering in here, isn't it?" She was an impish delight. No way had she intended to help him cool down any.

"Yeah, well it has something to do with my dance partner. I've never danced with someone who had such sizzling moves."

Again her lips tweaked into a smile as they took their seats at their table.

"Is it something about this place, Kat? Something that's making you less...inhibited?"

Her brows raised as her smile grew. "You...the music...the lights. I love it in here."

"I guess you won't want to return early to my parents' place to swim."

"We're staying until the place closes down for the night."

"I'll get us a drink. What would you like?"

"I already have one."

"The ice cubes have all melted. I'll get you a fresh one. What were you drinking?"

"Tom Collins."

PRESCOTT LEANED over and kissed Katrina's cheek, then hurried off to the bar. She was alone. Was this the time? She looked around the room for any sign of Starla and Camden. They headed toward the outer door. Undoubtedly, they'd had a fight. Or at least she assumed so. Starla folded her arms, and both scowled at each other.

Katrina hurried across the dance floor, avoiding the dancers swirling in her path. Prescott had forgotten the golden rule. Keep her in his sights. He was too hot not to get something to quench the fire she'd stirred deep inside of him. She smiled at the notion. A cool drink wouldn't do the trick.

Had he really wanted to marry her? Or was it just something he said because he wanted to get really cozy with her in his bed?

Her thoughts quickly shifted to Camden and Starla when she stepped outside of the club. The air was cooler than inside the building where the heat of all the warm bodies had worked up a sweat to the mesmerizing music.

Immediately, her instantly cooled skin tingled with apprehension. She heard their voices some distance away in the parking area. But where? A deceptive mist cloaked the area, resulting from the warm day, turned perceptibly cooler.

She concentrated on Starla's high-pitched whine. "I haven't said one word about wanting to be with Prescott. I don't know why you assume that! Then to find you here with that...that fortune teller!"

Camden laughed.

The lights in the parking area seemed to fade to black, and Katrina saw it in her mind's eye. The raven-colored SUV waited, spoiling to leap through the white lace of mist, flexing its muscles to strike.

fter Prescott paid for the drinks, his body chilled with worry. He turned to ensure Kat still sat at the table. She wasn't.

As quickly as he could, he headed for their table, slammed their drinks down, then surveyed the writhing bodies on the dance floor. What was he thinking of? She wouldn't have danced with anyone else. Well except maybe with Camden. That's who'd danced with her for the first dance already after all. The notion chilled his blood.

Then he hurried through the crowds to the ladies' room. His mind was totally muddled. She might have been in the restroom. It wasn't time to panic...yet. He took a deep breath, trying to calm his worry and refocus his efforts. But he saw no sign of her, or Camden and Starla either, for that matter. He wasn't waiting around at the ladies' room any longer.

Then he remembered she was supposed to save Camden. How could he have forgotten? He'd been so concerned Camden was after her again. And Kat...why she'd bewitched him too. *Damn!* His heart thundered erratically as he barged through the bodies in his way.

As soon as he burst into the cool air outside the club, his hot skin turned clammy. He focused on the parking lot devoured by a thick, white fog, illuminated eerily by the lantern lights high above.

Camden spoke somewhere in the distance, far across the parking area. "You pretend to want to be with me when all you can do is search for Prescott. And you were never that engrossed in him when you were going together. It's his interest in Lee that bothers you so."

Camden stood with Starla and argued. But where was Kat in the darkness? Prescott reconsidered the club. Had she only been in the ladies' restroom?

"Look out!" Kat screamed, making Prescott's adrenaline shoot to an all-time high.

He sprinted across the parking area in the direction of her voice. The slippery soles of his shoes clattered on the asphalt as his blood pounded in his ears.

Then an engine turned over in a truck-sized vehicle. The deadly SUV? He had to reach her before she was injured. Never before had he been filled with such dread. He couldn't lose her... not now, not ever.

KATRINA COULDN'T REACH Camden in time. Why she threw herself in front of the vehicle, never even occurred to her. All she could think of was stopping it. What made her believe she could halt the ton of black metal lurching forward? She hadn't time to ponder the situation. The bumper touched her leg, and she collapsed.

The blackness just like in her vision, surrounded her, no sounds, no light, no sensation of any kind. Then screams and shouts filled the air.

A hand on her wrist brought her partially to. "She's got a pulse," Prescott said, then touched her cheek. "Kat! She's coming to."

She rubbed her temple to still the pounding inside. "Is Camden all right?"

"Damn it, Kat! Camden's fine. You're the one who was almost killed!"

"I feel all right." But she had no visions. She stared blankly at Prescott.

"Lay still. The police and an ambulance are on their way."

"Oh, no, Scotty. I'm fine. Really. I don't want to go to a hospital." Her voice sounded meek like a child afraid she'd receive an immunization shot.

"You're going to do whatever anyone in authority says. This time we have evidence someone's out to do someone harm, and we'll do this by the book."

He spoke with firmness, and she hadn't the strength to argue with him further. Someone had covered her with a blanket, and the soft flannel fabric warmed her. She glanced around her to see several of the club's patrons gathered to watch.

She touched her forehead again as her temple ached with a vengeance. "Is Camden all right?" The look on Prescott's face made her fear she'd asked something wrong. Was he jealous?

Prescott's mouth opened slightly, but only in surprise, not to speak, and his forehead wrinkled even deeper.

Camden crouched down on the other side of her. "I'm right here, Lee. I'm just fine."

Prescott shook his head with concern. "She's repeating her questions. She doesn't remember what's been said."

"Trauma," one of the bystanders said.

"Can you wiggle your toes, Kat?"

"Scotty, I'm fine. I think I've got a bruise on my leg. But there's nothing wrong with me. I feel like an idiot lying here on the ground like this." Tears formed in her eyes. "I...I probably ruined my beautiful dress."

Prescott choked on his words. "I'll get you another...a hundred more. Don't worry."

She wiped away a tear dribbling down her cheek. He held her hand, but she couldn't focus on his thoughts. "What's wrong, Scotty?"

"I'm worried about you."

"But I can't tell." She closed her eyes.

"Kat?"

"Maybe we're no longer linked." The notion she was no longer linked with Prescott formed a knot in the pit of her stomach. She needed to know what he thought. For the first time in her life, she felt really alone.

"Where's the car, Scotty?"

"Sped off before anyone could react." He patted her hand.

The sound of sirens pierced the night air. He leaned over and kissed her cheek as the ambulance and police sedans pulled into the lot.

The paramedics climbed out of the ambulance as she tried to lift her head.

"Lay still," Prescott said.

Soon the paramedics checked her over for injuries as the police questioned Camden and Starla.

"Miss, do you hurt anywhere? Your back?" one of the paramedics asked Katrina.

"No really, I'm fine. Just maybe a little bruised."

"She was knocked unconscious."

Katrina frowned at Prescott. There was no way she wanted to go to the hospital. "Maybe I closed my eyes for a bit."

"She repeated her questions. She was unconscious for several minutes," Prescott said, still frowning and looking anxious.

"We'll take you to the hospital, miss and have you all checked out."

If she could have, she would have socked Mr. Prescott Worthington, he angered her so. She absolutely did not want to stay in the hospital.

PRESCOTT DROVE his car to the hospital after the police finished questioning him. He couldn't believe her Aunt Meg thought Kat could handle the problems they faced all on her own.

Then when the police asked if the four of them had any enemies, Camden had mentioned Kat and her encounter with the schoolteacher at the dance, astounding Prescott. The jealousy crept back in again. Why hadn't she told him the man had bothered her at the club already? The creep who had taken her to the drive-in maybe? The one Sascha had alluded to?

He'd have to ask her for more details. Camden didn't know a whole lot, though it irritated him, his brother knew more than he did. But his brother didn't know the creep's name. And then there was the man at the diner...Lucky. He couldn't believe she'd had the nerve to confront him on her own like she'd done.

Of course Starla had to add her half-brother to the list after the scene he'd made at the Galleria. There was no one else they could think of. Except...except for the man who'd actually embezzled the funds from Starla's family's business. The one she had covered up for and blamed her half brother for the crime.

Somehow, he had to find out who he was. He really didn't think the embezzler would have tried to run him over. Why would he have?

He pulled into the hospital parking lot and parked the car. He ran his fingers through his windblown hair. What if Starla's half brother, Thomas, thought Prescott embezzled the funds? He had been her boyfriend after all until Kat came along.

The first two incidents involved the attempted murderer trying to run him down. So it had to do with him. Then Thomas showed up at the Galleria. How did he know Starla would be there if he had just arrived in town if he hadn't been following her already? And in the parking lot at the dance club in the mist it would have been hard to tell if it was Camden or him with Starla. He rubbed his chin. However, her half brother might have figured Camden was her old flame, and maybe he'd been the one seeing her earlier.

Prescott shook his head. He didn't know what to think.

He climbed out of his car and headed into the hospital. Soon afterward, he knocked at Katrina's door. He couldn't believe after seeing her Aunt Meg in the hospital, he'd have to visit Kat in one.

When she didn't respond, he peeked into the room. Kat wore a hospital gown already and appeared to be sleeping as she reclined in the bed. He sat down on a chair next to the mattress and reached for her hand.

"You shouldn't worry so much, Scotty." She smiled as she opened her eyes.

"Are we still linked?"

"We seem to be."

Overwhelming relief flooded his system. He couldn't believe how overjoyed he was that she could still read his thoughts. She held a part of him inside her always, and the feeling warmed him. Her smile broadened. "Adjusting to the idea I see. But it could be over any minute."

He squeezed her hand. "Then you'll just have to do another reading for me, Kat. How are you feeling?"

She wrinkled her nose. "I'm fine. Just like I said. If you could have read my mind, I thought how much I would have liked to punch you for making me come to the hospital."

"You're one of the most stubborn women I know." He took a deep breath. "Did they run tests?"

"Yes. And I'm fine."

"But you're staying here overnight?"

"Under observation. And it's all your fault."

"Yes, well, I would rather you were home with me, but tonight, I'll feel better you're here."

"Without you. Visiting hours are long past."

"Yes, well, I'm staying. They'll have to get a police escort to remove me."

She smiled. "I'm not going to be much company, I'm afraid. They've given me something for the headache, and I'm really awfully drowsy."

"Just close your eyes, Kat, and get your rest. I'm not going anywhere."

"What about you? You need to get your rest too."

"Tomorrow. After I take you home with me."

"I guess swimming is out." She rubbed her temple and frowned.

"What? Not another vision."

"No, what if I have a job tomorrow?"

"You're not going anywhere tomorrow...just home with me."

Her eyes fluttered closed. "If the bed was a little bigger, you could warm me up a bit."

"Are you cold?"

"Yeah. My flannel gown would be welcome right about now."

"They always keep these places like refrigerators. I'll get another couple of blankets from the nurse."

She took a sleepy breath. "Thanks, Scotty."

He leaned over her and kissed her cheek. "Be right back."

"I'll still be here when you return. And it's all your fault."

He chuckled on his way out. Keeping Kat warmed up sounded really good to him. Only he imagined the hospital staff wouldn't have gone for what he had in mind.

THE NEXT DAY, Katrina was feeling much better and Prescott checked her out of the hospital and drove her back to his parents' place. "I'd drive you to mine, but I promised my folks I'd watch theirs while they were gone."

"I like the gardens here. Maybe later I could sit in them." She felt much better. Her head grew clearer, and she remembered most of what had happened the previous night.

He walked her into the house and headed her to his bedroom. She smiled. "Uhm, my room," she said as she pointed to the first door, "and your room."

"Yeah, they're both ours." He took her to his room.

She wasn't sure why he had done so, maybe to show Camden she was Prescott's girl. But she sensed he took a great deal of pleasure in moving her into his bedroom, no matter what the reason.

"I've been in bed all day and—"

"And the doctor said you should take it easy. More bed rest. Easy does it."

He unzipped the back of her red dress and held her arm as she slipped it to the floor. She pushed her heels off, and he pulled the bedcovers back for her. His gaze rested on her strapless lace bra and bikini panties. He sighed. She would have shaken her head at him, but she was afraid her head would begin to ache again.

She climbed into bed, and he covered her up.

"I was so out of it last night, I don't remember if I told Sascha what happened."

"I'll call them. I didn't catch your Uncle Jimmy's last name though."

"Brighten." She gave him the phone number.

"All right. I'll give them a call."

He walked out of the room. That's when she noticed he had a phone on his bedside table. Why didn't he call from there?

She waited a few minutes, then lifted the receiver. Nobody was on the line. She punched in the first three numbers, and the phone went dead.

Now what?

She closed her eyes and drifted off, but heard someone walk into the room, and she opened her eyes to see him carrying a tray of ice water, orange juice, and crackers. "It may not be as fancy as the hospital provides."

She smiled outwardly, but inwardly she tried to read his thoughts. What went on with the phone call to her uncle? She lifted the orange juice off the tray. "Did you get hold of my uncle?"

"Sascha, luckily. I'm not sure I want to speak with your uncle again."

Was he afraid of him? And did he really call at all? Maybe he worried that her uncle would have her spirited away to his own home.

"What did she say?"

"She was pretty upset. Your Aunt Meg's back home, but Sascha's staying with them a while longer." He sat down beside her on the bed and ran his fingers through her curls. "What I don't understand is if your aunt and uncle have such a nice big place, why the two of you don't live with them. I know you've told me you don't want to feel obligated, but..."

"It's just our way. When you get to be a certain age, you become independent...support yourself. Eventually have a family of your own if you can."

"But you and Sascha barely make enough to live on."

"So? We're happy. Much happier than if my uncle paid for everything, and we had to live strictly by his rules. Do you think I would have been allowed to go to the drive-in with you if I'd been living at home still? He's really controlling. He'd have had a first-rate FBI check done on you first. And when he learned you didn't have any of our...abilities...that would have been the end of that."

Katrina put the glass of orange juice down on the tray as she noticed Prescott's back stiffen.

"What's wrong?"

"I know about the man who'd attacked you. I want to know about all of it."

She swallowed hard. "Darrel Spencer was his name. I guess Camden told you."

"Yeah, but he didn't know the bastard's name." He took her hand in his and caressed her fingers. "What about him, Kat?"

"I already spoke to the police about him. I don't want them to think he was the one driving the SUV...not without proof. He was a creep when we were on the date, but if he's wrongly accused of attempting to run you over, he'd lose his teaching job."

"What happened?" Prescott's voice was so dark, she was afraid he'd decide to go after the guy himself.

"Nothing. Not really. He got overzealous in the car when we watched a movie, and I said no."

Brows furrowed, chin tilted down, he looked like he didn't believe her. "And that's it?"

"He wouldn't stop. Finally, I had to get out of the car, and he left me there. Stranded."

"Attempted rape."

"He didn't take it that far."

Prescott still looked skeptical. "Okay, so what was he doing at the club?"

"Dancing? I don't know. I told him to get lost. When Camden returned to the table, Darrel left. I never saw him after that."

"I'm sorry to bring it up now, when I'm sure you're not feeling the greatest." He leaned over and kissed her cheek.

She hadn't wanted to tell anyone about Darrel. Only Sascha had known what had happened. Not even her aunt and uncle. She'd kept the incident a well-guarded secret. Until now.

Prescott said, "Okay, so we have him as a suspect. Starla threw in her half-brother as an additional culprit. He'd been arrested at the mall, so that made him an easy choice."

"You think Darrel is angry that I'm seeing you?"

Prescott's brows rose. He probably wondered why she was talking about Darrel again. She hadn't even considered he could be a suspect until she had seen him at the club.

Prescott said, "Yeah, I think that's a possibility. Camden said you had seen him a couple of times at the elementary school where you substituted."

"Yes, but I never spoke to him."

"How did he act toward you?"

She ran her hand over the covers.

"Kat, how did he act?"

"Like he was interested. Like he wanted to take up where we left off. It wasn't going to happen. I had nothing to do with him. I never spoke a word to him the whole time I taught at the school."

"Okay, then he's still a definite suspect."

"Why try to run Camden over in the parking lot? That doesn't make any sense."

"He thought Camden was me? Camden and I look very much the same, you know. In the dark parking lot shrouded by mist, it would have been easy to mistake us for one another.

Both times before, it was dark. You were with Camden tonight when Darrel met him face to face. Maybe he thought you were seeing him now, if he realized there were two of us. He might be jealous when you're with anyone. It would explain why he might have gone to your apartment. He knew where you lived. He's been watching you...stalking you."

"But I had to save you the night of the fair. I saw it in my vision." She rubbed her temple as the tension pooled in it. "We weren't seeing each other before this. Why would I have gone to the ball otherwise? I had no intention of going there until the vision came to me. I pictured it in your future."

"Kat, early on you told me you could see what I wore, but then the next time you couldn't. You said it was like you were in the person's mind as they saw what happened to them, but not the first time. Why not? With Starla, you knew what she wore because she looked at herself in a mirror-like window. With me the first time, you knew I wore a tux. Why?"

"I don't know." She shook her head. The more she thought about it, the more confused she got.

"Okay. I had another thought. What about the fellow you said Starla was covering for? The one who embezzled from her parents' company?"

"I have to do a reading. I have to see if I can find out who the man was."

"But you've done two before with Starla. Nothing came of it."

"I'll have to link with her, as much as I'd hate to. It's the only way. Unless she just decides to tell us all she knows, which I highly doubt."

"Would that be dangerous for you, as we're already linked?"

"It might be. I'd ask Sascha to do it, but her powers aren't fully restored."

Then she thought of the phone conversation Prescott had

with her family. She grabbed up the phone. "I'll call her and see what she thinks of the idea."

"That phone doesn't work half of the time, Kat. I don't know why my folks don't just throw it out." He handed her his cell phone.

She took a deep breath. She was becoming paranoid. Taking the phone in hand, she punched in her uncle's number. "Hello? Sascha, how are your powers coming along?"

"I'm fine, not fully up to speed, but having a wonderful time of it. However, Prescott told me what happened last night. Of course, Aunt Meg already knew. Uncle Jimmy is having a fit that you're not staying with us, but Aunt Meg said to leave you be with Prescott for the time being."

"Good. We're trying to sort out a list of suspects. We have Darrel Spencer—"

"Ugh, he's a great one to add to the list."

"He was at the dance club last night."

"That doesn't sound good."

"Nope. Okay, then we have Starla's half-brother who got into a fight with Camden at the Galleria."

"Why would he be a suspect?"

"Maybe he thought Camden embezzled the money from her family's business. He accompanied Starla after all. Then we have the real embezzler...the one she covered for."

"Why would he want to hurt Prescott?"

"He dated her before she got involved with Prescott perhaps? Maybe the embezzler grew jealous. They broke up. But he still had a thing for Starla."

"And?"

"I'd have to link with her to find out who he was. It's the only way I can think of. If I bring up the subject, she's sure to think of him. I'll get the image and we'll know."

Sascha cleared her throat and Katrina knew what she'd say before she said it. "You can't do it, Katrina."

Katrina took a deep breath. "Because I'm already linked with Prescott?"

"Yeah. It's a dangerous business. Your mind might not be able to handle it."

Katrina sighed. She had to do it. She couldn't think of any other way. "It's too bad you can't help."

"You're right. Not until I'm fully recovered."

"And Uncle Jimmy—"

"No way. You know how he doesn't ever link with folks. It brings on a terrible temper."

Grinding her teeth, Katrina could think of only one other possibility and because of the current circumstances, that was out also. "Aunt Meg can't with her recent head injury either."

"You'll have to think of another way."

"Yeah." Only there was no other way Katrina could think of that would work.

"I mean it, Katrina. You can't link with her."

"All right, all right, I hear you." Katrina was going to do what she had to do.

"Let me speak to Prescott."

Katrina made a face. She knew Sascha would tell Prescott not to allow her to link with Starla.

"Katrina, I know he's sitting next to you."

She expelled her breath in an exasperated fashion, then handed the phone to Prescott.

His gaze never strayed from her. He nodded, his face serious. "I understand, thanks, Sascha. You bet. I'll keep her safe." He handed the phone back to her.

"Bye, Sascha. I'll see you soonest." She clicked off the phone and handed it back to Prescott. "Traitor."

He shook his head. "Not only are you linked to me, but you've suffered a head injury also like your Aunt Meg."

"Nonsense. It's barely anything like hers."

Prescott snorted. "You had a mild concussion. Can you think of anyone else?"

"We have three probable suspects."

Then his brow furrowed deeply. "And Lucky."

"Yeah, well he's definitely connected. But I couldn't find out who he was because Camden interrupted us."

"Do the police know—"

"I'd already told them about him and gave a detailed description and all. I just added about the meeting last night, and how he was involved in my aunt's mugging. I don't know for sure, but I'm certain he knows about my family's powers. I thought at first he was just hired to blackmail us and didn't really know about our abilities, maybe was told it was something else we were hiding. But not now. Not when he was afraid for me to touch his hand."

Prescott took a deep breath. "Do you know of anyone else who might be upset with your dating me?"

"How many times have I told you...this all started with you. It hasn't anything to do with me...except I've had to save you and your brother's lives," she said, giving him a pointed look.

Prescott didn't look convinced.

PRESCOTT KNEW something was wrong with the scenario of Katrina's rescuing him that first night. Everything had to have a reason...even if one had special abilities, didn't it? Something just wasn't right that she knew what he wore, not if she normally didn't see such a thing. He sensed she felt it, too, but for some reason, she just couldn't grasp what was amiss with the situation.

"Call Sascha back." He handed her the phone.

"Why?" she asked, sounding puzzled.

"Just call her."

Kat frowned at him. Her face indicated her irritation with him, but he had to find out who else might have not wanted her to date him. Just as a precautionary measure. If she was right, there'd be nothing to it. If she was wrong, they had to consider other suspects.

"Hello? Sascha? Prescott has a question for you. It seems he thinks it's some bent-out-of-shape boyfriend who doesn't like it that Prescott is dating me." She smiled. "Yeah, well, you can tell him. I haven't dated anyone in a good long while. He doesn't believe me." She handed the phone to Prescott.

"Hello, Sascha? Who else has Kat dated?"

"Nobody but Darrel in over a year. It's kind of hard to meet folks. Of course that doesn't mean she hasn't been asked."

"Who?"

Kat grabbed at the phone, but he jumped off the bed and walked away.

"Baldy... Baldwin O'Dell, booth coordinator for fairs he manages all over the United States. He's got a real crush on Kat. In fact, he rescued her from the drive-in when Darrel left her without a ride home."

"Baldwin O'Dell. Thanks. Looks like we've got a new suspect." He smiled at Kat as her mouth turned down. "Anyone else?"

"Sorry, nobody else that I can think of. If I do, I'll certainly get in touch with you. But, Prescott, Aunt Meg says she wants this over quickly. That there's not much time."

"What does she mean?"

"Aunt Meg's kind of cryptic sometimes. Well, actually I

should say we all have this problem...see bits and pieces. All she says is Katrina needs to put a stop to this fanatic before anyone else gets hurt."

"Does she see anything more?"

"No, sorry. I think her injury is causing her problems. She's on pain medication for the severe headaches. Fogs up the thought processes. Just tell Katrina to be careful, all right?"

"Sure thing, Sascha. Thanks."

Her family had to be crazy to think Kat could handle the attempted killer on her own. The idea perturbed him as worry tugged at his heart. He pocketed his phone.

Turning to Kat, he said, "Baldy. The one I saw at the fair ogling you. And when I tried to pay you the money for a second reading, he watched us. He's a suspect, Kat. Whether you think so or not."

15

Now Katrina was mad. Her head hurt with the tension built up from fuming over the matter. Why couldn't Prescott get it into his thick skull that whoever was after the Worthingtons had nothing to do with her? She served as their guardian angel, so to speak.

"Okay, take me home, Scotty." She would show him the truth of the matter.

He folded his arms across his chest. "No. You'll stay here until the police catch the criminal. It's much safer with the security measures we have in place here then it would be at your apartment complex."

"If I'm the reason for the threat to you and your brother, then I'm the problem. Take me home, and we'll test your theory."

He smiled. "I didn't say you *had* to be the reason. Only that we should consider the scenario in the event you *are* part of it."

"You haven't even considered vengeful employees or business associates, your competition. Nothing."

"I have. But we have an excellent staff of employees. No one has quit without good reason, like a couple of women who followed their husbands' careers. One man joined the service.

Another moved because he had to take care of aging parents. None have been discharged because of misconduct, nor have any left because of being disgruntled over their jobs for at least a year."

"Oh." Well, she was glad he had checked into the matter further. She relaxed her tense spine a bit. But she still knew it had nothing to do with her. "Baldy is the nicest man you'd ever want to meet."

"But you don't date him. Why not?"

She couldn't help the smile that crept across her face. She touched the covers over her lap. "I can't help it. I like a man with a lot of hair on top of his head. Running my hands through it while I'm kissing him, gives me a lot of pleasure."

"You don't say." His teeth shown this time in a toothy grin.

"I do. So for that reason and a couple of others, but not to do with him being unlikable, I haven't dated him. If I weren't so picky, I might find out he's my soul mate."

"Picky, eh? No way is he your soul mate, Kat." He crossed the floor to the bed. "The notion of you running your hands through my hair when we kiss, is giving me ideas, though."

"Don't get me started, Scotty. Getting hot and heavy on the dance floor is one thing where it's perfectly safe, but—"

"Hey!" Camden hollered. "How's my favorite girl?" Prescott groaned.

Katrina laughed.

Camden poked his head through the doorway. "Can I come in? I'm not interrupting anything, am I?"

"Yeah, you were." Prescott folded his arms again.

"Come on in," Katrina said. Camden would keep Prescott and her from doing what they ought not. She pulled her covers higher. "Do either of you own a long sweatshirt or T-shirt?"

"I do." Camden nearly ran out of the room in his enthusiasm.

Prescott walked into his closet, rummaged around, then pulled out a flannel long-sleeved shirt. Before Camden could return, Prescott slid the shirt over her arm, then the other.

A final drawer slammed in the room next door, and Camden barged into Prescott's bedroom, holding a Harvard sweatshirt.

"Sorry, Camden. Prescott beat you to it."

She breathed in the spicy scent of Prescott's shirt and pulled it close around her in a bear hug. She could sense Prescott wished he wore the shirt at the moment with her hugging him that way instead of just his clothing.

Camden dropped the sweatshirt on the bed. "If you need it for later." He pulled up a chair.

Prescott sat down next to Katrina on the bed and put his arm around her. She snuggled against his chest.

Camden said, "Okay, so the police are searching for a black SUV—no license plates."

"I bet it doesn't have license plates yet. I bet it's brand new," she said. "Then when he makes his move, he hides the temporary tags."

Prescott caressed her arm, sending a thrill through her. He either tried to irritate his brother or he just couldn't keep his hands off her. Maybe both.

"The police need to know who the man was who bothered you at the club last night," Camden said.

"They questioned me at the hospital this morning already."

"They did?" Camden asked.

"Yes, while Prescott signed the paperwork to get my hospital release."

Camden nodded. "Okay, then he'll be checked out. Anyone else you can think of?"

Katrina buttoned her borrowed shirt. "We need to find out who Starla helped to embezzle from her parents' business."

Camden cleared his throat. "The police won't touch it. They

say it's a family affair...as it was assumed her half-brother stole the money. Her parents didn't want to press charges so the police couldn't do anything about it."

"We're going to have to get the truth out of Starla then," Katrina said.

"That's easier said than done." Camden straightened his back. "Of course, Prescott knows her better than I do, but I don't believe she'll talk, will she?"

Katrina smiled. "Maybe we can induce her to."

"You're not going to link with her," Prescott said firmly.

The wrinkle in Camden's forehead indicated he was thoroughly confused. "Linking? What are you talking about?"

"Kat has linked with me. She sees images of what I see, not all of the time, but sometimes. And she can tell what I'm feeling."

"Damn."

Camden looked at her with new respect, though she was surprised he'd believe it. Especially after the time she'd had convincing Prescott.

"She had this notion she could link with Starla, and then ask her questions about the embezzlement. If Starla thought about the man, Kat could know who it was, possibly."

"Sounds like a great idea."

Prescott shook his head. "The catch is, it's dangerous for her if she tries it while she's already linked with someone else."

"Oh." Camden's gaze slid to Katrina, his brows slightly furrowing.

"Plus, she's had this head injury."

"My head is just fine." She pulled a curl behind her ear in annoyance.

"Anyway, she can't do it," Prescott said, ignoring her protest.

"I agree, Lee. It's too dangerous to even consider," Camden said.

Katrina rubbed her temple. "There's something else that's bothering me though."

"What?" Prescott ran his hand over her arm as if to sooth her concern.

"The vehicle. I saw it in Starla's future, only it was spotted with water. And in Camden's, it was dry. Last night there wasn't any rain. The vision with Starla has to be another day."

Camden shook his head. "No rain in the forecast anytime soon."

"Heck," Katrina said, "half the time the forecaster doesn't know when we're going to get a sudden shower."

"She's right, Camden."

"Or maybe he's run the car through a car wash," she added. Although she couldn't imagine Miss Hoity-Toity going to a car wash and cleaning her vehicle herself.

"Okay, so what about Starla?" Camden asked.

"Have you made up with her?" Katrina asked.

He squirmed in his seat. "She's not interested in me. She wants Prescott back."

She took Prescott's hand and squeezed it. There wasn't any way she would give him up to Starla. "We need to have her come to the house. Have a meal. Maybe have a séance. You never know what might happen."

Prescott gave her a stern look. "No linking, Kat."

"I won't. There are other things I can do. I'm very good at playing games."

"You won't hold hands with her." Prescott shook her hand with determination.

"Is that how she does it?" Camden asked.

"She holds your hand and does a reading. Only I sort of forced the link on her by accident."

"Yeah. And then Starla almost did too. That's why I yanked

my hand away from her when she grabbed hold of it the other day."

"All right. Tonight then?" Camden asked.

"The sooner the better," Prescott said. "We need to stop this maniac before anything else happens."

THE ONLY GOOD thing about the night's activities was showing off his cooking skills to Kat. Otherwise, Prescott wasn't interested in seeing Starla any further, and the last thing he wanted was Kat getting anywhere near her. He was certain she'd try to link with Starla as determined as she was to stop the attempted killer in his tracks.

Camden had promised him he'd keep Starla away from Kat in the event Prescott was busy with his cooking and couldn't keep an eye on her. He still didn't trust Kat as determined as she could be.

They started off with margaritas on the back patio. Though he worried how things might go for the night, once the heated pool caught his eye, his thoughts drifted to Kat's bikini.

She grabbed his hand and led him to the pinstriped umbrella-covered table where Camden and Starla had just taken seats.

"Later," she whispered to him.

He knew then, she was well aware of what he thought. They were definitely still linked.

"Are we swimming later?" Starla jiggled a navy bag. "I brought my suit, just in case."

"Sure." Kat squeezed his hand. "Prescott just bought me a new one so I can't wait to try it out."

He groaned inside. No way did he want Camden to see her dressed in the bikini. Then he realized she was shy about having anyone see her in it. She must have been referring to the one-piece.

"Is your head feeling all right?" Starla asked her. "It must have been some kind of a shock to know that SUV ran right over you. It was a good thing you collapsed like you did. Imagine trying to stop that thing. I guess you must have had a little too much to drink."

Camden shook his head. "I hadn't even thanked you, Lee, for saving my life. Before I knew it, you'd crumpled to the ground right in front of that SUV. I thought he'd killed you for certain. He slammed on the brakes, hesitating for a moment...well, we all did, then he roared off."

"I don't remember. As soon as the bumper hit my leg, everything went dark. That's all I can recall." She took a sip of her drink.

Prescott reached his hand out to hers and locked his fingers between hers. He didn't want to discuss the club incident any further. He'd nearly died when he thought Kat was seriously injured.

Even now his skin grew sweaty and goose bumps dotted his arms.

"So what's your degree in?" Starla asked her.

Prescott's stomach muscles tightened. Starla attempted to show how inadequate Kat was compared to her. He could have strangled his former girlfriend.

Instead of being defensive, Kat smiled, to his astonishment. "You can't earn a degree in the kind of knowledge I have. But if I could, I'd have top honors, rest assured."

Starla's smirk said it all. Kat was a nobody, and she would prove it. "Oh, really. Well, tell me, what are you so knowledge-able about?"

"You, for one. Your mascara smeared just below your right

eyebrow this morning. You swore and threw the wand in a gold wastepaper basket."

Everyone turned to see how Starla would respond to the comment. Her steely face showed no reaction. She tilted her chin up an inch. "Okay, so can you bring back the dead?"

Kat raised her brows. "Now that would be something. Do you mean can I converse with spirits?"

"Whatever."

"Normally, I like to deal with the living. They're much more interesting."

"Then you can't do it."

Prescott sensed Kat was uneasy with the notion. Her hand had tightened around his, and he assumed she didn't want to call on the dead. But he was shocked she could even do such a thing. "How does everyone like their steaks?"

Kat patted his leg in an attempt to reassure him. "I can, Starla. But sometimes folks don't like what dead relatives have to say to them."

"I'm not afraid of any ghosts. Let's do it."

Even Camden shuffled his feet. Prescott figured he was concerned about Kat too. His brother probably didn't like it Starla was goading her on either.

"So what do we need? Absolute darkness? Candles? More ambience?" Starla asked.

"Poolside is fine."

Prescott leaned over and kissed Kat's cheek. "Are you certain?"

She took a deep breath and nodded. He was sure she wasn't ready for the task. Was it the link between them that concerned her? Her reserved behavior was what bothered him the most. If she hadn't been worried, she would have met Starla's challenge head on like a bull pitted with the red cape-flagging matador.

Starla shifted in her seat. "So what do we do? All hold hands? What?"

Prescott immediately noticed the problem and as he caught his brother's eye, Camden jumped up from his seat and moved his chair around so that he would hold Starla's right hand and Katrina's left. "Boy, girl, boy, girl," he said. "Better to catch spirits with a mix like that."

Kat smiled.

Prescott chuckled inwardly. They'd foiled her first attempt at linking with Starla. Had she acted reluctant to do the ghost hunting trip, to throw them all off? She was good at playing games, he could see. Camden and he would have to be on their guard all night.

"Holding hands is really not necessary, but if everyone wants to play it that way—"

Camden grabbed her hand. "I know I do."

Prescott frowned. Maybe he'd had her all wrong. If she didn't need to hold hands, she probably hadn't intended to. She must have smiled because the notion tickled her that he and Camden thought she was trying to link with Starla.

"You don't need any spooky music?" Starla asked.

"She can't handle a lot of distraction," Prescott said.

Starla resituated her chair, pulling it closer to Prescott. "So what happens now?"

Kat closed her eyes. "Everyone must be quiet while I concentrate."

THE PRESSURE WAS REALLY ON, and Katrina hated it. Doing séances was part of what she was known to do well in family circles. But she really despised them. The dead could bring back painful memories. Why did she want to dredge up sad pasts?

Being linked with Prescott, she found her thoughts immediately searched through spirits looking for relatives or friends of his. No dead people that he knew. She looked for Camden next, figuring he might have had a friend who'd possibly died young. Nothing there either.

Much relieved, she sighed. Her thoughts shifted to Starla, but Katrina's own dead relatives attempted to hold her attention. "Great Aunt Matilda." She nodded her head in greeting as the silver-haired woman stretched out her hand. She floated away.

The woman had died well before she was born but was the family greeter. Always the first vying for attention whenever Katrina did a séance.

Then a teenager appeared. "Chris Watkins," Katrina said.

Starla grunted. "Idiot. He wouldn't wear a helmet when he rode his motorcycle."

"He says hi to you, too, Starla."

She snorted her response.

Katrina couldn't see anyone else, just shadowy figures wandering around in the distance, idle spirits searching for solace.

Her attention moved out of the spirit realm. What nobody knew was she could still link through Camden or Prescott to Starla. At first, she'd been reluctant to try, but knew she had to find out who the embezzler was. Was he the connection to their troubles? If so, she had to at least attempt to learn who he was.

She had to clear Prescott's concerns about her from her mind first though. She squeezed his hand. "Scotty, count sheep."

He chuckled.

If he knew what she was going to do next, he would have stopped the séance immediately. She had to act quickly. The only way she could get Starla's mind off the motorcycle ride she'd shared with the young man who had died was to introduce a new topic. As soon as she did, Prescott and Camden might figure out what she was up to.

She had to do it with subtlety. Thomas, her half-brother was the key. "Thomas was his friend. He misses Thomas."

"Yeah, the jerk." Starla's thoughts focused on her half-brother and his relationship with the dead boy. They golfed at the country club while Starla watched from the golf cart.

"They liked to golf, but you didn't."

Starla didn't respond. Katrina had to move the topic closer to the present. Two years ago was when Thomas left Dallas. So then must have been when the embezzlement took place. "How old is Thomas now?"

Complete quiet followed except for the gurgling of the water in the pool as the warm water poured out of the jets. Katrina tried to relax as she realized her hands gripped the brothers' too firmly. Would they sense what she was trying to dredge up?

"Twenty-eight."

"The accident happened when the boys were sixteen, twelve years ago."

"Yeah."

Good. She'd kept it focused on the dead boy, in part. She'd brought Starla to the current time frame as she tried to calculate his age, but she'd instantly reverted to the distant past, and she needed to come forward again.

Then Katrina had an idea. It was only a guess, but it would have to do. "There was someone else who took his place...the dead boy, I mean. Someone else who showed you a good time."

"Jeremy? You mean he's dead too?" Starla sounded a little shocked. Not upset or saddened, just disbelieving.

It wasn't working. Jeremy was just another sixteen-year-old. She didn't want to lie and say he'd died, but Prescott was sure to figure she fished for something else. She took another long shot. "He was a friend of the dead boy too."

"Oh, yeah."

Katrina's hands grew clammy with perspiration. The whole linking experience wore her out. She wasn't certain she could last much longer at it. Prescott *wasn't* counting sheep. He analyzed everything she said, and so did Camden. Their thoughts muddled her ability to think properly.

"And the one after that?"

Too many years existed in between. She could never get through all of the boyfriends the woman undoubtedly had, and still link them to the dead boy. Somehow, she had to mention the embezzlement. Maybe she'd get a flash concerning who the embezzler was before Prescott and Camden stopped her.

"I don't think the next one knew David," Starla said.

"There was one...he was well-to-do, like you."

Prescott's hand tightened fractionally on hers. She knew she was proceeding much too slowly.

With a snotty tone, Starla said, "They all were."

"But this one you liked especially well. You would have done anything for him."

Prescott cleared his throat.

Katrina said, "David, the dead boy, he said you hated Thomas with a vengeance."

"My father preferred Thomas over me. First and only son, sort of thing."

"Maybe it's time for me to throw on the steaks," Prescott said.

Katrina ignored him. "But one cared for you above all others."

"Prescott said he did."

"Someone before Prescott. Someone who had wealth, too, but would do anything for you. You thought if he did something really important for you, he'd be tied to you forever."

Starla remained silent. Katrina tried to force the image of the man, but Starla fought it. Why? Her mind was blank. Why was there no image of the man? "But he left you. He didn't stay with you as you presumed he would. He took the money and ran."

Starla pulled her hands away from Prescott and Camden breaking the link.

Both the brothers stared at Katrina as if they waited for some kind of revelation. She blinked twice, then smiled. "Medium rare, Scotty. That's how I like my steak."

He didn't move from his seat.

She downed the rest of her drink. "And I'll have another margarita. Great stuff."

"Are you okay, Kat?"

"You bet, Scotty. But I'm thirsty. Who's the bartender around here?"

"I'll get us a fresh round." Camden rose from his seat. His slow actions made her figure he was afraid he'd miss out on something as soon as he returned to the bar in the den.

"Aren't you going to feed us?" Kat assumed Prescott was reluctant to leave her alone with Starla.

"Come on, Kat. Help me get some of the stuff for the meal."

Starla tapped her fingers on the glass patio table. Her voice showed her annoyance. "I guess I'll just wait for everyone to get back."

Prescott grabbed Katrina's arm with a firm grasp and hurried her inside the house. As she crossed the living room toward the kitchen, she knew he was anxious to ask her what she'd found out. He was angry with her, worried she might have injured herself with trying to link through them to Starla. He didn't say a word, and she figured he wanted to make sure Starla couldn't hear them.

When he pulled the porterhouse steaks from the refrigerator, she was surprised he still didn't say anything. Wasn't he in the least bit curious?"

"I already set the spices over there on the countertop, if you'd get those for me, Kat."

"Sure thing, boss." Hmm, it appeared when he was really angry, he didn't say anything. She could live with that. The strong, silent type. She picked up the spice jars.

She was still linked with Starla, and she wasn't sure why it hadn't bothered her, unless, the brothers had provided a buffer for her. She wasn't certain what had happened.

Starla hadn't cooperated with her one little bit, but Katrina hadn't ended the game either yet. Next move was Kat's.

16

Prescott attempted to keep his cool. He knew Kat only tried to stop anyone from attempting murder, but he hadn't wanted her injured in the process. He'd never thought she could link to Starla through them. Though he'd been thoroughly monitoring her conversation in the event she slipped a question in about the embezzlement, she'd still managed to do it. *Subtly.*

The only peace of mind he had in the whole matter was that she seemed so cheerful. The linking hadn't harmed her as they'd feared it might.

Still, he had a devil of a time curbing his anger. He figured she sensed this too. He couldn't help how he felt about her. Didn't she realize he'd do anything for her, but jeopardize her life?

They headed back toward the patio. He couldn't brooch the subject of the linking business with Starla either. Did Kat know who embezzled the funds? He assumed she would have told him if she knew. She must not have been successful. That meant she'd have to be watched further. He was certain she'd make another attempt.

He glanced at her as she carried the spices beside him. Unless she already did know, and she planned on investigating the matter further on her own. He wouldn't put it past her. He groaned. She raised her brows.

He couldn't still his thoughts. Certain she read them, he figured she knew just what he thought. Served her right. She ought to know this too. He wasn't letting her go it alone. He'd be her shadow.

She smiled back at him.

Was that vixen smile of hers her way of saying he had no control over her? Or was she amused he planned to stick to her like a tack to a corkboard?

"Sorry, Scottie. I didn't find out who he was."

"You shouldn't have been trying to, Kat. What if you'd been injured?"

"More harm's coming our way if we don't find out who he is."

"But he might not even be part of the whole equation."

"You're right, of course."

"You really didn't find out anything?"

She leaned over and kissed his cheek.

He dragged her into his arms and kissed thoroughly, deeply, tongue to tongue, his hardness pressed against her silky softness. "Don't try to smooth things over with me. I mean it. You're not going to link with her anymore."

"Right, Scotty."

His muscles tightened with tension. She would attempt it no matter how much he dissuaded her. He wanted to skip the steaks and return her to his bedroom. And then? He'd make love to her like he'd wanted to do on the dance floor, and every other time he'd been with her.

Instead, he had to act the host and ensure Kat didn't have another go at Starla. He walked onto the patio with Kat.

Camden grabbed the spices from her. "Your new drink is on the table, Lee."

"Thanks, Camden. You come in pretty handy."

"There are lots more things I can do well. Cook, too, but Prescott wanted to show off tonight." "Hmm, you both cook. That's good to know."

Starla snorted.

Kat sat down across from her as Prescott placed the steaks on the grill. He looked up to make sure Kat behaved herself. She winked at him, indicating she was up to no good.

Camden nudged him. "Is it all right to turn on some music?"

"Sure, that'd be a good idea. More distraction," Prescott said.

Prescott knew Camden thought the same thing. Kat would attempt to probe Starla's thoughts again. The music from the club had been a distraction. They needed the colorful lights to further the mood. Then he'd want to hold her close and dance again.

Camden turned on the music. Starla tapped her nails on the glass. The way Kat studied Starla's actions, was she reading her mind?

"How's your drink, Kat?"

"Great, Scotty. Camden's a super bartender."

Starla's mouth curved down. "Mine's great, too, if anyone's interested."

Camden grinned. "All these compliments will go to my head."

Prescott took a sip of his cocktail, nearly choking on the contents and wrinkled his brow. Camden had doctored the drinks up good with a lot of extra tequila. But would it keep Katrina from getting into trouble?

≈

STARLA'S NAILS clicked on the table in a rhythmic beat to the music. Katrina took another sip of her drink. It was strong...too strong. Did Camden think he could inhibit her powers? They had a strength of their own. She narrowed her eyes at Starla. "Why did he embezzle from your parents?" Her voice was low and calm, trying to draw out the truth.

"What?"

"They made him angry. Why?" Katrina couldn't see who he was, only that Starla thought about his anger. She wanted to control him for her own dark purposes. Pin the blame on her half brother...get him out of the way.

Starla leaned back in her chair. "Thomas didn't like it that his father remarried after his mother died. Then they had me. He wanted to continue to be the only child, I guess."

"Steaks are ready!" Prescott called out, undoubtedly trying to break Katrina's concentration.

She smiled at Starla. The woman proved to be a first-rate prevaricator. "Not Thomas. I'm talking about your boyfriend. He needed the money, but it wasn't just a matter of stealing it. He didn't feel he stole the money. Why?"

"I don't know what you're talking about."

Katrina took another sip of her drink as Prescott served the steaks. He frowned at her, and she smiled back.

Camden returned to the patio table with a potato salad and green beans, then took his seat with everyone else.

Katrina speared a green bean. "He didn't see himself as a thief. He took what rightfully belonged to him, didn't he?"

Camden scooped up a generous helping of potato salad from the crystal bowl. "Who are you talking about?"

"Starla's boyfriend."

"Rather she's talking about my half-brother, Thomas. Sure, he felt the money belonged to him, I suppose."

Katrina rubbed her temple. Starla was on to her. She refused to see an image of the embezzler. Had she realized Katrina could view it for herself if Starla just thought about him hard enough?

Probably. She was cunning...cunning enough to help with the embezzlement.

Prescott patted Katrina's leg. She ignored the sensation of warmth that rippled through her body. She had to focus on Starla's thoughts. No more distractions. If only she could use mind control also.

"The steaks are perfect, Prescott," Camden said.

"Yeah, they're great." Starla reached over and squeezed Prescott's knee.

Katrina closed her eyes as she controlled the urge to pummel Starla instead. If she laid a hand on Prescott again...

Then Katrina saw an image. Starla fought with her old boyfriend. But when and where? Recently. She wore the same black gown at the Worthington's invitation-only ball. She argued with him about something, and he had his back to her. He leaned over a table and ignored her. "You met him at the Worthington's ball. You fought with him. But you'd already had a row with Prescott first."

"Don't be ridiculous."

Katrina could see the man stand up in her vision. His red hair made her think of Damon. He turned to face Starla. It *was* Damon.

Katrina stood up from her chair. "I...I'll be right back."

She hurried off to Prescott's office, her stomach nauseous. Damon had been Sascha's lover...the one she'd fallen for and lost her powers over. *He* was the embezzler? Did Sascha know too? Prescott's footsteps followed behind her, and she turned.

"What's going on, Kat?"

"I have to call Sascha. Can I use your phone?"

"Who is he? I know you've found out who the embezzler was."

She looked down, twisting her hands together. "Damon."

When Prescott didn't say anything, she looked up at him. He shook his head. "We've got to call the police, Kat."

"No. He stole the money, but it really belonged to him. Starla's parents took it away from his own folks. Some kind of cheating scheme they became involved in where Damon's parents invested in the illegitimate business Starla's parents owned. Only they thought the venture was legitimate."

"Why would he want to harm us?"

"I don't think he does. But I've got to make sure. I have to ask Sascha what she knows about this."

Prescott pulled out his cell phone. "We're in this together."

She nodded and took the phone from him. After dialing her uncle's house, Sascha answered. "Sascha, I have to know about Damon."

"Yes, he embezzled the money."

Katrina knew then that Sascha's powers had fully returned. They'd always been able to know what the other thought before they even spoke the words...not until Damon had made love to Sascha, and her powers had vanished like a puff of mist.

"And the hit-and-run incidents?"

"No, he's not involved in this. I think Aunt Meg vaguely remembers...but she can't—"

"Recall. Yes, I know. I sensed that. Like she recognized the mugger, but she can't quite catch—"

"The image."

Katrina smiled. In a flash, they finished one another's sentences. Their abilities drove their parents crazy. "Thanks, Sascha. I'm glad your powers have returned...full force."

"You don't know how happy I am either. I'm not taking any chances ever again."

But Katrina would. She knew now she would give them up, just to be with Prescott forever.

"You can't even think that, Katrina. You don't have a clue how that'll affect you."

Katrina reached over, grabbed Prescott's hand, and pulled him close. He wrapped his arms around her as she rested her head on his chest. His spicy scent, his body warming hers, and his steady heartbeat thumping against his chest stirred her desire. "I know how I'll be if I don't."

"Talk to Uncle Jimmy first."

"Got to go, Sascha."

She ended the call and handed the cell to Prescott. No way would she talk to Uncle Jimmy. He'd absolutely forbid her to have anything further to do with Prescott.

Prescott hadn't a clue what she intended to do. His thoughts still focused on the driver of the SUV. She had other notions. She wanted him to make love to her. Now for the first time, she knew how strong the pull was.

She wound her finger around his button. "Maybe Starla and your brother could take a hike."

Prescott lifted her fingers to his lips. "What had you in mind?"

"Swimming."

"Starla said she brought her swimsuit too."

"So? Would you rather see her in one?" She unfastened one of his buttons. "Or me?"

He stilled her fingers. "What's going on in that unique mind of yours, Kat?"

She grinned at him. She knew she turned him on something fierce, but he seemed reluctant. "Just getting you ready to take the plunge."

"You're not talking about swimming, are you?"

"I don't want to wait."

He smiled and pulled her close. "As much as I'd like to give you what you want from me as I want to have from you, we must be sure. You know that."

She sighed deeply. "I don't want to be sure. I just want to enjoy every bit of you." His touch made her whole body tingle with anticipation.

"What would your uncle do to me, if I made you lose your powers? What did he do to Damon?"

Katrina tried to pull away from him, but he wouldn't let her go.

"What, Kat?"

"It's family business."

He walked her over to his desk and sat down, then pulled her onto his lap. "Tell me, what did Uncle Jimmy do to Damon?"

PRESCOTT WASN'T REALLY afraid of what her Uncle Jimmy might threaten him with if he and Kat made love, and she lost her powers. He worried more about taking such an extraordinary gift away from her that she lived with on a daily basis. How could he do such a thing? He couldn't. But even still, he wanted to know how powerful her uncle really was.

"Kat?"

She ran her fingers over his, tantalizing him to the nth degree. Was she trying to get him to switch the topic?

"Tell me, Kat."

"Damon has to marry by month's end."

"So that he doesn't try to make the moves on Sascha again?"

Kat shook her head. "Sascha and Damon deeply care for each other. They're just not meant to be together, is all."

"Then why does he have to marry?"

"We have a troublesome cousin, Lucy. Aunt Meg's daughter. Damon has to marry her."

Prescott couldn't believe what she said. "Nobody can force anyone to marry someone."

"If Sascha knew about Damon's embezzlement from Starla's parents' company, Uncle Jimmy will know this too. He could threaten him with prison."

Prescott wasn't buying it. "Kat, there's some other reason."

She turned her face to him, her green eyes as expressive as ever.

"What, Kat? Tell me why Damon would marry someone he wouldn't love."

"A curse."

The notion made him want to laugh, but Katrina's set jaw curbed his amusement as he attempted to take her seriously. "A curse."

"Yes."

"Your Uncle Jimmy would cast a curse on Damon."

"No, Aunt Meg would."

"Oh. And the curse?"

She squirmed on his lap, making him groan inwardly. Lap dancing. Now that was an idea. He tried to keep his mind focused on the important issue at hand. "Kat, what kind of curse?"

"You don't want to know." She shoved a curl behind her ear.

"You know I do, or I wouldn't be asking."

"He can't...well, it won't...the thing is he can never have pleasure with it again."

He thought he got her drift, but he wanted to know for certain. "Can you be a little more specific?"

"No."

"He can't have any children?"

"You could say that." She tugged at his shirt. "He couldn't ever find pleasure with a woman, you know, because a certain bodily part…" She took a deep breath. "Wouldn't function properly any longer."

Prescott chuckled. He couldn't help himself. The whole idea was so ludicrous.

"I'm serious, Scotty."

He kissed her cheek. "I know you are. I don't know what came over me…really." But if her Aunt Meg truly could put such a curse on a man, his notion of having Kat faded fast.

"But, Kat, I thought you said your Uncle Jimmy had threatened him."

"Sure. But Aunt Meg would do the actual deed. Now Damon has to marry Lucy or pay the consequences."

"Does she have powers?"

"Yes."

"And if he's not her soul mate?"

"Lucy is a quarrelsome woman. Aunt Meg has given up on her. If Damon turns out not to be Lucy's soul mate, she'll lose her powers. The family will be satisfied."

"But not Damon."

"He'll have to live with the consequences of his actions, one way or another. Sascha paid for hers."

"But not forever."

"He doesn't have to be married to Lucy forever either."

"Oh. So he'll have a reprieve from his prison sentence after how long?"

"Two years."

"And if he doesn't marry her?"

"He'll lose his…*powers* forever."

"It doesn't seem fair."

"Life isn't fair, Scotty. You ought to know that."

"You didn't tell me about this…before."

"I wasn't sure how you could handle it."

"Well, I guess it puts a different light on the situation."

"Yeah."

"That's why you didn't want to tell me."

"Yeah."

"I love you, Kat. I want you to know that, first and foremost. I love you with all my heart."

She smiled, but her smile wasn't sweet...it was wickedly sensuous, and he knew what she still had in mind. He turned a sweet gypsy into a sex-craved enthusiast.

She laughed.

He smiled back at her. They were still linked.

17

K atrina and Prescott turned their heads toward the office door as Starla's voice elevated from the hallway as she spoke to Camden. "I'm sick of this business with this gypsy fortune teller who's ensnared you with her witch's claws."

Katrina chuckled. She tugged at Prescott's hand. "I haven't been called a witch in years." She and Prescott stepped into the hall to see Camden following Starla to the front door.

Camden said, "Nobody's keeping you here, Starla."

As soon as she stormed out of the house, Katrina saw the return of the image of the SUV in Starla's mind's eye...sprinkled with water. It was in Starla's future that the wet vehicle appeared. She'd see it on her way out of the estates. Katrina was certain. She ran past Camden before he shut the door after Starla's speedy exodus.

"Get a gun, Camden!" Prescott shouted to him, then sprinted after Katrina. "Wait up, Kat! What do you see?"

Starla's sports car peeled down the brick drive, screeching to a halt at the security gates.

Katrina's heart pounded as she ran to catch up to her. The air was dry, no sign of clouds in the black velvet night. Why did the deadly SUV appear wet?

As if in answer to her question, the automatic sprinklers shot out, spraying a fine mist over the entire landscape.

The security gate opened. Katrina saw the black SUV waiting out front, its hood dribbling with water droplets, its engine silent through Starla's eyes.

Then Katrina saw it for real. But as soon as she reached the gate, the black wrought iron metal spears drew shut, effectively blocking her path. The vehicle idled for a moment, then the SUV roared into action, dashing down the road in a fit of rage.

She grabbed the gate, her head hazy as her thoughts grew muddled, and slid to the ground. Prescott pounded the brick drive behind her as Camden's footsteps followed from farther away.

"Kat!" Prescott hollered, his voice filled with panic. He ran up to her, then dropped to his knees and pulled her close. "Are you all right?"

"Take me to your bed and make love to me." Her voice was weary.

He kissed her cheek and hugged her with all of his strength. He felt warm and protective, but she wanted his loving more than anything else right now.

"Is she all right?" Camden asked as he reached them, gun readied.

"Yeah. I think the linking and séance has taken its toll on her." He lifted her in his arms and walked her to the house.

"And him?" Camden waved his arm at the road behind them.

"We'll have to deal with him later."

"*I'll* get him later, you mean." Katrina was serious. She knew she had to get him.

"Sure, Kat." Prescott kissed her forehead. "Whatever you say."

He didn't believe her, but it didn't matter. She'd get the maniac. Soon.

AFTER TUCKING Kat into his bed, Prescott left her alone in the dark, and then called Sascha, worried about Kat's condition.

"She'll be all right, Prescott," Sascha said over the phone. "Whose idea...forget it. I know whose idea it was. Really, it wasn't a bad thought, but...well, séances can be draining for her. That's why she doesn't like doing them. They make her feel powerless afterward. And Prescott?"

He suspected what she'd say before she even said anything. "Yeah, Sascha?"

"Don't have sex with her. I know she wants it and is willing to give her powers up for you, but she doesn't really have a clue what it would be like. You don't know how badly the family will react either when they learn of it. Has she told you anything about it?"

"Yes, about Damon. So it's all true then?"

"Yeah, our family doesn't mess around. Got to go and get ready for another birthday party tomorrow. Take care of her. Don't let her get hurt."

He knew she meant more than just from whoever was targeting his family. "I won't."

"Thanks, Prescott. I hope you're truly the one for her. Give it time. Night."

"Goodnight, Sascha."

They disconnected and he pondered her words. First and foremost, he wanted to keep Kat safe. He wanted to take down the bad guy. He wanted to be the one for her. And he wanted to do all of it now, damn it.

He joined Camden by the pool, his brother furrowing his brow at him in concern as he paced at the edge of the water.

"She'll be fine by morning, I'm certain. I checked with Sascha to be sure, and she said she's always drained when she has a séance. That's why she doesn't like to do them," Prescott said.

"Lee should have told us that earlier." Camden rubbed his chin, his brow still furrowed.

Prescott nodded. "I agree. Is it over now between you and Starla, Camden?"

"The woman wants you, not me. Now if you'd go back to Starla, I'd pursue the matter with Kat."

"You don't have a chance with Kat." Prescott couldn't help the snap to his voice.

Camden smiled, almost looking as though he thought Prescott was in for it now. "So are you going to marry her?"

"I want to, but the issue of marriage is kind of a complicated one."

"Tell me about it. I've already been through two."

Prescott turned his attention to the pool. Was he ever going to resolve the issue of being Kat's soul mate? "Listen, I'm going to retire a bit early to bed."

Camden chuckled. "If she waited for me, I wouldn't have left her alone for a minute."

"I meant to sleep."

"Yeah. I know what you meant."

Prescott frowned at him. "See you in the morning, Camden."

"I'll be going in to work early. What about you?"

"I'll be sticking close to Kat. She can come in with me to the office. Or we'll stay at home and work out of the office here. I don't want her to be alone."

"I don't blame you there. I called the police about the SUV. Still no word about who it might belong to."

Somehow, he had to stop the madman. "Night, Camden." Prescott headed for the bedroom and stripped down to his boxers. Then he slipped under the covers with Kat and wrapped his arms around her, pulling her close. She snuggled sleepily against his wired body, instantly making him hard.

She whispered, "Make love to me, Scotty."

"Sure thing, Kat."

But for now...only in his dreams.

EARLY THE NEXT MORNING, Prescott got a call from Sascha, and he was glad to hear Kat had gotten a job, but she wasn't going to work alone.

Already dressed, he leaned over the bed and kissed Kat on the cheek. "Wake up, sleeping beauty. Our cook made ham and cheese omelets. You have a job this morning."

Kat sat up in bed and wiped the sleep from her eyes. "What?"

"Sascha called. Perrytown Elementary School needs a kindergarten teacher for today."

Kat jumped out of bed. "Where's my dress?"

"Hanging in my closet. You know, I'll have to move a lot more of your things in there. Well, actually into my condo."

"Fat chance. My uncle wouldn't allow me to move in with a fellow." Kat sounded like she was teasing.

Or not. Sometimes he couldn't tell.

She fumbled around in the closet looking for her dress.

He smiled. He could see how much she must have enjoyed teaching children. Or was it that she needed the money so badly?

He took a deep breath. He'd provide her with all of the material wealth she'd ever need.

"I love teaching children, Scotty."

He laughed. They were still linked. "All right, well then you know I'm going with you."

"That should be fun."

He was glad she didn't disagree with him.

She walked out of his closet, already wearing the floral dress. She wiggled her burgundy shoe from the night of the ball in the air. "My shoe?"

"We'll have to bring the other over here so this one doesn't get lonely."

She chuckled and slipped into the pair of sandals.

"You can have an assistant at school, can't you?" he asked. If she couldn't, she wasn't going to the job. Simple as that.

"Sure, parents often come in to assist. We'll make believe you're a parent. I'll put you in charge of finger painting. Do you have an old shirt you could wear?"

He patted his blue and white pinstriped, button-down collared shirt. "This is as old as they get."

"Bought a week ago, yesterday, right?"

He smiled, then he pulled her close. She sure had him pegged. "You were awfully restless last night. I had to hold you tight to make your nightmares go away."

"I liked your dreams better."

"You saw?"

"Yeah. You make some pretty good moves. When are you going to use them on me?"

He laughed. "We're still linked. I hope I wasn't the one disturbing your sleep too much."

"Not with pleasant thoughts like you had. Hmm-hmm. Pretty good moves." She turned her mouth up to meet his. "I guess you're afraid to make them on me, under threat of a curse."

He grinned back at her. "Time for school, Kat. We'll discuss curses later." He pressed his lips against hers, but she quickly pulled away.

"Sorry, you can have more if you want it later, Scotty. Can't be late for school." She tugged at his tie.

He linked his fingers with hers and walked her to the kitchen.

After eating the cheesy omelets, they headed to Perrytown. Slightly anxious, Prescott worried how he would fare at school. He hadn't been in a school for years!

Before long, he leaned over pint-sized desks, showing five-year-olds how to match pictures in columns. He hadn't any idea how attentive little kids like that could be. When he looked up to see what Kat was doing, he found her grinning at him. Then without being able to help it, he thought of how he wanted to join her in the swimming pool after their hard work-out at school. She shook her head, her smile still stretching across her face.

When recess time arrived, she led the class out single file while he walked beside her. "You know, Mr. Worthington, the class isn't used to having a man teaching them. This is the quietest I've ever seen this group."

He chuckled.

"I think working with the kids kind of suits you. You're not having any headache at all."

"Yeah, well, I hadn't realized how much fun finger painting could be."

She touched his tie. "Good thing the paint is washable."

"I might have to leave the splotches on it...just so I can remember the day I worked hard as an assistant kindergartner teacher."

"Will you come with me again when I get to substitute?"

"Sure. When are they having the Easter egg hunt?"

"Turkey time is first. Everyone dresses up for the feast."

"Be sure and schedule me for that."

"I may not have a substitute position around that time, though one of the teachers is pregnant and plans to take some time off from work before then. So I might have a job for about four months."

"Is this what you want to do full time?"

"Eventually. I have to be certified first though."

"I'll pay your way."

She squeezed his hand and two of the girls said, "Oooh."

Prescott and Katrina laughed. She cleared her throat as they watched the kids play on the playground. "What do I have to do in return for it?"

He instantly thought of his bed, and she chuckled.

"Mr. Worthington."

"Marry me. Even if you don't, or can't, I'll pay for your education. I want to see you happy, Kat."

She took a deep breath. "I'll take you up on it. Becoming a bona fide teacher is all I've ever wanted. Uncle Jimmy said he'd pay for my courses, with strings attached. He never does anything for free. I wouldn't want to even know what that would entail."

"Hmm, the notion of strings attached makes me think of one thing."

"Swimming, I know, Scotty. Your thoughts distract me from my work."

He laughed as he had a devil of a time keeping his mind off her. "Yeah, well, you can't blame me. If I'd had you as a teacher for kindergarten, I probably would never have learned my ABCs. I would have fallen in love with my teacher and wanted her to tutor me after hours."

He shifted his attention to a blond-haired man eyeing them with envy about fifty yards from where they stood, his hands on his hips as his mouth curved down. Was that the man who'd offended Kat at the drive-in?

"Darrel Spencer, I presume." Prescott ran his finger over her arm.

She glanced over at Darrel, then turned back to watch the children. "Yeah, just ignore him."

Prescott wasn't in the mood to discount the man who'd attempted to molest Kat. Not only did he want this Darrel to know Kat was with him now, but he was willing to have a show-down with him. Normally he wasn't a fighting man but throwing down the gauntlet was just what he had in mind when Darrel tried to stare him down.

Kat kissed his cheek. "Come on, Scotty. Remember, I know just what you're thinking. Fighting on school grounds isn't allowed. Not for the kids and not for the adults either."

She clapped her hands and directed the children back into the school. "You know, I loved my kindergarten teacher, and most of the others after that. I always wanted to teach."

He realized she was trying to change the subject, but he couldn't still his thoughts about Darrel. He gave a backward glance. The man had folded his arms and watched them, egging him on. "Jerk," Prescott said under his breath.

Kat touched her finger to his lips. "Shhh. We're in school now. You have to set a proper example for the class."

He didn't want to do what was right. He wanted to kick Darrel Spencer's butt. He'd teach him to treat a woman improperly.

A chuckle escaped her lips. "Yeah, I wouldn't mind seeing you do that either. But not on school property."

After they returned to the classroom, she had the students sit on the polar bear reading rug. Then she pulled up her chair and grinned when Prescott sat between the children. They were just as thrilled to have him in class as he assumed she was to have him there.

Singing was the next order of business, and the kids loved trying to teach him the words of a new song they'd just learned. His being way out of tune tickled everyone.

When the afternoon class ended, he escorted Kat to his car. He had never had so much fun with children in his life, and the hope that he and Kat would have twins pleased him no end. She just had to be the one for him.

As soon as they left the school building, he saw Darrel headed for her car, and Prescott could think of only one thing— giving the creep a message that he couldn't miss.

As PRESCOTT ESCORTED Katrina out of the school toward his car, Darrel Spencer walked up next to it. Katrina could have punched Darrel herself for trying to make a scene at the school.

"What do you want, Darrel?" she asked, as Prescott bumped him out of the way and pulled her door open for her.

"There's a school social. I thought maybe we—"

"You thought wrong."

She slipped into the passenger's seat, and before Darrel could press the issue with her, Prescott closed the door. She smiled when Prescott scooted into the driver's seat. "Do you think he got the message?" she asked.

"I was ready to give him a less subtle one if we hadn't been in the school parking lot."

"I bet you never ever fought over a girl in your life."

"You're right," he said, as he backed the car up barely missing Darrel, who acted as though he wanted to show how tough he was as he stood firm. "That must mean you're mine for keeps."

"Yeah."

As Prescott drove Katrina through the district near her apartments on the way back to his parents' home, she spied Sascha's stolen car pulling in front of them.

"That car! It's Sascha's! Follow it," she said, pointing at the red vehicle with the personalized license plate, Wildcat.

"Wildcat?"

"Damon bought the plate for her. Hurry, don't let it get away."

"Get my cell phone out and call the police."

Katrina reached into Prescott's pocket and pulled his phone out. When she punched in 911, only static met her ear. "Something's wrong with your phone."

"I haven't had any problems with it. Try it again."

The vehicle turned in front of oncoming traffic, making Prescott brake his car, while Katrina held her breath. "Don't let him get away."

"Him?"

"Whoever." She punched in the numbers again. Still nothing but static sounded. "Nothing. It's not working."

By the time they turned to follow Sascha's car, the vehicle had vanished.

Prescott grabbed his phone and dialed 911. Instantly, a woman's voice came on the line, and he gave the information to the police about Sascha's car.

Katrina stared at him in disbelief. "It wasn't working, really."

"Probably a concrete overpass or mountains nearby obstructed the signal."

She frowned at him. Neither obstacle existed anywhere in the vicinity.

"Okay." He hung up the phone. "They've got a squad car looking into it."

"We lost him." Katrina folded her arms, so angry that they had lost sight of the car she could scream.

By the time they arrived at Prescott's parents' home half an hour later, she was feeling less irritated and more in the mood to have some fun. "I have a bathing suit now."

"Uh-huh."

"A while back, you mentioned boating. What about if we take a boat ride across the lake?"

"The lake."

She knew he thought more on the line of the pool where he could see her in her string bikini. "Yeah, I've never been boating on the lake. You offered before. Then Camden took Starla. I wondered if you'd like to take me for a zip around the lake."

He smiled. "Okay. Then later this evening...the pool."

She knew she wasn't going to get out of modeling the two-piece for him. For now, she really had an urge to go boating. She patted his leg. "Maybe you could show me your place in the meantime.

"It overlooks the lake."

"I know. That's why I thought you could show it to me."

"Oh. I thought you had something else in mind."

"Yeah, what you were dreaming about this morning."

He chuckled. "Well, I know we can't, Kat, but I can't help dreaming about it."

She ran her hand over his thigh. "You sure made a great assistant today in school. You'll make a great daddy."

"Are you sure you can't find out from your Aunt Meg about us?"

"Not until she stops taking that medication. Her mind is too foggy. I just can't make any sense out of it. Yet she's trying to tell me something. I feel it, like a gentle nudging at my temple. But I can't decipher her thoughts."

Prescott spied his brother's car parked near the garage. "Camden."

"What's wrong?"

"I hope he doesn't ask to go along."

"Just say no."

He walked her into the house. "Sometimes that's easier said than done."

"Hey!" Camden said in greeting as he walked out of the kitchen. "How was school?" His smile indicated he was totally amused as he figured Prescott would have had a lousy day playing kindergarten with a bunch of five-year-olds.

"The most fun I've had in a good long while." Prescott pulled Katrina close. "She made learning really enjoyable."

Camden shook his head. "What are you up to now?"

"Scotty's taking me for a boat ride."

Camden glanced down at Prescott's newly painted tie. "Uhm, I thought the paints were supposed to stay on your fingers."

Katrina patted Prescott's tie. "Lovely colors, don't you think? The kids thought it was great." She headed for the bedroom. "I'm getting changed."

"I guess I'll run out for a bit, myself." Camden punched some numbers into his phone. "Hello, Candy? Are you free this afternoon? Do you want to go to a show? Super! I'll pick you up in twenty." Prescott slapped him on the shoulder, then hurried after Katrina.

"Guess Starla's old news."

She tugged him into his bedroom with his tie. "Yeah. I knew it would happen sooner or later."

She grabbed her jeans, shirt, and the one-piece bathing suit.

He eyed her with interest. "Not the two-piece?"

"Later, for the pool. If I wear it on the boat, it'll get wet and..." She frowned at him. "I meant from swimming."

He laughed. "I can't help what being with you brings to mind."

When she headed out of the bedroom, he stopped her. "You really don't need to go next door."

"Yeah, I really do."

He kissed her lips, and she pulled him close. "Do you want to skip boating?"

"The pool," he said.

"Later. Take me boating first. I want to see the lake by boat. I've never done that before."

"Like me and the drive-in."

"Yeah. Maybe we could try that again after the fortune-telling party on Friday."

"I'd like that. Okay, get dressed and I'll take you for a spin around the lake."

PRESCOTT HAD to curb his feelings for Kat somehow. He was bound to get them both into a whole lot of trouble otherwise. But everything she did made him that much more determined to have her for his very own.

He grabbed an ice chest, loaded it with sodas and ice, then hauled it out to his car. When he was done, he picked up some beach towels and suntan lotion, though it was past the burning part of the day already. Still, he wanted to be prepared.

Then she appeared in her T-shirt and jeans. When they stepped outside, he tugged at her shirt. "Got something on underneath that?"

She laughed. "Do you want to see?"

He glanced over at the gardener who shoveled bark mulch around a tree nearby, pausing his work to see what Prescott's answer would be. "No, not around here."

He hurried her into the car and before long, they parked at the boat dock. He could tell by Kat's wide eyes and smiling face she was as enthusiastic as a little kid on her first train ride. "You've never been on a boat, Kat?"

"Never."

"I'll have to take you on a really big one."

"A yacht?"

"A cruise ship."

"I'd better check this out first. What if I'm just a landlubber at heart?"

He laughed. "All right." He pulled her to a yacht that made her blink her eyes.

"This is yours?"

"My parents'."

"They don't mind you playing with their toy?"

"Only if we're very careful." He helped her to climb on board.

"Thank you, Captain."

"You're welcome." He pointed to the ice chest. "You can serve the drinks while I take us out."

She lifted the lid of the ice chest and stared at the ice. In her vision, fog lifted from the cooler, thick and cold. There was something else, hiding in the mist. Something she couldn't make out. Was it him? The maniac who plagued them every day?

"Is anything the matter, Kat?"

She looked up at him. Her face must have been as white as the fluffy sheep on her granny gown, the way his brow wrinkled immediately with concern.

He cut the engine, walked across the deck, and pulled her close. "What do you see, Kat? What happens now?"

18

Katrina let out her breath in exasperation as the boat rocked on the lake. "I see a fog and I believe he's hiding in it, Scotty, but I can't be certain. I don't know why else I would see the image."

"When?"

She shook her head as she pulled her T-shirt over her shoulders. He took a deep breath as she revealed the skintight leopard fabric stretching over her breasts, showing her buxom cleavage in ample proportion. She smiled as she caught him gaping at her.

"I don't know when this is." Setting her shirt on one of the chairs, she looked out across the lake and sighed. "For now, I'm in heaven. This," she said, waving at the lake and the boat, "is really fun. I don't want to think about the other." She turned around and squeezed him tight.

He kissed her lips, and she parted them for him, stirring his blood with desire. His hands ran through her curls caught in the breeze as she rippled her fingers through his. "Better than Baldy?"

Prescott loved the way she touched him, hungrily with

resolve. Then his gaze dropped to the dip in her bathing suit, cut nice and low on the bodice.

"Much. But for now," she said as she caught his roving hands as they worked their way down her shoulders, "captain the boat. I want to sail around the world." She unzipped her zipper and slid out of her jeans.

He couldn't help watching her every move as if she did a striptease just for him.

She grinned. "Your tongue is hanging out again." She turned and reached down to get their drinks. Her bottom wiggled suggestively as she wriggled the cans out from under the ice. Without looking up at him, she said, "Listen, with thoughts like that, you're going to have to marry me."

He chuckled as he yanked off his shirt. "I can't help it. That bathing suit looks too darn good. By the way, the boat doesn't have any sails, honey."

She handed him his drink, then wrapped her arm around his waist. Her soft skin felt so good against his. He wanted to feel every bit of it against his own.

She chuckled. "Sailing sounds classier than just plain boating."

"More work too." He pulled her to her seat, then started up the engine. As he piloted the boat, he pointed out the sights, including his place overlooking the lake, woods surrounding it all the way down to the water's edge, only a shadowed view of it as if it was part of the landscape and not some monstrosity of a house sitting on a manicured lawn like some of the homes were.

"It's lovely."

"I'll take you up to it after we stow the boat." He couldn't help but watch her closely. He tried to ensure if she had another one of her visions, he'd know and learn what she'd seen. She didn't seem to want to hide anything from him any longer, and he assumed she wanted him to help with the problem. Then for the first time he realized what she'd said. Was it a slip up or was the guy gunning for Kat now also?

"Kat, you said he waited for us. Not for me, but us."

"I'm always with you. Well, I mean, you won't let me be by myself."

Prescott nodded. "Damn right."

"Well, for that reason alone, we'll be together when he comes for us again."

"At the dance club, you knew you would be alone. You said so."

"Yeah." She captured the hair blowing in her eyes with her hands. "I did. This time we'll be together. I just feel it. I haven't had any kind of a vision, but I just know it."

Hell, he hated that she'd be anywhere near the madman. Trying to get his mind off the impending threat, he asked, "Do you want to cool off a bit?"

"Sure."

He stopped the engine and dropped anchor. Before he could remove his pants, he heard a splash and looked over the side.

She popped out of the water and smiled. "It's just right."

He grinned back at her and shook his head. He nearly fell as he tried to pull his feet out of his pants he worked in such a hurry. She laughed at his struggles.

"You'll be sorry," he said, then dove in after her.

She swam away from the boat, but he soon tackled her.

His wet mouth covered hers as he kicked with his feet to keep them afloat, and she wrapped her legs around him. "We've got to get married."

"Yeah, we do. I can't see that my family would object to my losing my powers if you're not my soul mate, but we get married first."

He frowned. "I don't want to be the one to make you lose

your powers. Besides, you said that Sascha couldn't marry Damon as he wasn't the right one for her."

"It'll be my choice. Sascha chose not to marry Damon once she lost her powers. She knew it would be forever if she stayed with him. She didn't want to lose them forever. My aunt and uncle felt Damon pressured her into having relations with him in the first place. He hadn't, but they figured he was ultimately responsible. That's why they feel he deserves the curse if he doesn't marry their daughter. Besides, they'd get her off their hands."

He shook his head. "We've got to talk to your Aunt Meg first. I want to make this right with your family, one way or another."

"All right."

"Now."

Her smile warmed him, and then a fish nibbled at his toe. "Come on, Kat. Let's give her a call."

"Still, she might not be able to tell me anything." She climbed up the steps on the boat, then grabbed a towel as Prescott followed her.

He wrapped his arm around her towel-covered body. "You don't mind my sharing your towel with you, do you?"

"I've never shared a towel this way before, but I kind of like it."

"If you want to take your bathing suit off and get into something dry—"

She laughed. "That's okay. I'll just dry off a bit while you drive the boat."

"Suit yourself. I'm going to change."

She folded her arms and watched him.

Now he felt like a stripper with an audience. He yanked off his wet suit and slipped into his boxers.

Grinning, she clapped her hands, and he chuckled. He had to marry her. That was all there was to it.

On the drive back to his parents' home, Katrina stared at the side view mirror for some time, then rubbed her forehead.

"What do you see, Kat?"

"I don't know. I can't see anything really. He's there, just waiting for us. I know it, but I can't visualize anything clear about him. In fact, well, it's like the fog we had at my place the other night. He must have been there waiting, cloaked. Only that time, I couldn't see him at all...not in a vision or anything."

"But you say you can't see him now either."

Chill bumps covered her arms. "No, you're right. I can't, but I know he's there."

"It's been hot enough, and the temperature's bound to drop tonight. A Canadian cold front's supposed to roll in later. That'll most likely create some fog."

"You mean we'll miss our swim in the pool?"

"Not on your life. It's still hot out, and the pool is toasty warm. Tonight, much later, we'll have to do some serious snuggling to keep us warm."

She smiled and patted his leg. "I'll call Aunt Meg later to see if she has any idea about us."

When they drove into the garage, Prescott couldn't have been more delighted. Camden still wasn't home. He didn't want to rush her...well, yes he did. He hurried her into the house. "A dip in the pool, and then we could get Chinese takeout?"

"I thought you'd never ask."

"You know what I have in mind to do."

KATRINA NODDED. She knew Prescott wanted her more than anything else in the world, and she him. They couldn't wait any longer.

"What are we going to do about us, Kat?"

"Have you something you want to ask me?" She raised her brows.

"I want you to marry me. You know I do. But what if we're not meant to be soul mates and you lose your powers?"

"Then I'll have to live without them."

"I can't ask you to give them up for me, and I don't want things to change between us because of it."

They walked into the house and headed for his bedroom. "Nobody says you're asking me to give them up. It's my decision." In the room, she pulled the bikini from the sack.

"What if you resent—"

She held her finger to his lips. "If you want to know if I'll marry you, my answer is yes with all my heart." She wiggled the bikini in the air. "I'll change in the guestroom."

"Don't mind me."

She laughed.

When she finished dressing in the guestroom, Prescott waited at her door, perusing her from head to toe. "I like it even better now, when I have you all to myself."

"Maybe we ought to call Camden and have him chaperone us. Or better yet, Uncle Jimmy."

He shook his head, took her hand, and walked her out to the pool. "Not Uncle Jimmy."

"Sascha will tell him what I said. He might be on his way here to take me back home already."

"We won't let him in."

She walked down the steps into the pool while he dove in. She swam out a way, but he soon wrestled her, and she screamed in delight.

He pulled her close, their bare wet skin warming one another. "Hmm, this is kind of like our dancing at the club."

"Only no music or lights."

"Don't need any distraction tonight." He touched the straps to her top.

"What are you up to, Scotty?"

"Absolutely no good."

She grinned at him. He was hard in all of the right places, and she wanted every bit of him. The wet ties were giving him fits as his brows knit, and she touched his temple. "Your headache is returning."

"We're still linked?" He chuckled. "Ah."

The string around the neck came undone, and she shook her head, a smile stirring on her lips. The phone rang. They ignored it. He struggled with the ties to the back of her suit.

Katrina closed her eyes as the answering machine turned on, and her Aunt Meg said, "Katrina, dear, now I know you're there. Pick up the phone."

Prescott ran his tongue along Katrina's neck, licking off the water droplets dribbling down her skin.

"Katrina, I have to tell you, he's the one, but for heaven's sake, you have to wait until after you're married."

Katrina pulled away from Prescott and swam to the stairs in a panic. He was the one? Truly? The answer to her prayers? Her heart couldn't be stilled this time. She climbed out of the pool, holding her bikini top in place, then ran across the patio and grabbed the phone. "Hello, Aunt Meg?" she asked.

"I knew you were there, dear."

"Prescott's the one?"

"Of course, dear. Are you still linked with him?"

"Yes, but—"

"Well, he's the one and that's why you're still linked. But he has to marry you, first, before you can take the relationship any further."

"I thought you only said that because you didn't want Sascha and me experimenting."

"No, dear, you must be married."

Katrina frowned.

"Promise me."

Prescott headed for the stairs.

"I promise." She took a deep breath as Prescott joined her, wrapping his arm around her waist and pulled her close.

"We will."

"Good, I can hardly wait to hold your twins in my arms."

"They *were* mine all along."

"Yes, dear. Tell Prescott what I've said. He must marry you first."

"Yes, Aunt Meg. Thank you." She hung up the phone and looked up at Prescott.

"I'm the one," he said, unable to hide the enthusiasm in his voice.

She grinned. "That's what my Aunt Meg says." His gaze dropped to her swimsuit, and she shook her head. "She also says we have to wait until after we're married."

"But we don't have to wait to get married." He hurried her into his bedroom. "Get dressed. We're making a quick trip to Las Vegas."

"You never told me you were a gambler, Prescott."

"This is one gamble I'm willing to take."

"But your parents—"

"Hurry, Kat. I'll make plane reservations, and we'll be out of here."

"But won't your parents—"

"They'll be delighted I finally found my soul mate. Now if you could only help Camden find his, they'd even be more thrilled. After two divorces, they figure he'll never settle down with the right woman."

In the guestroom, she slipped into her floral dress, then dried her hair with the dryer. When she was done, Prescott joined her, carrying a small leather bag. "We'll drop by your place and get you a change of clothes. Then we'll have just enough time to drive to the airport. Let me scribble a note for my brother to let him know where we're going."

He hurried off to his office while she hung her bathing suit up in the bathroom to dry. When he returned for her, they headed for the garage.

As soon as they walked outside, Katrina shivered. The air had grown cold and a blanket of mist cloaked the whole region in a cover of white. "I'll have to pick up a sweater at home."

The mist...just like in her vision. It had arrived, and now so would the threat. She shook her head as she noticed Prescott watching her. "It's the fog from my vision all right. I don't see anyone yet."

The Worthington's place was too well protected. If the killer attempted to harm them, it would have to be along the road somewhere. Just like when she poked around in the ice chest... the mist that enveloped them was frigid.

He opened the car door for her, then hurried around to the other side of the vehicle. When he climbed in, he started the engine and turned on the heater. "It'll be warm in Las Vegas, most likely. Do you want to stay an extra day or two?"

"We have to get back for the party for your parents."

"I almost forgot about them." He headed down the drive, and when the gates opened, he drove onto the road. "I can't believe your Aunt Meg finally told us."

"The medication wore off enough." She rubbed her temple.

"What's wrong?"

"She still doesn't know who struck her...but...damn, it's the same person who's after us. I'm almost certain. She knew we were meant for each other, and he must not have wanted her to tell us. The memory of who it was still eludes her."

"Then you were the key all along, and it was that he didn't want me dating you."

"Worse, he has to be someone who knows my family and our abilities." Katrina tapped her fingers on the seat as she sucked in a breath. "He's behind us, Scotty."

"Now?" He glanced in his rearview mirror. "How can you tell? There are lots of headlights back there."

"He's there."

Prescott drove off the exit ramp and headed underneath the overpass.

"Where are you going?"

"Back to the house."

The lights of the vehicle drew closer, and she knew he'd strike them. She felt the impact before it ever happened. "He's going to hit us." She tried to keep her voice calm, but to her annoyance, she sounded frightened. She braced herself for the blow.

Prescott missed most of the force of the collision as he sped around the turn. The SUV veered off south, then tried to realign itself behind their car.

She knew they'd never make it against an SUV...not unless they had a bigger truck to fight it. Or a gun.

"You don't happen to have a gun on you, do you, Scotty?"

"At home, I'm afraid."

He handed her his cell phone. "Call the police."

She dialed 911. The phone was dead. "Batteries are out."

"It can't be. I recharge it every night."

"It's not working."

"Hook it up to the lighter and charge it. The cord's in the console."

She dug around in the console, then pulled out the cord. After hooking it up, she tried the phone again. "Nothing." She glanced back at the SUV that lurked behind them some distance. "He can't have powers, too, can he?" she said under her breath.

"What?"

"If he knows my aunt knew we were soul mates, he might have some of our abilities. Or other kinds, that I don't have."

"Like?"

"Maybe make communication equipment inoperable."

Prescott shook his head. She knew he didn't believe her. It really didn't matter. Then her skin crawled with recognition. The phone hadn't worked before this. Once when she tried to use it as they chased the person who drove Sascha's car. He had to be the same who followed them now. "Are we passing over water?"

"Shortly."

He would force them into it. Did he know she now knew Prescott was her soul mate, and he would attempt to kill her too?

19

"Stop the car, Scotty," Katrina demanded in a panic.

"Why?"

"He won't try to kill us if I leave you."

"No."

The SUV struck them, and Katrina let out a muffled scream in surprise. They were nearly to the bridge. They wouldn't make it.

"He's going to send us through the railing." Tears filled her eyes. She couldn't see what happened afterward...only that she and Prescott would be in the water once more that day...only not to play in this time.

The SUV plowed into them again, just as she predicted. The front bumper crashed through the railing. The air bags exploded out of the dash. Seconds later, the white filmy material deflated. Grabbing Prescott's arm as they sailed through the air, Katrina bit her lip hard, drawing blood. Instantly, Scotty hit the window buttons, rolling them down for their escape if they survived the crash. Then with a powerful bang, the car slammed into the water. The seatbelt yanked her back in place, bruising her.

As the car sank, he yanked his seatbelt free, then grabbed Katrina's. "Kat!"

She heard his voice from far away, her mind filled with the man's thoughts. "He's coming to join us," she murmured.

"Kat!" he said grabbing her arm and pulling her toward his window. "We have to get out. Are you all right?"

"He's coming."

The man wanted to join her in a watery grave. He told her so.

With an explosive crash, the SUV soared through the air and landed in the water near them. Prescott pulled Katrina away from the SUV and toward the shore, most of her concentration on their would-be killer.

"He's not going to make it," she whispered. "He doesn't have the will to live."

"Kat," Scotty said, trying to draw her out of the fog she was in, but she couldn't help it. The man was calling to her, in pain, his emotions of despair and longing swamping her.

She felt the ground beneath her feet as they reached the bank, barely aware she'd half swum, half been dragged to the shore.

Prescott sat her down, both soaking wet, his brow furrowed, worried for her. "Kat, are you all right?"

"He's drowning." She was numb. She couldn't feel anything for the man who had attempted to kill them both.

Prescott kicked off his shoes and yanked off his socks. "I'm going in after him. Will you be all right?"

She nodded, but she knew the man would never make it. "There's no use."

Scotty waded out anyway, her hero to the rescue. His bare feet splashed as he swam back to where the SUV's metal rack on top of the SUV still poked out of the lake. Shivering, she rubbed her arms.

"Prescott," she whispered, when he dove under.

After a few seconds, he resurfaced, then dove under again.

She stood. "The car doors are locked," she said under her breath.

More splashing followed, and Prescott returned to her, unable to get to the driver of the vehicle.

"He doesn't want any help. Certainly not from you," she said.

Prescott took a heavy breath. "I couldn't let him die without trying to help him. The doors are locked and—"

"He's speaking to me." She stared at the dark lake without seeing the water. "He says I wouldn't go out with him. But he was always there for me when I needed him. He says you'll have your fun with me and throw me away. That your type would never marry someone who's not rich like you."

Prescott pulled her into his arms and held her tight, warming her marginally.

She rubbed her temple and frowned. "He's in pain. He's dying, but he doesn't care. Not if he can't be with me. He says you won't share with the likes of us. That he didn't want you to hurt me. Not like that other guy did." A tear rolled down her cheek. "It's Baldy, and he's not going to make it."

"I've got to get you warmed up, Kat. You're shivering uncontrollably. I'm afraid you're going into shock."

Her heart raced like the ocean tide pulling out to sea. She nuzzled her face against Prescott's wet shirt. "He's dead." Shivers continued to wrack her body as the cool breeze stirred their dripping wet clothes.

He walked her back up to the road. Before he could wave anyone down in the thick fog, a car pulled up, and to Katrina's horror, Lucky got out.

She took a step back. "Lucky," she said under her breath as she shuddered. Prescott pulled her close, protecting her against the new menace.

Lucky lifted a phone to his ear, eyeing them. "There's been

an accident. Some folks need medical attention. Two cars in the water, one man dead." He gave the location, climbed back into his car, and drove off.

Prescott rubbed her arm as he held her tight against his body, still trying to warm her. "Who the hell was he?"

"He was Baldy's cousin. Baldy had coerced Lucky to try to keep me away from you whenever Baldy attempted to kill you. Lucky really hadn't any interest in revealing the family's secrets. Not when his own family had the same kind of secrets. That's how he knew about my family. His threats were only a ruse."

Prescott pressed his body against hers in a gorilla grip, attempting to stop her shivers, to no avail. "Hold on, Kat. Someone will be here soon." He lay her down on the ground where the land sloped slightly, pointing her head downhill.

"What are you doing?"

"Attempting to warm you." He lay on top of her, heating her body with his.

Time seemed to stop, yet she couldn't quit thinking about Baldy and what he'd tried to do. Sirens sounded in the distance and colorful lights approached.

Prescott kissed her forehead. "The cavalry has arrived." He climbed off her and waved to the police as they pulled off the shoulder and hurried to help them.

"My fiancé is in mild shock."

One of the officers brought out a blanket and wrapped her up in it.

"The driver of the SUV is still in the lake," Prescott told the police as he directed them to the location of the accident. Katrina listened in silence as Prescott told their story...every bit of it, except for the part about her family's abilities.

～

LATER THAT EVENING, Katrina and Prescott cuddled in his condo before a fire, watching the flames flicker in the pink brick fireplace without a word spoken between them. She held his phone for half an hour, as she leaned her back against him. His arms wrapped around her while his fingers stroked her velour robe tie. Taking a deep breath, she finally punched in the numbers.

"Aunt Meg, it's over."

"Yes, dear. I know."

She sighed another ragged breath, her hair still damp after showering off the scum from the water they had swum in earlier. "I have to ask you...why did I see Prescott dressed in a tux in my first vision where I had to rescue him?"

"It was *your* future you foresaw, not his."

"But how did Baldy know I'd go to the dance to see Prescott? I mean, why would Baldy have attempted to kill him if I hadn't been dating Prescott? If I hadn't seen Baldy try to run over him in my vision, I wouldn't have been there in the first place."

"Baldy knew Prescott was the one."

"How?"

"I guess he was so focused on you when he saw Prescott first meet you at the fair, he knew before the rest of us did. Anyway, he had to get rid of his competition."

"And you? Why did he attack you?"

"He came to speak to your Uncle Jimmy about Prescott Worthington. He told him you needed to be with a man who had special abilities. Your Uncle Jimmy happened to agree. But I sensed Prescott might be the one. I figured he worried I'd tell you, and you'd marry Prescott. So Baldy helped me to lose my powers for a while, believing he could get rid of Prescott in the meantime. He assumed by the time I regained my abilities, Prescott would no longer be a threat to him."

"When did you know this?"

"I called as soon as I realized, but there wasn't any answer.

You must have already left the house by then. You must delay the inevitable and get married first."

Katrina smiled and kissed Prescott's cheek when he nuzzled his face against hers.

"Katrina, tell me you didn't."

"I have to go, Aunt Meg. Talk to you later." She hung up the phone, then handed it to Prescott. "Yeah, I'd like to do that again too."

"We're still linked?"

"You bet, Scotty. Forever and ever."

PRESCOTT LINKED his fingers with Kat's as he walked her back to his bedroom. "You know, I would have waited until after we were married. If you had lost your powers..." He shook his head. Being linked with Kat, made him better than whole. Losing that connection...he didn't even want to consider such a thing.

He backed her up to his bed, pinning her legs against the edge of the mattress as he drew her close.

She ran her fingers along the inside of the waistband of his silk boxers stirring his groin with renewed gusto. "Yeah, well, we'd missed our flight to Las Vegas. The next isn't for another three hours even. I couldn't wait that long. Not only that, though Aunt Meg tried to hide the truth from me, the fact of the matter was we could make love as long as we were soul mates, and I wouldn't lose my powers, whether we were married or not. The notion slipped into her thoughts briefly. There was no way I was waiting any longer." She chuckled. "She did it with Uncle Jimmy before they were married too."

Smiling, Prescott untied Katrina's belt. "You could have told me, you vixen." His fingers slipped inside her robe, then touched her breasts with eagerness. The satiny soft curve and feel of her firm breasts cupped in his hands made him sigh. He was in heaven.

Lost in his touch, she nearly purred her satisfaction as her hands ran over his silk-covered buttocks. Then she responded, "I wouldn't have waited, even if I hadn't known."

She ran her fingers along the length of his erection in his silky boxers, sending a surge of white-hot heat through him. "I need you." She smiled a look of the devil in her expression. "And it looks like you need me."

"Yeah, well," Prescott said as he slid her robe off her shoulders, "it's all your fault you're so tantalizing."

He swept away the dark curls collecting over her shoulder, leaned down, and touched his mouth to her bare skin. Her fingers grasped his boxers in response, and she tugged them down, stripping him, making him groan. "Slowly, honey."

She grinned. "I can't wait."

He chuckled as he leaned her against the bed. Immediately, she parted her legs for him, encouraging him to slip into her wet and willing feminine heat. He tried to savor the moment, his mouth conquering hers, their tongues competing in a mating dance, but she slipped her hands down his back, grasped his buttocks and pressed him against her greedy body.

Inwardly, he laughed. She wanted him, every bit of him, and satisfying her appetite was just what he needed in his life. But she wasn't going to force him to hurry this time. He sensed she was afraid to allow him to pleasure her too. More than anything else in the world, he wanted her to enjoy every bit of their love-making as much as he did.

Slowly, he touched her nipple with a playful sweep of his tongue. Her fingers swept through his hair with tenderness, but when he touched her at the source of her pleasure, she moved her hands to his back again, pressuring him to fill her with his love.

"Make love to me," she insisted.

"I am," he responded, totally amused. He would, but on his own terms this time. Straddling her leg, he maneuvered his body so he could touch her where he could give her the most pleasure.

"Oh, Scotty," she moaned as he dipped his finger into her, felt how wet she was for him already, and began to coax her into submission. Only she wasn't submitting. She arched against his questing fingers as he rubbed her mons, wringing her emotions from her, loving how quickly she became aroused to his touch.

His body was burning up, desperate to quench his thirst for her. His thickening arousal pressed against her leg, but he wanted inside of her now, her heat surrounding him, expanding for him, softening for him.

She arched against his fingers, parted her lips, said his name in such a wondrous loving way, "Omigod," after that, that he knew she was ready for him.

She was his...now and forever. Her body shuddered with climax and before he totally lost it, he slipped inside her warm, wet folds. "I love you, Kat."

All she could do was moan something inaudible, her mouth and his locked together, feasting, loving, as he slid his cock inside her sex, enjoying the bond that was more than just physical, but something that went much deeper.

Thrusting deeply, he kissed her mouth, his tongue tangling with hers, his fingers locked in her hair as she ran her nails down his back, gently scoring his skin. God she felt good.

Desperate to hang on, but unable to, he reached his peak, the exquisite feeling of pleasure and completion wracking his body as he spilled his seed inside of her, bathing her with his love and heat.

She grinned back at him as her hands swept over his shoulders. "I love you too, Scotty."

He kissed her lips firmly, their tongues dancing the tango briefly, then they parted. "You deserve to enjoy every bit of me as I do you."

Wrapping her arms around him, she gave him a firm embrace. "Okay, so when can we do it again?"

THREE DAYS LATER, Katrina hugged Sascha when she arrived to put on their fortune telling show at the Worthington place. Prescott watched them nearby, raising a champagne glass to the two of them as they looked in his direction.

"I understand you and Prescott are selling that condo of his. Have you found anywhere else to live?"

"Yeah, we're moving into the country. The place has a lovely carriage house. Do you want to live there? You know, I'll need some help with the twins when they arrive."

Sascha squeezed her with a warm embrace. "Thanks, so much, cuz. You know I'd love to."

"I know you'd do the same for me if the roles were reversed." She pulled a red curl away from Sascha's cheek. "Aunt Meg said she's concerned about you though."

"There's nothing to worry about, Katrina, really."

"She says you've been moping about ever since I got married."

"Nah, you know me. I think regaining my powers so all of a sudden made my hormones shift out of control. But tell me, did you do it before you got married? I have to know...if you make love with your soul mate, will you lose your powers if you're not married first?"

"Now you know what Aunt Meg said. You have to wait."

Sascha grinned at her. "You're hiding your thoughts on the matter." She nodded at a gentleman whose hair was as red as hers. "Got work to do. Remember, try to say something nice when you tell folks' fortunes. I want to come back here next year. The food's fabulous."

Katrina grinned at her cousin as she turned her attention to the redhead standing before Sascha. That's when she knew her cousin would be all right.

"Sascha the Sensation?" The redhead stretched his hand out to Sascha. "I've been waiting all evening to get a word with you."

She touched his hand. "My you have a very long lifeline, but..." She paused.

Katrina said under her breath, "Tonight your life will be..."

"Kat?" Prescott said interrupting her train of thought. "You've been so busy with fortune telling and the like, I've felt neglected. I thought we might sneak away for a few minutes from the crowd." His dark brown eyes clouded over, and she knew just what he had in mind.

"The guestroom or your room, Scotty?"

"I love it when you know just what I'm thinking. And for your information, honey," he said as he slipped his fingers between hers, "my room, *is* your room."

She glanced back at Sascha who still held onto the redhead's hand. She winked at Katrina and her orange lips turned up in a smile.

Katrina nodded, then pulled Prescott toward his bedroom. "Meghan, that's the name of our baby daughter, named for Aunt Meg."

He kissed her cheek. "I heard Sascha ask you earlier if you'd help her with her booth at the Crescent Fair this weekend. Do you mind if I come along?"

"Sure, I'll give you some tips on the biz."

"You want me to be a gypsy fortune teller?"

"It's all in the family, Scotty."

"And we'll have turkey legs and cotton candy for lunch?"

She led him into his bedroom, then he locked the door behind them. "Have I told you how much I love you?"

"In lots of creative ways." He leaned her against the bed. "Life just can't get any better."

She tugged at the buttons on his shirt.

"Well, maybe it can."

He pulled off her tank top. "There's only one problem, I see, Kat. Camden wants to know who in your family can find him the girl of his dreams."

Katrina smiled. "Pleasure first." She tugged at his belt. "Family business later."

ABOUT THE AUTHOR

Bestselling and award-winning author **Terry Spear** has written over a 100 paranormal romance novels and medieval Highland historical romances. Her first werewolf romance, *Heart of the Wolf,* was named a 2008 *Publishers Weekly*'s Best Book of the Year, and her subsequent titles have garnered high praise and hit the *USA Today* bestseller list. A retired officer of the U.S. Army Reserves, Terry lives in Spring, Texas, where she is working on her next shifter book, while enjoying her grandkids, her Havanese dogs, gardening, photography, and creating photo compositions and fantasy artwork.

For more information, please visit www.terryspear.com, or follow her on Twitter,
@TerrySpear. She is also on Facebook at http://www.facebook.com/terry.spear. And on Wordpress at:
Terry Spear's Shifters http://terryspear.wordpress.com/
Subscribe to Terry Spear's New Releases Announcement https://www.goodreads.com/author/show/421434

Excerpt from another romantic suspense now available by Terry Spear, *In the Dead of the Night.*

IN THE DEAD OF THE NIGHT

by
Terry Spear

PUBLISHED BY:
Terry Spear

20

IN THE DEAD OF THE NIGHT

"**A**re you sure the bastard is staying here?" Allan Thompson whispered to fellow A.T.A. agent, Dale Smith.

They hid in the shadows of the thirty square foot storage building, a good three hundred feet from the suspect's house. Terrorism was the new game in town. The newly formed U.N. sanctioned Anti-terrorism Agency had agents tracking down terrorist cells all over the world. But tonight, four special agents watched for signs of Thurman Wilson at the Texas redbrick, ranch-style home outside of Waco. When it came to extorting money for Columbian-based terrorist activities, he acted as a financier extraordinaire.

Dale stroked his red beard. "One of our agents sighted Wilson with the woman earlier today in town. Then she came directly back here. Our agent lost track of him though."

Allan fought the urge to break into Jenny Brant's house to ensure she remained safe. His black T-shirt dripped with sweat, not only from the eighty-five-degree heat and humidity that hung heavily in the air, but from the anxiety that plagued him concerning the welfare of Wilson's latest conquest. Then the woman appeared at the dining room window, her long red-blond curls cascading down her shoulders over a pale blue satin robe. She peered into the night as he and Dale stared at her in silence.

The cicadas and crickets sang their raucous chorus as an owl hooted from a nearby tree. The stiff breeze swished through fields of corn across the street and nearer by, the sound of cows moving about in the darkness added to the country melody in the dead of the night.

But the woman garnished all of Allan's attention for the moment. What kind of a woman would succumb to the charms of such a man? All of Wilson's lovers ended up dead. For the first time, Allan and his team saw one of his women alive before Wilson's thugs finished her off. Allan had an overwhelming desire to keep her safe. Not because of how pretty she was, but because he couldn't stand the idea they might be too late to save her, if Wilson decided tonight she would be history.

Yet, Allan couldn't jeopardize the case. If Wilson showed up, it would be the closest they'd ever gotten to apprehending the sick bastard.

Jenny reached her hand up to the side of the window and tugged at something. A white shade drew down, lower and lower, until all he could make out was the shadow of her petite figure against the fabric. Then she moved away from the window and stood at another. Each time, she gazed into the dark. Was she looking for Wilson's return? Or was he in the house already? They couldn't be certain. By the time they located the place and scoped out the area, it had been too late to slip in a few bugs.

Allan's gut clenched with concern. Nothing felt right about the woman, or the situation. Was it because they'd found one of his lovers alive for the first time?

After she shut the remaining shades, the lights in the house turned off, first in the kitchen, then the living area. The light in the bedroom flipped on after a few seconds.

Agent Cameron Polansky moved toward them in the shadows, holding a thermos of coffee and a stack of Styrofoam cups. Ruggedly built, with a cleft in his chin the size of the Grand Canyon, the man exhibited a pillar of calm under any circumstance. "See anything?"

"Ms. Brant pulled all the shades shut, then turned out the lights," Dale said. "No sign of anyone else in the house. Though we can't be absolutely certain he's not in there. One of the agents thinks Wilson sighted him in town earlier today and may have spooked him."

"What's her involvement in all this?" Cameron asked.

Dale poked his boot into the grass. "Probably a pawn like the last one and all the others. Wilson likes a steady diet of young women, only they normally don't live long enough to tell any tales."

The light from the bedroom turned off.

Agent Samuel Stevens joined the group and nodded in greeting. "The house is quiet. The woman must have gone to bed."

Allan and the others watched for any sign of movement on the roughly ten-acre sized lots, the land split between each home in long narrow rectangles, making for acre-sized front yards and nine-acre long backyards. Live oak and native mesquite dotted the land, breaking up the level terrain. Next door a handful of cattle stood sleeping. The occupants of the brick home there also slept. At two in the morning, it was to be expected. Allan glanced over at the wood framed house on the other side of hers. No lights on inside there either.

What was she doing up so late at night? Was she an insomniac? Or was she worried because Wilson hadn't returned home? The notion sickened Allan. How could the beast worm his way into these women's lives, then destroy them in an instant? If they knew how his henchmen would use a few expeditious carvings of a knife to remove their identities afterward...

Bastard.

Allan shifted his attention to the surrounding area again, trying to get his anger under control. Stark security lights hung from twenty-foot-high poles, stretched faint fingers of illumination into the countryside estates. But farther out where the A.T.A. agents stood, the area remained pitch black.

Wrought iron lights on the front and backsides of Jenny's house provided additional security. But for the agents tonight, the lights gave them a pretty good view of any movement at the front and back of the house. From the blueprints they'd obtained, the garage on the east side of the house had no windows, but on the other, two windows gave access to the master bedroom, both cloaked in darkness.

Still, they watched the area for any movement with night vision goggles.

Allan shifted his weight. "What do we know about her?"

Cameron studied the house. "Tax accountant, twenty-four, red-blond hair, green eyes, a real looker. You know, the way he likes them."

"Only after he's done with them, they're not much to look at." Dale shook his head. "Sicko. We've got to get him this time."

Allan frowned. "I've seen the photo of her." Catlike green eyes and a smile that wouldn't quit. Heart-shaped face with creamy skin and dimples to boot. Great figure, and silky curls that rested on her shoulders. A heart breaker. He knew what she looked like, and she was way out of his league. The type of woman who had a string of boyfriends, had to have. What he wanted to know was what else did they know about her?

"Personal habits? Friends?"

Cameron poured steaming hot coffee into a Styrofoam cup

and handed one to Dale. "Best friend, Roxie Adams, works with her in the tax office. Known each other since they were in kindergarten. Both graduates of Baylor University, both have master's degrees in accounting. She and her friend volunteer at the animal shelter, soliciting support for homeless pets and adoptions for them."

Allan frowned. The whole scenario didn't seem right. None of the other women Wilson had been involved with had been that well educated. They didn't own their own homes or have decent jobs. They were young, pretty, and unattached like her, but Jenny didn't fit the rest of the profile at all.

Cameron passed a cup to Samuel. "Jenny's parents are retired army, live in Florida. She'd been engaged to a man for a year, and they broke up. He'd been seeing someone else on the sly. As far as we know, she's been seeing this clown for three weeks."

"That's a record. Are you sure there's not something more to his interest in her?" Allan accepted the cup of coffee Cameron offered him. "I've never heard of him sticking with a woman that long. Chances of his getting caught are increased tenfold."

"Yeah, well, maybe he's really got a thing for this one." Cameron shrugged a shoulder. Tall and rock-solid, he was Allan's six-foot height and a crack shooter with any kind of a gun he got his hands on.

"Right," Samuel said, sarcasm dripping from his voice. "The man can't have a long-term commitment with any woman."

"Oh, and the lady's got a permit to carry a concealed weapon," Cameron added.

"Why?" Allan asked.

"For self-protection, I suppose, living alone in the country."

Samuel shook his head. "It won't do her any good against Wilson and his thugs. Why don't folks leave it to us trained professionals to handle?"

A four-legged critter moved on the property to the east, and the men all turned to face it.

"Damned cows," Samuel said. The blond-haired, chunkier built, ex-marine, born and raised in Sacramento, California, didn't care for country stakeouts.

"It's a horse," Allan said, amused at his partner's mistake.

Dale and Cameron chuckled under their breaths.

"Whatever," Samuel grumbled.

Cameron motioned to the cornfields across the road. The stalks reached six foot and swayed in the hot breeze as if they danced to some musical beat, the wind whistling with a whoosh through their golden leaves. "Come on, Samuel. Let's move back into the field so we can watch the front of the house and get away from the *cows*." More chuckles ensued.

The two men moved off in the dark, skirting the homes and the lights and disappeared.

"So what do you think, Allan?" Dale finished his coffee, flattened the cup, and stuck it into his shirt pocket. "I mean, about the woman. Think he wants her for some other purpose?"

Allan had never heard of Wilson taking a woman into his organization to serve as a terrorist member. Love them and dump them...dead, was his practice. "I'm not sure what to think. But it doesn't sound like his usual M.O." Uneasiness gripped him, and he was certain it was all due to the fact that she was still alive, and he feared she wouldn't be for long.

Headlights from the road caught their attention. The tension in Allan's gut mounted. "We might have company."

Though they were already hidden in the dark, they crouched down, waiting to pounce like panthers, their muscles tense, their guns drawn, readied for their prey.

The pickup truck drove on past in a westerly direction. Dale cursed under his breath.

Allan sighed deeply, trying to take the edge off his raw

nerves. He preferred a firefight to staking out a house any day. In this instance, he'd rather be inside, guarding Jenny, than watching from a distance. He couldn't shake the disconcerting notion that one of Wilson's henchmen might still slip into her house unnoticed and turn her into another statistic. If Wilson *was* aware the A.T.A. agents were breathing down his neck, he'd place Jenny on the terminal list immediately.

Another fifteen minutes passed, and they heard two men whispering to one another as they approached from the west, their footsteps crunching on the graveled circular drive, still cloaked in darkness.

Allan touched Dale's shoulder and motioned for him to head west. If it wasn't Wilson, the terrorist was sending a couple of his thugs. If that was the case, Jenny's life was in danger of being terminated, quickly.

Harsh, hushed words woke her from her sleep. Jenny rolled over on her side in the queen-size bed. She touched the empty place where Thurman Wilson usually slept this time of night. Their relationship had been horribly strained for the last day and a half. He wanted to marry her at once, but she had to delay it as long as she could, hoping he wouldn't become suspicious. Before long though, she knew she'd have to act, one way or another.

She glanced at the clock. Nearly half past two. Then she recalled Thurman hadn't come home.

Had she been dreaming that she'd heard voices? Or was he home now, talking to himself or speaking to someone on his cell phone?

She pulled her covers aside, sat up, and yawned. Thank God tomorrow was Saturday, no work.

The sound like the popping of firecrackers went off outside. She shook her head. Idiot neighbors. It didn't matter the time of year, they were always shooting off fireworks or shooting dove or something. Though the hour seemed a little odd.

She tucked her hair behind her ears and rose from the bed. The central air conditioner clicked on, humming as it worked, spinning a cool breeze about her head.

Half asleep, she padded barefoot out of the bedroom and down the carpeted hallway. "Thurman?"

By habit, she never turned on lights as she moved around in the dark, not wanting to wake herself up. She knew where everything was, as long as Thurman didn't move anything. The back outdoor lights provided a nightlight kind of illumination in the living and dining area through the shades on the windows. But when she stepped into the living room, she realized at once something wasn't right. It was too dark. One light bulb might have gone out, but all three at one time?

Before she could investigate, the doorknob twisted to the French patio doors leading out of the living room and onto the trellis-covered porch. A chill ran down her spine. She stood frozen in the middle of the living room with indecision.

Thurman was the only other who had a key to her place. It had to be him. She relaxed.

Then the door burst open with a bang. She couldn't see who it was in the dark, but it had to be Thurman. Unless...

She didn't want to think of any other scenario. He wanted her and badly. He wouldn't harm her. Not yet.

"Thurman?"

As soon as she spoke, footsteps hurried toward her, but not from the back door, instead from the kitchen. Panic filled her instantly. She turned and dashed for her bedroom, trying to keep her wits about her. If she could reach her gun in the bedside table...

Blood pulsed in her ears and her skin crawled. How could she have been so foolish?

"Damn it!" a man's dark voice said, as a chair crashed in the living room.

"Shit, Blackie!" the other exclaimed, as he evidently tripped over the first, who'd spoken in the dark.

Blackie yelled back, "The damned cops are all over the place! Bernard got hit already. I'll take care of the girl. Get to the vehicle and bring it here or we'll never get out of here alive."

Jenny slammed her bedroom door shut and locked it. She sprinted to the nightstand. After nearly yanking the drawer completely out of the chest, she shoved her hand inside. Nothing but papers.

"Ohmygod." On the verge of hysteria, her voice sounded unnatural to her ears. When heavy footsteps ran toward her door, chill bumps freckled her skin.

Where's the gun? She'd just moved the gun from its hiding place in her closet to the nightstand that morning before work. Thurman couldn't have...

The doorknob to her bedroom door twisted violently.

She fumbled with the light switch to the crystal lamp sitting on the nightstand, her fingers shaking so hard she couldn't locate it.

Something slammed against her hollow core door, caving the whole thing in with a crash. She let go of the lamp, and yanked the bottom drawer open, though she was certain the gun had been in her top drawer. She slid her hand over the papers and other paraphernalia inside. No gun, damn it!

Her whole body prickled with a chill as she tried to think.

She jerked the lamp's cord out of the wall. Unable to see the intruder in the dark, she imagined he couldn't see her either, but all the noise she'd made would have clued him in. Still if she could use the nearly three-foot tall, heavy crystal lamp on him...

Hurried footsteps closed in on her. His clawing onion breath and sweaty body odor suffocated her. She swung the lamp at the figure. The lamp connected with his solid body, resulting in a thud. He yelped in pain, then swore at her.

Grabbing her arm, he jerked her backward. His jagged fingernails dug into her bare skin. He'd kill her for sure now.

A scream she didn't recognize, full of terror and panic, issued from her. Her heart beat spastically before a painful blow to her head radiated outward. The darkness filled her skull, shutting out the pain, the smells, the world.

In the Dead of the Night is already available online now.

ALSO BY TERRY SPEAR

Heart of the Cougar Series:

Cougar's Mate, Book 1

Call of the Cougar, Book 2

Taming the Wild Cougar, Book 3

Covert Cougar Christmas (Novella)

Double Cougar Trouble, Book 4

Cougar Undercover, Book 5

Cougar Magic, Book 6

Cougar Halloween Mischief (Novella)

Falling for the Cougar, Book 7

Catch the Cougar (A Halloween Novella)

Cougar Christmas Calamity Book 8

You Had Me at Cougar, Book 9

Saving the White Cougar, Book 10

Big Cat Magic, Book 11

≈

Heart of the Bear Series

Loving the White Bear, Book 1

Claiming the White Bear, Book 2

≈

The Highlanders Series:

Novella Prequels:

His Wild Highland #1, Vexing the Highlander #2

Winning the Highlander's Heart, The Accidental Highland Hero, Highland Rake, Taming the Wild Highlander, The Highlander, Her Highland Hero, The Viking's Highland Lass, My Highlander

Other historical romances: Lady Caroline & the Egotistical Earl, A Ghost of a Chance at Love

Heart of the Wolf Series: Heart of the Wolf, Destiny of the Wolf, To Tempt the Wolf, Legend of the White Wolf, Seduced by the Wolf, Wolf Fever, Heart of the Highland Wolf, Dreaming of the Wolf, A SEAL in Wolf's Clothing, A Howl for a Highlander, A Highland Werewolf Wedding, A SEAL Wolf Christmas, Silence of the Wolf, Hero of a Highland Wolf, A Highland Wolf Christmas, A SEAL Wolf Hunting; A Silver Wolf Christmas, A SEAL Wolf in Too Deep, Alpha Wolf Need Not Apply, Billionaire in Wolf's Clothing, Between a Rock and a Hard Place, SEAL Wolf Undercover, Dreaming of a White Wolf Christmas, Flight of the White Wolf, All's Fair in Love and Wolf, A Billionaire Wolf for Christmas, SEAL Wolf Surrender (2019), Silver Town Wolf: Home for the Holidays (2019), Wolff Brothers: You Had Me at Wolf, Night of the Billionaire Wolf, Joy to the Wolves (Red Wolf), The Wolf Wore Plaid, Jingle Bell Wolf, Best of Both Wolves, While the Wolf's Away, Christmas Wolf Surprise, Wolf Takes the Lead, Wolf on the Wild Side

SEAL Wolves: To Tempt the Wolf, A SEAL in Wolf's Clothing, A SEAL Wolf Christmas, A SEAL Wolf Hunting, A SEAL Wolf in Too Deep, SEAL Wolf Undercover, SEAL Wolf Surrender (2019)

Silver Bros Wolves: Destiny of the Wolf, Wolf Fever, Dreaming of the Wolf, Silence of the Wolf, A Silver Wolf Christmas, Alpha Wolf Need Not Apply, Between a Rock and a Hard Place, All's Fair in Love and Wolf, Silver Town Wolf: Home for the Holidays

Wolff Brothers of Silver Town Wolff Brothers: You Had Me at Wolf

Arctic Wolves: Legend of the White Wolf, Dreaming of a White Wolf Christmas, Flight of the White Wolf, While the Wolf's Away

Billionaire Wolves: Billionaire in Wolf's Clothing, A Billionaire Wolf for Christmas, Night of the Billionaire Wolf

Highland Wolves: Heart of the Highland Wolf, A Howl for a Highlander, A Highland Werewolf Wedding, Hero of a Highland Wolf, A Highland Wolf Christmas, The Wolf Wore Plaid,

Red Wolf Series: Seduced by the Wolf, Joy to the Wolves, Best of Both Wolves,

Novellas: A United Shifter Force Christmas

Highland Wolves of Old: Wolf Pack (Book 1)

∽

Heart of the Jaguar Series: Savage Hunger, Jaguar Fever, Jaguar Hunt, Jaguar Pride, A Very Jaguar Christmas, You Had Me at Jaguar

Novella: The Witch and the Jaguar

Dawn of the Jaguar

∽

Romantic Suspense: Deadly Fortunes, In the Dead of the Night, Relative Danger, Bound by Danger

∽

Vampire romances: Killing the Bloodlust, Deadly Liaisons, Huntress for Hire, Forbidden Love, Vampire Redemption, Primal Desire

Vampire Novellas: Vampiric Calling, The Siren's Lure, Seducing the Huntress

~

Other Romance: Exchanging Grooms, Marriage, Las Vegas Style

~

Science Fiction Romance: Galaxy Warrior

Teen/Young Adult/Fantasy Books

The World of Fae:

The Dark Fae, Book 1

The Deadly Fae, Book 2

The Winged Fae, Book 3

The Ancient Fae, Book 4

Dragon Fae, Book 5

Hawk Fae, Book 6

Phantom Fae, Book 7

Golden Fae, Book 8

Falcon Fae, Book 9

Woodland Fae, Book 10

Angel Fae, Book 11

The World of Elf:

The Shadow Elf

Darkland Elf

Blood Moon Series:

Kiss of the Vampire

The Vampire...In My Dreams

Demon Guardian Series:

The Trouble with Demons

Demon Trouble, Too

Demon Hunter

Non-Series for Now:

Ghostly Liaisons

The Beast Within

Courtly Masquerade

Deidre's Secret

The Magic of Inherian:

The Scepter of Salvation

The Mage of Monrovia

Emerald Isle of Mists

Made in the USA
Las Vegas, NV
13 November 2023

80717354R00184